VANISHING POINT

PATRICIA WENTWORTH

ISIS

LARGE PRINT

Oxford

First published in Great Britain 1965
by
Penguin Books

Published in Large Print 2010 by ISIS Publishing Ltd.,
7 Centremead, Osney Mead, Oxford OX2 0ES
by arrangement with
Hodder & Stoughton
An Hachette UK company

British Library Cataloguing in Publication Data
Wentworth, Patricia.
  Vanishing point.
  1. Silver, Maud (Fictitious character) - - Fiction.
  2. Detective and mystery stories.
  3. Large type books.
  I. Title
  823.9'12–dc22

ISBN 978–0–7531–8646–6 (hb)
ISBN 978–0–7531–8647–3 (pb)

Printed and bound in Great Britain by
T. J. International Ltd., Padstow, Cornwall

CHAPTER
ONE

Rosamond walked in the dark wood. The trees were leafless overhead, and the earth soft and damp underfoot with the thick carpet strewn there by the autumn winds. There had been so much rain in the last few days and nights that the dead leaves no longer rustled as she walked. The wood lay at the bottom of the garden, but once you had passed the two great oak trees which guarded the entrance you might have been a hundred miles away from that, or from the house, or the road which lay beyond the winding drive. Out of sight, out of mind. What the eye does not see the heart does not grieve over. Those were old true proverbs. If you could not see the road, what did it matter who travelled along it? If you could not see the house, what did it matter who lived there? Whether it was the long-ago Crewes who had their time of fame and fortune, or Lydia Crewe who had been born too late for it and spent a grey life mourning for the loss, or whoever was to come after her, whether it was Rosamond and Jenny Maxwell, or another? Once you were in the wood, it didn't matter at all, because there wasn't any house to be compassed with observances and served with bended knees. There wasn't any past or future. There was only the earth which had brought forth the trees, and the sky which made an arch above them. And that was why Rosamond walked in the wood. She could slip out of the everyday life in which she rose at six and worked with hardly any moment free, until at the end of the long day she lay down upon her bed and slept. For which reason she had somehow found the means to hoard or snatch these moments of escape. She had realized long ago that if she did not have them she would not be able to go on. She must be able to get away to where she was no longer just someone who answered bells, wrote letters, did the shopping, gave a hand here, there and everywhere, and generally kept things going. She must be able to get away . . . But there was someone whom she could not leave behind her. She could never leave Jenny, because Jenny was in her heart, and you cannot leave your heart behind you however far you go. So now as she walked in the wood, the thought of Jenny came with her and walked there too. A foolish loving picture, because the real Jenny would have hated to walk in a damp wood with only leafless boughs between her golden head and the night sky. Jenny loved warmth and colour and light; Jenny loved voices and music, and the bright glow of the fire. She could never understand why Rosamond left these things to go down through the dripping garden to walk in a lonely wood. But then she had long ago made up her mind that grown-up people did very odd things. Now when she was grown-up herself she had quite made up her mind what she would do. She wouldn't stay stuck down in the country — not once she could choose for herself. She would go up to London, and she would live in a flat right on the top of the highest house she could find and whoosh up and down in a fast exciting lift — the sort where you press a button whenever you want to and it's just like flying. And she would write books that would sell for thousands and thousands of pounds, and her back wouldn't bother her any more, so she would go dancing every night and have the most wonderful dresses in the world. Of course she would give half the money to Rosamond, because Rosamond would have to come too. She couldn't do without her. Not yet — not till she was quite grown up, and that wouldn't be for another five or six years, till she was seventeen or eighteen. It seemed a terribly long time to wait.

Down in the wood Rosamond watched the tracery of black branches against the soft deep grey of the sky. She had been standing quite still for a long time. Something small and furry ran over her foot. An owl swooped. It was as white as a cloud and it made no sound. It swooped, and it was gone as if it had never been. Very faint and far away the clock of the village church struck six. She drew in a long breath of the cold, damp air and went out between the oak trees into the everyday world again.

CHAPTER
TWO

She came in by a side door and along an unlighted passage to the hall, where a single bulb diffused what did not amount to much more than a glimmer. The big fireplace was a black cave, the stairway plunged in gloom, the door with its massive bolts like something to keep a prisoner in, or a true love out. Jenny used it constantly in the tales she wrote. She had a secret fear of it, as she had of the shadowy ancestors who stared down from their portraits upon the hall where they had walked, and talked, and laughed, and loved, and hated in the old days.

These were Jenny's thoughts, not Rosamond's. Once she had come out of the wood Rosamond had no time for fancies. The hall was dark because electric light cost money, and having spent what she considered a vast sum on putting it in, Miss Lydia Crewe was at some pains to ensure that it should be as little used as possible. How much money there really was, no one had any idea but Lydia Crewe. The house was to be kept up, but there was no money for what she considered the fantastic wages of the present day. The old furniture must be polished, the old silver must be bright, and since Mrs Bolder in the kitchen and the couple of village girls who came in by the day could not possibly achieve the standard she demanded, it was Rosamond who must make good what they left undone.

She was crossing the hall, when there was a knocking on the heavy door. If the bell had rung, Mrs Bolder might have heard it, or she might not. In the face of a good deal of pressure she retained a strong conviction that it was not her place to answer the front door bell. There should have been a butler to do that, or at least a parlourmaid. That Miss Rosamond should answer it really shocked her. It wasn't what she had been used to, and she didn't know what things were coming to. But as to herself, farther than the back door she wouldn't demean herself, not if it was ever so.

Rosamond, being fully aware of these sentiments, concluded that the bell must have been ringing for some time, and that the now continuous knocking was a last desperate effort to attract attention. As she drew back the bolts she wondered who could be there, since anyone who knew the ways of the house would come round to the west wing where Lydia Crewe kept her state and she and Jenny were tucked away.

She opened the door and saw Craig Lester standing there — beyond him the vague shape of a car. What light there was showed him big and solid in a heavy coat. When for a moment he said nothing, the height and bulk of him began to seem oppressive. There was something strange about the way he just stood there and looked, as if there were things to be said between them and he could not come by the words. The impression was there as she drew in her breath, and gone before she could take another.

And then he was saying in a deep, pleasant voice, "Is this Crewe House?"

It might be someone asking his way. But apparently it was not, for right on the top of her "Yes" he was asking for Jenny — Jenny!

"I've called to see Miss Jenny Maxwell."

"Jenny?"

"I am not speaking to her, am I?"

He did not think so for a moment — it was the obvious thing to say. Her "Oh, no," was what he expected.

As she spoke she turned a little, her hand still on the door, and with what light there was no longer directly behind her, he could see that there was really no mistake. He hadn't expected her to be Jenny Maxwell, and he had no idea who she was now, but that she was the original of the photograph he could not doubt. The tall, graceful figure, the dark clustering hair, the way she held her head — all these had brought conviction even before she turned. Now, looking from the darkness of the porch, he saw her face in the faintly glowing twilight which filled the hall. It was rather like seeing a reflection in water, because he could only guess at the colour which a fuller light would show. The eyes were shadowed. They might be brown, or grey, or a very dark blue. But the brows over them were the brows of the picture, strongly marked, with the odd lift and tilt which gave the face its own decided character. Another woman might have the wide generous mouth, the line of cheek and chin, but those lifting brows could belong to no one else. They certainly didn't belong to the Jenny Maxwell who had written to him. He said,

"It is rather a late hour to call, I'm afraid, but I was passing this way, and I hoped that it might be possible for me to see her. I ought to have been earlier, but I had a puncture, and then lost my way in your winding lanes."

She took a step back.

"Jenny?"

"Miss Jenny Maxwell. She lives here, doesn't she?"

"Yes . . ."

Her voice had a doubtful tone. A perfectly strange man coming in out of the night and wanting to see Jenny — it didn't seem to be the sort of thing that happened, and here it was, happening. She said with a simple directness which he liked,

"I am her sister, Rosamond Maxwell. Do you mind telling me why you want to see Jenny?"

He said, "She wrote to me."

"Jenny wrote to you?"

He nodded. "She didn't tell you?"

"No — no —"

"And you don't know who I am?"

He produced a card and held it out. She read, "Mr Craig Lester." Under the words a second name was added in pencil — "Pethertons".

Rosamond began to understand. She stood back a little farther. He came across the threshold, took the door from her hand, and shut it behind him.

"You mean you are from Pethertons the publishers? Jenny wrote to them?"

He laughed.

"I seem to be betraying a confidence! But she isn't very old, is she?"

Rosamond said, "Jenny is twelve — and she should have told me. I am just wondering where we can talk. You see, most of the house isn't used — it will all be dreadfully cold. My aunt has her rooms, and Jenny and I have a sitting room, but I would rather talk to you first, if you wouldn't mind its being not at all warm."

He was so much intrigued that he would have accepted an invitation to the Arctic circle. Certainly he would have done a good deal more than follow her across the glimmering hall to a door which opened under the sweep of the stair.

As she switched on a single overhead light, the room sprang into view, small, with panelled walls whose ivory tint had deepened with age almost to the colour of cafe-au-lait. There were cracks in the paint, and there were worn places in the pale flowered carpet. That was the first effect that struck him, the cool pallor of the room — brocaded curtains and coverings so faintly tinted that they might have been wraiths of their own forgotten beauty — mirrors framed in tarnished gold, the glass too dim to reflect anything more substantial than a mist. But there was no dust on the exquisite old china which graced the mantelpiece, on the William and Mary cabinet, on the elegant pie-crust table between the windows. If the room breathed the very atmosphere of disuse, it was to the eye most beautifully

8

kept. Craig Lester's eye was a discerning one. At a single glance it provided him with a good deal of food for thought.

He saw Rosamond seat herself, took the big winged chair which she offered him, and observed with satisfaction that her eyes were, as he had hoped, not brown or grey, but that very dark blue. But, like the room, she was pale. Her lips should have been redder, and there should have been colour in her cheeks. And she was thin — the delicate line of the cheek fell in a little. He saw that her clothes were shabby — an old tweed skirt, an old blue jumper, thick country shoes. The shoes looked damp, and there was moisture caught in her hair. He felt suddenly ashamed of his own warm coat. If she had been out in those thin clothes, and he was sure that she had —

To her "You really won't be too cold here?" he found himself replying roughly,

"But it's you. I've got a coat, but what about you? If you've been out with no more on than that —"

There was something about the way she smiled that wasn't like anyone else. It had a quality which eluded him. Afterwards he thought that it was kindness.

She said, "It was only to the bottom of the garden. There's a wood there — I like to walk in it."

"In the dark?"

"Oh, yes. It's so restful."

He knew then how tired she was. She was pale because she was tired. An extraordinary fierce anger sprang up in him. It left him astounded at himself, and with the feeling that what had started out as a momentary whim was about to turn, or had already turned, into a dangerous venture. He said nothing, because there was nothing to say, unless he said too much. To have come here at all was an act of incredible folly. Or the wisest thing he had ever done in his life.

She looked at him, a little surprised, a little doubtful. The impression she had had of him when she opened the door was borne out now in the lighted room. Some of the bulk was accounted for by the heavy tweed coat, but there was breadth and strength beyond the common. His features too were broad and strong, and very deeply tanned under thick dark hair so closely cropped as almost to defeat a vigorous tendency to curl. Almost, but not quite. Dark eyes, dark eyebrows, and, at the moment, a dark angry look. She did not know how it was possible for her to have offended him, but it certainly seemed as if she must have done so. Yet she had only spoken of the room being cold — and of walking in the wood. Now why had she done that? The wood was her secret place, the only place where she could think her own thoughts and be alone. She did not know why she had spoken of it to Craig Lester, or why it should have angered him. Her thoughts showed in her face — doubt — a shade of timidity just touched by surprise. And then she was saying,

"You wanted to talk about Jenny. You said she wrote to you?"

The dark look vanished. Laughter sparkled in his eyes. She liked the way they crinkled at the corners.

"She sent us some of her work."

"Oh . . . " The soft sound breathed dismay.

"She wrote — a very precise and grown-up letter. She didn't say how old she was — after all, one doesn't in a business letter. It was rather on the lines of, 'Miss Jenny Maxwell presents her compliments to Messrs Pethertons and begs to submit the enclosed manuscripts for their consideration'."

Rosamond's eyes widened, her lips twitched. She said,

"Oh dear!" And then, "That's rather the way my aunt writes business letters. She is my great-aunt. She dictates to me. There was one a little while ago about a lease — the last bit sounds as if it had come out of that. She was writing to her solicitor, and she begged to submit it for his consideration."

He threw back his head and laughed. She said at once in a tone of distress, "You won't laugh at Jenny — not when you see her, will you, Mr Lester? She's proud and sensitive, and her writing means a tremendous lot to her. It would upset her dreadfully if you were to laugh at it, and it's bad for her to be upset. You see, she was in a very bad motor smash two years ago. At first they thought she would die, and when she didn't, they thought she would never be able to walk again."

He saw the muscles of her face tighten and the moisture come to her lashes. He began to speak, but she put out a hand to stop him.

"I don't know why I said that — they don't think so now. My aunt offered to take us in, and Jenny has got on so wonderfully here. She can walk a little now, and they say she is going to be perfectly all right, only she must have a quiet, regular life, and she has got to be kept happy. If she is worried or upset she slips back again, so she mustn't be worried or upset. And the chief thing that keeps her happy is her writing. You see, it's dull for her. There aren't any other children, and if there were, she wouldn't really be up to playing with them, but when she writes it's like going into another life. She can make her own companions, and she can do all the things which she hasn't been able to do since the accident. You don't know how thankful I've been —" She broke off and looked at him, her colour risen, her eyes dark and bright with tears. "You won't laugh at her, will you, or say anything to discourage her?"

He said, "No, no, of course not. But I am afraid —"

"I didn't mean anything about publishing what she sent you. Of course you can't do that — she's much too young. But if there is anything you could say —"

He laughed.

"Oh, there's quite a lot! Of course at present she's copying most of the time — picking the plums out of other people's pies. But every now and then there's an original turn. If she was to start observing for herself and putting it down in words of her own" — he sketched a gesture — "well, I don't know, but she might get somewhere. This whole business of the infant phenomenon is as tricky as you please. I've seen quite extraordinary verse produced by a child of five or six — a couple of fragments, and never another line. It generally happens when they are emerging from the nursery and before the deadening influence of education gets going on them. Practically every child of that age can act, and quite a lot of them can produce some kind of highly original work, but the minute they get to school it's all over. The herd instinct asserts itself, and from then on the most frightful thing in the world is not to be exactly like everyone else. Jenny is past the usual age, but she has been segregated from the herd, so if she has any originality it may survive."

She leaned towards him a little.

"Mr Lester — what do you really think about her work?"

"I've been telling you. What do you really think yourself?"

"She doesn't show it to me. I told you she was proud. She won't risk criticism, and whatever I said, she would know what I was thinking."

"If she is going to be a writer she will have to face criticism — and accept it."

She said very directly, "If she is going to be a writer — don't you see, that is what I want to know. She hasn't got anyone but me. I want to know how much I ought to encourage her. Anything she takes up is bound to be more important to her than it would be if she were able to join in all the things that other children do. Ought I to encourage her to think of it as a career or . . . "

He said, "Or?" and saw a flush come up into her face.

"No, there isn't any or. I couldn't discourage her. She hasn't got enough for it to be possible to take anything away."

He found himself sharing her mood, instead of being able to stand back from it and criticize. They were being ridiculously intense. All right. And so what? He supposed he had it in him to be intense as well as the next man. He said, speaking with deliberation, "I can't tell you what you want to know, because, as I have already said, these things fizzle out. But I don't see why that should trouble you. There isn't anything that could be published now. All that you've got to do is to let her have her head — let her go on writing. She will anyhow, until she finds out — we all find out — whether she can make a good job of it, or whether she can't. Meanwhile see that she has the right things to read — don't let her fritter away her taste on trash. I suppose there's a library in a house like this?"

She gave him a rueful smile.

"Very old-fashioned."

He laughed.

"Scott — Dickens — and the other Victorians!"

"She won't read them."

"Starve her till she does. Stop the rubbish. If she doesn't get it she'll be hungry enough to fall to on wholesome food. By the way, what does she read? No, you needn't tell me — I know. 'He pressed a long burning kiss upon her lips. "My love, my love!" she cried.' All that sort of thing!"

The dark blue eyes widened.

"Oh! Did she write that?"

He grinned.

"And a lot more like it, only in one place she made it a bitter kiss. And there was something about 'tears salt on the lips'. That mightn't have been copied."

"But — she oughtn't to be writing about things like that. I mean, if it's just copying, it doesn't matter so much, but if she thought of that for herself . . . "

He had another of those unpredictable spurts of anger. Her look of distress had been poignant. What did she know about kisses washed in tears?

She said doubtfully,

"I suppose you had better see her."

CHAPTER
THREE

They came out into the hall again and across it to a long dark passage. The light which Rosamond switched on was up in the ceiling and as faint as candle light. There was no sound anywhere, until quite suddenly an electric bell buzzed, and went on buzzing. The sound came from behind a door on the left. It was perfectly plain that somebody wanted something and would go on ringing until the want was supplied. Rosamond stood still and said in a low voice, "It's my aunt. I must go. I won't be any longer than I can help." And upon that was gone. The infernal buzzing stopped. He heard a harshly-pitched voice and a murmuring low one which presently ceased, while the other voice went on. He thought Rosamond Maxwell was being scolded, and that either from habit or discretion she took her scoldings in silence. He found himself disliking the owner of the scolding voice.

He walked away from it, and had almost reached the end of the passage, when the door which faced him was jerked open and a girl in a green dress looked out at him. She had one hand on the door, and with the other she leaned across and clutched the frame. A long faded shawl in a mixture of colours now practically extinct hung from her shoulders and trailed upon the floor. Above it there were features which would have been pretty had they been less pinched, eyes of a startling blue, and a shining aureole of hair. The face was a child's, but the eyes were harder than a child's eyes should be. He had never seen anything like the hair in his life. It was the colour of bright bronze. It stood away from her head in springing waves and curled into delicate tendrils about the temples and ears.

He said, "Miss Jenny Maxwell?" and she took her hand from the door to catch at her shawl and said,

"Yes, of course. But who are you?"

There was neither shyness nor discomposure. He said, "Your sister was bringing me to see you."

"Where is she?"

"A bell rang. She went into a room half-way along the passage."

Jenny nodded.

"Aunt Lydia's bell. It rings all the time, and she can't be kept waiting a minute. She is Miss Crewe, and this is her house. I suppose you know that." She took a halting step backwards. "If you were coming to see me you had better come in."

Everything in the room was shabby. Curtains frayed at the edges. A carpet with a disappearing pattern. Old sagging chairs. A Victorian sofa darned where the upholstery showed, but for the most part hidden by the rug which Jenny had thrown back and by a litter of books and papers. She sat down, pulled the rug over her, and pointed.

17

"You had better have that chair. The springs want mending, but I don't suppose you'll go through."

"I hope not."

The brilliant eyes watched him with interest. They were not soft and deep like Rosamond's. They had the brightness and glitter of sea water under the sun. After surveying him at her leisure she said, "I suppose you are a doctor. I have seen so many of them. At first they thought I was going to die. They didn't say so, but of course I knew. Now they say I'm a Remarkable Case. It's a bore being an invalid, but you meet some very interesting people, and it's nice to be a Remarkable Case."

"I shouldn't think it would make up for not being able to run about. But you are going to be able to do that too, aren't you?"

She pursed up her mouth.

"I expect so. You haven't told me your name. Are you one of the famous ones? The last man who came to see me was. He came over from Paris on purpose, and I can't remember his name, because I think it was Russian. It sounded like a sneeze, and the Russian ones do, don't they?"

"I'm afraid I'm not a doctor at all."

"Oh? Then why did you want to see me?"

"Well, I was passing —"

"How did you know there was anything to pass, or anyone to come and see? Did you know my father and mother? If it was my father, Aunt Lydia wouldn't be at all pleased. She has always been angry because my mother was a girl, and because my father wouldn't

18

change his name when he married her. If he had, we should have been Crewes and carried on the family, and now there's no one. It makes her wild to think of Maxwells living in Crewe House, so perhaps she'll just leave it to the nation, and Rosamond and I won't have anywhere to go — like Vera Vavasour and her child in *Passionate Hearts*. Have you read *Passionate Hearts*? It's by Gloria Gilmore."

"I don't think I have."

"Oh, you would know if you had. It's marvellous! I cried so much over the seventeenth chapter that Rosamond took it away. But she had to give it back again, because I wouldn't stop crying until she did!"

He controlled his face.

"Why do women always like something that makes them cry?"

He had nearly said *girls*, but perceived that it would have been a mistake. Jenny was preening herself. His last-minute substitute couldn't have gone down better. As she continued to discourse upon her favourite books, he was conscious of disappointment. *The Heart's Awakening, Lady Marcia's Secret, A Sister's Sacrifice* — If these were Rosamond's choice! He said, "That's the sort of thing you like?"

She was flushed and eager.

"Oh, *yes!* Haven't you read any of them?"

He shook his head. "They are not very much in my line."

"What a pity! They're lovely! But it's so funny, Rosamond doesn't care for them. She wants me to read dreadfully stuffy things, and why should I if I don't like

19

them? When I've got a Gloria Gilmore I just don't care about anything in the world — not about my back or anything. Then there's Mavis la Rue. She's marvellous, but Rosamond has got a regular down on her, I can't think why. She makes you feel as if even dreadful things could be beautiful, if you know what I mean. Rosamond didn't. And she took *Passion For Two* away from me even after I'd told her that. I didn't think she would be so unkind, but she was. And I believe she had a row with Nicholas about letting me have it, because the books haven't been nearly so exciting ever since."

So Rosamond was not responsible for Gloria Gilmore. He experienced a ridiculous sense of relief. As he inquired, "Who is Nicholas?" Jenny made a casual gesture.

"Cunningham," she said briefly. "He works at that place the other side of the village, Dalling Grange. Experiments for aeroplanes, you know — or perhaps you don't, because it's all frightfully secret. Aunt Lydia says they'll blow us all up some day, but I expect she's thinking about atom bombs. Anyhow I asked Nicholas, and he only laughed and said his lips were sealed."

"He is a friend of yours?"

She sat up straight and pulled in her chin.

"I used to think he was, but now I'm not so sure — because of his giving in to Rosamond like that. He's in love with her, you know. At least I suppose he is, because he looks at her that way, and it's all right in a book. Gloria Gilmore and Mavis la Rue make it sound lovely, but when it's someone you thought was your friend, and then you find out he is nothing but a trampled worm, it just looks sloppy."

So Nicholas was sloppy about Rosamond. Craig was finding Miss Jenny Maxwell quite informative. The theme fascinated him. He pursued it.

"There's a general consensus of opinion that people in love are apt to look silly — except to each other."

"Rosamond isn't in love," said Jenny with the extremity of scorn. "She wouldn't have time, for one thing. It's Nicholas who is in love with her. I don't suppose she even notices it. Aunt Lydia adores him, so he comes in and out a lot. The aunt he lives with is one of her oldest friends. They both adore Nicholas. The Cunninghams are just next door. Much too close for another house really, but it used to belong to the Crewes — a dower house for the old ladies of the family, with a way through to the garden so that they could come in and out and the family could drop in and visit them. People didn't seem to get bored with their relations as much as they do now, and everyone thought it was a very nice arrangement. But when the money began to go wrong Aunt Lydia's father sold the Dower House, and of course Aunt Lydia minded dreadfully. She would mind if she had to sell a pebble off the drive, so you can imagine what she felt like when it was a whole house absolutely bang next door where she could see strangers going in and out. So it was just as well that she made friends with Miss Cunningham, wasn't it? There was a brother too, and she fell in love with him — like Romeo and Juliet, you know. And then something happened. I don't know what it was, because people won't tell you. That's one of the really horrid things about being young, and it's no good their saying it's the best time of your life, because it's very — very . . . " She cast about her for a word and came out with "*frustrating!*"

Craig laughed.

"Cheer up — it will pass! 'Youth's a stuff will not endure'."

She made a child's face at him.

"That's what people always say about the things they don't have to put up with themselves! What was I saying? Oh, about Henry Cunningham. Nobody knows what happened — at least if they do they won't tell. But he went away for more than twenty years, and Aunt Lydia never got over it. It's frightfully difficult to think of anybody as old as Aunt Lydia ever having been in love, isn't it? And very depressing too, because there's a picture of her in the drawing room quite nice-looking, and she's pretty frightful now."

It was at this rather embarrassing moment that Rosamond Maxwell opened the door. Her quiet manner held, but it had been shaken. She was even paler than she had been. He guessed at the effort which steadied her voice as she said,

"My aunt would very much like to see you, Mr Lester."

Jenny made an abrupt movement.

"What on earth for! He's come to see me, hasn't he!"

"I'll bring him back, Jenny. You can go on with your talk afterwards. I think Aunt Lydia would like to see him now."

22

Jenny's spoilt-child expression warned him that he had better get out of the room as quickly as possible. Her protests followed him as he shut the door.

A little way along the passage he stopped.

"She seems to think I'm a doctor."

Rosamond said, "Oh —" And, "You haven't talked to her then?"

"Oh, yes, we've talked."

He wondered what she would say if she knew how frank that talk had been.

"But not about her writing —"

"Mostly about how much she admires the great works of Miss Gloria Gilmore."

Rosamond threw up a hand.

"What can I do! She does love them so, and they are really quite harmless. It is Nicholas Cunningham who brings them. His aunt has shelves and shelves of them, but I've told him not to bring any more of the la Rue woman's stuff. *Broken Vows* and *Passion For Two!* Jenny was so cross when I took them away, but they were really nasty. I don't think the others will do her any harm."

He made a wry face.

"Children like sugar."

Her smile came and went. It was a little tremulous.

"Don't say that to Jenny." Then, on an urgent note, "We mustn't stand here talking. Aunt Lydia doesn't like to be kept waiting."

She took him along to the door which she had opened before, went a little way in, stood aside for him to pass her, and said, "Mr Lester, Aunt Lydia."

He was never to forget his first impression of Miss Crewe's room. At a glance two things emerged — it was grey, and it was crowded. He was to discover later on that the original colour of the hangings, the striped wallpaper, and the faintly patterned carpet had been a delicate shade of blue. Under this light and the lapse of years they were now as grey as dust. And so was Miss Lydia herself.

She sat in an upright chair, a hand on either of its massive arms, and dominated the scene — tall, stiff, with thick iron-grey hair taken back relentlessly from a high, narrow brow and bony features. He found himself wondering what she could have looked like when she was young. The bones were all good. With bloom and colour there might even have been beauty there. The thin, stiff figure might have had its curves — it had none now. The right hand lifted and was extended to him. Stones flashed in half a dozen rings — diamond, emerald, ruby, sapphire. The fingers that wore them were as cold to the touch as bone. She said, "How do you do, Mr Lester? I understand that you have come down to see my niece. Pray sit down."

It was definitely alarming. No, that was wrong, the word should have been *indefinitely*. He wasn't a boy, to be intimidated by an old woman who had outlived her world and retreated into a solitude of her own making. Absurd to have any feeling except compassion. For her — or for Rosamond Maxwell? His former anger rose in him as he took the chair to which she had pointed and said, "I happened to be passing. But I must apologize for troubling you at this hour. I must confess I lost my way, and then when I was so near . . . "

There was an overhead chandelier bright with faceted lustres. The electricity so sparely used in the rest of the house blazed from it upon a room full of old and undoubtedly valuable furniture, upon the bookcases and cabinets which lined the walls, upon every description of chair and every kind of small occasional table, upon the china which filled the cabinets, the innumerable small objects which littered the tables, and upon Miss Lydia herself in a grey velvet wrap lifting the hand with the sparkling rings and saying, "You came to see my niece. I am told that you are in a publishing firm. I believe she amuses herself with scribbling, but you will not ask me to believe that you take that sort of thing seriously."

Her tone affected him in a singularly unpleasant manner. It carried so final a dismissal of Jenny's childish ambitions. They might have no value in themselves, and yet mean all the world to a crippled child.

"She had no business to trouble you," said Lydia Crewe.

He achieved a smile.

"Well, that is what we are there for. I didn't know how young she was. Of course there could be no question of publishing any of her work at present, but I thought I should like to see her, and perhaps give her a little advice. She obviously loves writing, and since she isn't very strong, it is probably a great pleasure to her.

It is much too soon to say whether there is any real talent."

"And so you came down here to say that. Very obliging of you, I am sure. Can we offer you some refreshment?"

She was the great lady condescending. It pricked him. He said, "No, thank you," and got to his feet.

"You must be getting on your way? Perhaps we can direct you. Where are you making for?"

He had been aware of Rosamond in the grey room behind him. She came forward now, threading her way between the tables. Resistance sprang up in him. He was being dismissed, and he was in no mind to take his dismissal. He said with a kind of pleasant firmness, "Thank you very much. Perhaps you will tell me how to get to the village. I suppose there is one, and that it has an inn of some kind. I can't have much farther to go, and there's no real hurry. I don't feel like wandering in any more lanes tonight. Then, if I may, I could perhaps see Jenny again tomorrow. If she really wants to write she ought to start on a regular course of reading."

Lydia Crewe lifted her puckered lids and gave him a long cold look. Her eyes were deeply set, and deeply shadowed by the arch of the brow. He thought they must once have been fine. She said with abrupt irrelevance, "Are you related to the Lesters of Midholm?"

"Why, yes."

She nodded.

26

"You have a look of them. They were all big men. There is some slight family connexion. My great-grandfather married Henrietta Lester in 1785. She died young." Her tone dismissed Henrietta as a failure.

He was surprised, therefore, when she said quite graciously, "Very kind of you, I'm sure, to take so much trouble about Jenny. She will naturally be delighted to see you. Rosamond will show you the way out and direct you to the inn. It is quite small of course, but Mrs Stubbs is a very good cook. She used to be with the Falchions at Winterbourne. Goodbye, Mr Lester."

He touched the cold hand again and made his farewells. He found himself outside in the passage with relief.

"Do I see Jenny again now?"

Rosamond shook her head.

"Better not, I think. If she is too excited she won't sleep. Can you really come back in the morning?"

"Oh, yes. What time shall I make it? Ten — half past?"

As they went back towards the hall, she gave a sudden soft laugh.

"Are you really related to those Lesters?"

"I really am."

"And do you know exactly how? Because Aunt Lydia will certainly cross-examine you. She knows everybody's family tree much better than they do themselves."

"I'm word perfect. My grandfather was a brother of old Sir Roger Lester's. The present man is my cousin Christopher."

She had opened the front door and was saying, "If you turn left at the foot of the drive, the village is not much more than a quarter of a mile. The name is Hazel Green, and the inn is the Holly Tree. Mrs Stubbs is a pet — " when he broke in after the manner of someone who has not been listening.

"Do you dust all that damned china?"

When she thought about it afterwards it occurred to her that she ought to have snubbed him. Rosamond wasn't very good at snubbing people. She said in an apologetic voice,

"The daily women aren't careful enough. Aunt Lydia wouldn't trust them."

There was quite a cold air coming in, but neither of them felt it. He said with anger, "Do you know what I would like to do? I'd like to put all that stuff in the middle of the floor and smash it with the poker!"

And all she did was to look at him and say, "Why?"

He obliged with a copious answer.

"Because you're a slave to it. There isn't a speck of dust on the wretched stuff, or anywhere else that I could see. And who does the dusting? You every time! And mind you, I know about dusting. My sister and I had to help at home. My father died, and the first thing my mother did was to get rid of practically all that sort of stuff. She said there wouldn't be anyone to do anything except ourselves, and she wasn't planning for us to be slaves to a lot of irrelevant crockery, so she made a clean sweep of it. This house is cluttered till you can't move, and you're worn to a shadow trying to cope with it."

It was the most extraordinary conversation, and perhaps the most extraordinary part of it was that she found it quite impossible to be angry. Strangers oughtn't to speak to you like that. He didn't feel like a stranger. He broke all the rules and he broke down all the fences, but it wasn't for himself, it was for her. He was angry because she was tired — because there was too much china and too much furniture and her work was never done. It was so long since anyone had cared whether she was tired or not that she was shaken, but not with anger. She felt a weakness and a warmth, and got no nearer to an answer than a faint tremulous smile.

He said, "Why do you do it?" and she lifted her head and spoke gently.

"Most women have a good deal to do in their houses nowadays, you know. It doesn't hurt one to be tired at the end of a day's work."

"It hurts to be given a hopeless task and kept at it till it breaks you! Three quarters of that stuff should be put away! Why don't you say so and go on strike until it's done?"

The smile was gone. She straightened herself a little.

"Please, please — you mustn't. My aunt has been most kind in taking Jenny in, and it has meant everything for her. We really had no claim. Anything I can do in return —"

"I know, I know — and it's not my business, and all the rest of the conventionalities! Let's take them as said and get down to brass tacks. It is really impossible for you to have a sensible talk with Miss Crewe? After all, she can probably remember how many women it used to take to do what she expects you to take on single-handed."

"It was a different world, a different life. She hasn't the least idea how long anything takes to do. There was a cook, and a kitchenmaid, and a between maid, and a woman up from the village three times a week to scrub, and a butler, and a parlourmaid, and two housemaids. And everything went like clockwork."

"She tells you all that, and she can't see?"

"No, she really can't. She just thinks they were lazy and overpaid, and that there is no entertaining now, so of course it is all quite easy." A light shiver went over her.

He said impulsively, "You're cold — I mustn't keep you. But I haven't said anything like all I'm going to."

A big warm hand swallowed hers up, held it a moment, and then let go. He went out on to the porch, and down the steps, and into his car and drove away.

CHAPTER
FOUR

Mrs Stubbs's cooking was all that Miss Crewe had said. The parlour at the Holly Tree was warm and bright and comfortable — old leather chairs well broken in, a red tablecloth to replace the white one when his meal had been cleared away, and a row of fascinating objects on the shelf over the fireplace. Craig sat gazing at them and considering how much he preferred this homely warmth and comfort to the dreary bygone grandeurs of Crewe House. Sèvres and ormolu were all very well in their time and place, but for everyday fireside comfort give him the yellow cow with a lid in her back which was really a cream-jug, the milk being put in at the lid and pouring out of the mouth; the cup and saucer of copper lustre with its bands of raised fruits and flowers on a ground of bright sky blue; the mug with Queen Victoria and Prince Albert in lilac and grey, the Great Exhibition in the background, and the date 1851 displayed in silver. There were also some rather intriguing wooden candlesticks with what looked like little heaps of cannon-balls piled at the four corners of the base, and a tall pottery jar with a picture of a khaki-clad soldier of the South African War and the dates 1899-1901. Below on either side of the hearth there were two very large pink shells which took him back to his boyhood, when he used to stand in front of a dreadful little muddle-shop which he passed on his way to school, looking in and coveting just such another pair.

Mrs Stubbs came in, hoped he had everything to his liking, and stayed for a cosy little chat. The shells were brought back by a great-uncle who had taken to the sea. The cow and the lustre cup and saucer had come down from her great-grandmother. "And I don't hold with all this throwing out and putting in a lot of silly rubbish. New it may be, and the fashion it may be, but I don't hold with it. When the young people come in they can do as they choose, and I suppose when I'm in my grave I shan't mind, not even about my granny's yellow cow that she used to allow me to stroke Sundays for a very particular treat. Oh, well, every dog has his day, as the saying is, and no use troubling oneself that I can see. Makes your blood go sour, and then what are you like to live with! Better laugh as long as you can and hold your tongue when you can't!"

He went up to Crewe House in the morning, and Rosamond let him in. He found Jenny bright-eyed, flushed, and very grown-up indeed.

"How do you do, Mr Lester? You must have thought it very silly of me yesterday to mistake you for a doctor, because of course you are not in the least like one. Rosamond has told me about your coming down from Pethertons, and she says I mustn't expect you to publish anything. But then I never did — not really. Only you will talk to me about it, won't you, and not

32

just say it's no use and I must wait till I'm older. You don't know what a curse it is being young and have everybody say you can't do any of the things you want to do because of it."

He said, "I shan't do that, because there's quite a lot you can do now, and I'd like to talk to you about it very much."

Her hands were at her breast, painfully clasped. The brilliant eyes answered. Rosamond, leaning over to lay a hand on her shoulder, was vehemently pushed away.

"Well," he said, "writing is a trade. If you want to write you'll have to learn it. Take any conversation. There are the words, there is also the way people look and move, and the tone of voice they use, and when you come to write that conversation down all you have got is the words. And they are not enough. Somehow, by hook or by crook, you have got to make up for colour, the life, and the sound which you can't transfer to paper."

"How?"

"That's what you'll have to find out. For one thing, written dialogue has got to be better than the ordinary stuff that people talk. It must have more life and go in it. The colours must all be brightened. There must be more individuality. The clever people must be cleverer and the silly ones sillier than they would be in real life, or you won't get them across at all, and your book will be dull. Then you want to watch your reading rather carefully. Don't read too much of any one author, or you will find you are copying him, and that is fatal. You'll have to read the standard authors, because they lay down a good foundation and you won't be able to do without it. And as you read, just notice how they get people in and out of rooms, or from one place to another — how they produce what is called atmosphere — that sort of thing. They all do it different ways, so you won't be in danger of copying any one in particular."

Jenny nodded vigorously.

"And then — you probably won't like this, but it's important — write of things you know something about."

Jenny's already feverish colour deepened.

"If everyone did that, there would be a lot of dull books. I don't want to write about the things that happen every day — I'm bored with them! What can I write about *here?*"

Dangerous ground. He hastened away from it.

"Well, you live in a village, and a village has people in it just the same as a town has, or a South Sea island, or a castle in Spain. It's the people and what goes on in their lives that makes things interesting — or dull."

For the first time her hands relaxed. The flush began to fade. She said slowly, "Sometimes you can't think what was in their minds. Nobody could with Maggie."

"Who is Maggie?"

"A person in the village. She just walked out of the house one evening and never came back."

Rosamond threw him an uneasy glance. He ignored it.

"Why did she do that?"

"Nobody knows why."

He said, "Tell me about it in your own way — as if it was a story you were writing."

"I don't know how to begin."

He laughed.

"That is always one of the difficult things."

She thought for a bit, and then shook her head vehemently.

"I can't do it like that. I can tell you what happened."

"All right — go ahead."

She nodded.

"You mustn't think about it being a story — it's just something that happened. But it's not interesting, or romantic, or anything like that — it's just a bit frightening. Maggie lived with her father and mother in a cottage in the village. You can see it from the bottom of our drive, only they don't live there now. The father and mother were quite old, and Maggie wasn't at all young, or nice-looking or anything like that. And about a year ago, at eight o'clock in the evening when it was quite dark, she finished her ironing and said to her mother, 'I'm just going out for a breath of air. I won't be long'. And no one ever saw her again."

"You mean she disappeared just like that?"

Jenny nodded.

"I told you it was rather frightening. And if I was writing it for a story I should stop there, because the end rather spoils it."

"What was the end?"

"Oh, she wrote — twice. On a postcard to her mother, and to Miss Cunningham. She was the daily at the Cunninghams', and their card just said, 'Away

35

temporary'. But the one to her mother was longer — something about being obliged to go away and coming back as soon as she could. That's what she wrote, only she never did, and they never heard any more. The postmark on the card was London. And in the end they went to the police, but they couldn't find her. Nobody knows what made her do it, because she had always been such a good daughter. And when she didn't send any money or anything, the poor old Bells had dreadfully little."

"You say they don't live here any more?"

"Oh, no. They're dead. Maggie oughtn't to have gone away and left them."

Over Jenny's head Rosamond gave him one of those looks. All right, he was a blundering fool, and Jenny oughtn't to be encouraged to dwell upon village tragedies. Let her stick to her Gloria Gilmores and life as it never was. Only if you were going in for fairy tales, he preferred *Beauty and the Beast*, *Cinderella*, and the *Twelve Dancing Princesses*, with the warp in folklore and the weft in fantasy. He gave back Rosamond's look with as much hardihood as he could muster and said, "Yes, that's the sort of thing I mean. Only it needn't always be tragedy, you know. Queer things happen in villages, just as they do everywhere — and nice things and interesting ones." He even steeled himself to add, "Gloom is the hallmark of extreme youth."

Jenny flushed. He felt that he had been a brute, but Rosamond's eyes were thanking him.

She left him with Jenny after that, and presently brought in a tray with cups of tea and some of Mrs

36

Bolder's biscuits which melted in the mouth. She found the party going with a bang and Jenny chattering away nineteen to the dozen, after which she ate a great many biscuits and drank what was practically a cupful of milk.

"And if any of us was slimming, we shouldn't be able to, should we? So what a good thing it is that we're not, because Mrs Bolder does make the most heavenly biscuits. I expect it will be years, and years, and years before Rosamond and I have to think about that sort of thing. She runs about too much, and I can't run about enough. And anyhow it must be perfectly ghastly to think about everything you eat and feel perhaps you oughtn't to. Miss Cunningham is like that, you know. She doesn't eat this and she doesn't eat that, and she gets fearfully hungry. And then quite suddenly she can't bear it any more, and everything she's taken off comes on again, so what's the good? Anyhow she's quite old, so I don't see why she worries. Nicholas teases her about it, and she goes all pink and says, 'Oh, my dear boy!'."

Rosamond walked down the passage with him when he had said goodbye. He wondered whether he was to be summoned to Miss Crewe's presence again, but they passed her door in silence. As they came out upon a wide corridor which led directly to the hall, she said in a hesitating voice, "Would you care to see the house?"

He made no attempt to soften the tone of his reply.

"No, I wouldn't."

Her lips quivered into a smile.

"People do come and see it. There are some good pictures."

"No, thank you."

"Two Lelys and a Vandyck, and a pet of a Gainsborough — Miss Louisa Crewe, three years old, in a white muslin dress and a blue sash, with a puppy."

"Then in heaven's name, why doesn't she sell them and give you a human life?"

The smile went out like a blown candle flame.

"Aunt Lydia will never sell anything," she said. "And you — you mustn't say things like that."

"Then you had better not ask me to bow down to the idol which is destroying you all. I suppose it started as a perfectly good house put up to serve the needs of real live flesh-and-blood people. The sort of life they lived is over. The kind of houses they lived in just aren't wanted any more. They've either got to be put to new uses, or they'd be better pulled down. You know as well as I do that this house is nothing but a mausoleum, and that it's draining the life out of you. If you're going to ask me what that has to do with me, I'll tell you."

"But I'm not asking you."

"I'll tell you all the same. First of all, it's everyone's duty to prevent an attempt at suicide." He grinned suddenly. "That's not what you expected, is it? I'm on nice firm uncontroversial ground there. I see you about to leap from Waterloo Bridge, and I put out a restraining hand!"

"I think you are quite mad."

"No — only metaphorical. But cheer up — it gets easier as it goes on. In the second place, you keep doing something to me. You make me angry, and you make me tired. If I'm not in a rage with Miss Crewe for making a slave of you, I'm in a rage with you for letting yourself be made a slave of. 'A Sister's Sacrifice', that's what you are — a living embodiment of one of those Gloria Gilmores that Jenny wallows in. Do you know, I haven't been so angry half a dozen times in the last half dozen years! I wouldn't have believed it of myself, but there it is, and I expect you know what it means just as well as I do. And now perhaps we had better change the subject."

She had been watching him in a way that came across to him as aloof. Not exactly the Blessed Damozel looking forth over the gold bars of heaven, but perhaps the medieval damsel watching a furious lance being broken for her sake. There was a suggestion that men *would* play these rough games, and that there wasn't anything you could do about it. What she said was a plain inexpressive "Yes". And then, "I would like to talk to you about Jenny."

She took him into the hall and across it into the small pale room where they had talked last night. They sat in the same chairs, and talked about what Jenny should read, and what she should be encouraged to write.

It was Rosamond who spoke about Maggie Bell.

"I don't know what made Jenny bring that up. It's a frightening story."

"I don't suppose she found it so. There has been time for her to get used to it."

"I hoped she had never heard very much about it."

39

"In a village? What a hope! Besides children always know everything."

"Nobody has ever known what happened to Maggie. It really is frightening, you know. She was such a good daughter. She would never have gone away and left her father and mother like that if she hadn't been obliged to."

She was echoing Jenny's words. He guessed that they were not so much Jenny's as everyone's. They were what had been said so often that as soon as there was talk of Maggie Bell the words were there, all ready to be used again.

He said, "I suppose it was the usual thing — some man, and she couldn't face the talk."

"But there wasn't any man. She must have been forty, and she had never been about with anyone."

"Axiomatic," he said. "Girls who disappear or who get themselves murdered have never had any men friends — all their friends and relations say so. But that's an old story. Let us now give our minds to Jenny."

CHAPTER
FIVE

Chief Inspector Lamb sat back in his office chair and allowed his frowning gaze to rest for so long upon Detective Inspector Frank Abbott that that promising young officer began to wonder which of the crimes regarded by his Chief with particular disfavour he had committed this time. Whichever it was, the appropriate homily would undoubtedly be forthcoming. Since he knew them all by heart, from Thinking oneself Better than one's Superiors, Entertaining a quite False Impression that one's Opinion had been Sought or was Desired, through a long list to, last and not by any means least, the Using of Foreign Words where Plain English ought to be Enough for Anyone, he awaited the breaking of the storm with resignation, and was surprised that it should be still delayed.

Lamb glowered. His big face was florid. The heavy thatch of black hair, irrepressibly determined to curl on the temples, showed only the slightest tendency to become thinner at the crown. His prominent brown eyes were fixed in an unwavering stare upon Frank's tall elegance. The cut of his clothes, the harmony of socks, tie, and handkerchief, the shining perfection of the shoes, might individually or collectively provide the

41

theme of a discourse. But it was not until a respectful "Yes, sir?" had been interjected that the Chief Inspector broke this menacing silence. On a deep growling note he produced these unexpected words:

"Didn't you send me a picture-postcard from a place called Melbury sometime or other?"

Reflecting that it was rather long after the event for this to be brought up as a breach of discipline, and that to the best of his recollection the card itself had merely carried a photograph of the new Melbury housing estate, Frank replied, "It would have been about this time last year. I had a weekend, and ran down to see a cousin."

Lamb nodded, still frowning.

"Don't know why you sent me the card."

"People you mentioned — friends of one of your daughters who were moving to Melbury — I thought they might be interested in the housing estate."

Lamb grunted. He and Mrs Lamb had had a trying time last year with their daughter Violet. Why she couldn't take a decent young fellow and marry him and have done with it, he didn't know. This time it had been one of those long-haired cranks who want to do away with the Army, the Navy, the Air Force, and the Police, and then everything would be quite convenient for everybody. The fellow had some sort of job at Melbury, and Violet had actually got to the point of saying she wanted to marry him. But thank goodness it was all over now, and she was going out with the son of one of their chapel members, a very steady young man, and with good prospects in his father's business, which was

42

wholesale groceries. Not desiring to enter upon these details, he cleared his throat and said in a dogmatic manner, "Quite so, quite so. Melbury — exactly — about this time last year."

"Yes, sir?"

Lamb leaned forward and picked up a pencil. He wrote the word Melbury upon a piece of paper, and then said in a slow and meditative manner, "You were staying with cousins. What about staying with them again?"

One of Frank's pale eyebrows rose.

"Oh, I don't know them all that well," he said. "They asked me down, and I went." There was a faint gleam of humour in his eyes. "I have rather a lot of cousins."

Lamb said heartily, "A good thing family feeling. Pity there isn't more of it these days. Plenty of people don't know who their own great-grandfather was."

Inspector Abbott smoothed back the very fair hair which was already beyond criticism.

"My great-grandfather had twenty-seven children," he remarked negligently. "One or two of his brothers and nephews also helped to keep up the average, which is why I can find a cousin in most places if I'm put to it. Sometimes it's convenient."

Lamb began to tear up the paper upon which he had written the word Melbury.

"Well, I was thinking of that," he said. "And I was wondering how it would be if you were to look up these Melbury cousins of yours again." He dropped the torn-up bits into a large wastepaper basket.

It was borne in upon a young man with an irreverent turn of humour that his respected Chief was giving an exhibition of tact. He was reminded of Dr Johnson's reply when invited by Boswell to give his opinion on the subject of a woman's preaching. "Sir, it is like a dog walking on his hinder legs. It is not done well; but you are surprised to find it done at all." He said in a respectful manner, "Very good of you, sir, but I hardly think —"

The Chief Inspector made the sound which may be written "Tchah!" and came into the open.

"As a matter of fact I wouldn't mind having someone down in the neighbourhood without making an official matter of it. The whole thing may be a mare's nest, or it may not, and whether it is or whether it isn't is not properly our pigeon. But I had better begin at the beginning."

Frank Abbott murmured that it might be as well. He continued to prop up the mantelpiece.

Lamb pulled some notes out of a drawer, slapped them down on the desk in front of him, and looked up to ask a question.

"These cousins of yours — do they live right in Melbury?"

"I'm afraid not, sir. Did you want them to? They're a mile or two out, on the Hazel Green side."

Lamb nodded.

"You know Hazel Green?"

"I've passed through it. I was only down there for a weekend."

"Well, not so long after you were there a woman called Maggie Bell disappeared from the village. She went out one night for a breath of air and never came back again. About a week later there were two cards with a London postmark . . . Yes — let me see — Paddington. One was to her employer and said, 'Away temporary. M.B.', and the other to her parents, 'Coming back as soon as I can. Florrie will come in. Don't worry. Maggie.' The employer is a Miss Cunningham. Maggie worked there daily. The other members of the household are an elderly invalidish brother, Henry Cunningham, and a young chap, Nicholas Cunningham, who is a nephew. Now about half a mile out of Hazel Green and off the main road you have Dalling Grange which was taken over by the Air Ministry during the war and has been retained by them for experimental purposes. Nicholas Cunningham works there. The experiments are top secret, and the Security chaps get jumpy if anything happens within a hundred miles of the place. They got jumpy over Maggie Bell. She was forty years old and no looker. No one had ever seen her with a man. I know that's what the friends and relations always say, but in this case it really seems to have been true. After those two postcards there has never been anything more, and she has never been traced."

"What about the postcards — were they genuine?"

"I don't know. The parents didn't question them, nor did Miss Cunningham. Maggie was always at home, and the only specimen of her handwriting available was the signature on her identity card. The handwriting people wouldn't commit themselves one way or the other. The fact is, she wrote a horrid scrawl, and the pen used on the identity card must have been just about through."

"And where do we come in?"

"We don't, properly speaking. We're being dragged in — the Paddington postmarks — and if you ask me, a lot of fuss about nothing. To my mind the woman must have met with some accident. She had old parents, she was a good daughter, and she was the breadwinner. She wouldn't have gone off and left the father and mother to fend for themselves. The question is, what took her to London and kept her there for a week? If the postcards are genuine, it wants explaining. And if they are not, then everybody would like to know who wrote them, and why."

Frank Abbott said, "A bit late in the day, isn't it, sir? What exactly is the point of my going down to Melbury now?"

Lamb frowned heavily.

"The fact is, there's been a leakage of information. We're being asked to cooperate. We shouldn't send anyone down there officially, but it was agreed that it might not be a bad plan if you were to take a spot of leave and pay a private visit to the neighbourhood. There seems to be an idea that it mightn't be a bad plan to sift over the local gossip." He cleared his throat and added, "On the social side, as it were."

Frank Abbott straightened himself. A respectful and attentive expression gave way to an irrepressible gleam of humour as he murmured, "What you really want is Miss Silver."

The Chief Inspector's colour deepened, his brows drew together. But there was no explosion. Instead, with merely the hint of a growl in his voice, he observed that it mightn't be a bad thing.

"One of those cases where I don't say she wouldn't be useful. The fact is, people like talking, but they don't like talking to the police. That's where Miss Silver comes in. The only thing that stops people talking is being afraid. Well, no one's afraid of Miss Silver. She's a good mixer — makes people feel she likes them — sits there with her knitting and makes herself pleasant. And mind you, it isn't put on either. It wouldn't go down like it does if it was. She likes people and she takes an interest in them, and they fairly tumble over themselves to tell her things. Whereas if it was you or one of the locals coming in with a notebook, you'd have them stiffening up and putting everything away under lock and key. There's a lot goes on in a village that doesn't get talked about — not to outsiders. It gets known all right, and it gets whispered from one to another, but it doesn't get as far as the police, and if they come in and ask questions there isn't anybody knows a thing. I grew up in a village and I know. They've changed a lot since I was a boy — motor buses, and cinemas, and the wireless, and the young people going away to the towns — but they haven't changed all that underneath. You go and have a talk with Miss Silver and see if she hasn't got some old crony she could run down and visit in the Melbury direction. Mind, it's got to look accidental, or it won't be any good. The fact is, everyone wants this job finished off good and quick. If there's anything going on down there, they want to know what it is. And if there isn't anything going on, they want to be sure that there isn't before people get up asking questions in the House."

CHAPTER
SIX

Miss Silver was dispensing coffee in the flowered set which had been the Christmas present of a grateful client. The cups had a blue and gold border and little gay bunches of flowers, the saucers a similar border and an occasional scattered bloom. Frank Abbott, having duly admired them, enjoyed his coffee and awaited the moment to do his errand. Not in the house of any one of his numerous relations did he feel more at home than in Miss Maud Silver's flat, with its rather bright peacock-blue curtains, its carpet in the same shade adorned by floral wreaths, its workmanlike desk, and the Victorian chairs with their frames of bright carved walnut and the upholstery which matched the curtains. The pictures looking down upon the scene were all old friends — reproductions of *The Soul's Awakening*, *The Stag at Bay*, *Hope*, and *The Black Brunswicker*. Miss Silver herself, with her neatly netted fringe, her beaded shoes, the large gold locket which exhibited her parents' initials in high relief and contained locks of their hair, might have stepped out of any family album before the twentieth-century wars had shattered a Victorian and Edwardian world. In appearance, in manner and tradition she was miraculously a survival.

Even her dress, though lacking the sweeping folds of those earlier days, contrived to produce its own effect of being permanently out of date. The little net vest with its high boned collar suggested the nineties, and the stamp of the small dressmaker, "Ladies' own materials made up", provided every garment she wore with a family likeness to all those other garments fashioned laboriously in villages and back streets before the days when a gentlewoman could purchase or wear a readymade dress.

Frank Abbott found amidst these surroundings a sense of security which he could not put into words. It was with reluctance that he set down his coffee cup and returned to the world of crime.

"You do not happen to know anyone in Melbury, I suppose? Or do you?"

Miss Silver put her own cup down upon the coffee tray before she replied. She had at times a way of contemplating a new subject with the kind of bright attention with which a bird may be seen to regard a problematical worm. This was one of those times. Frank received the very decided impression that Melbury was a worm, and that she was so regarding it. She repeated the name on a slight note of inquiry.

"Melbury?"

He nodded.

"Do you know anyone there?"

"Not precisely in Melbury. But why do you ask?"

"The Chief would be glad if you did."

"My dear Frank!"

"He wants someone to feel the social pulse, not so much in Melbury itself as in the neighbouring village of Hazel Green."

Miss Silver said, "Dear me!"

This being her strongest expression of astonishment or concern, he was not surprised when she followed it with, "This is really quite a coincidence."

"Then you do know someone there?"

"I have an old schoolfellow in Hazel Green."

"My dear Miss Silver!"

She lifted a flowered knitting-bag from the lower tier of the small table which supported the coffee tray and, opening it, took out a pair of needles from which there depended a narrow strip of ribbing in an extremely pleasing shade. Little Josephine, her niece Ethel Burkett's youngest child, was now approaching her sixth birthday. A twin set in this delightful cherry colour would be very becoming. It used to be the fashion to dress a fair child in nothing but blue, but in this matter she applauded the modern trend. As she pulled on the cherry-coloured ball and began to knit she amplified her previous remark.

"I had really quite lost sight of Marian. It is not always possible to keep up with one's schoolfellows, and during my early days in the scholastic profession I was very fully occupied, but as recently as last year I came across her again at the house of another old school friend, Cecilia Voycey. She had invited her to stay, and thought it would be pleasant to have a little reunion. Dalling is not very far from Melbury, and I really was extremely pleased to see Marian again,

51

though rather sadly changed. She married into an old country family. They owned what was quite a show place, but successive death duties crippled the property, and during the war it was taken over by the government."

Frank Abbott cocked an eyebrow and said, "Not Dalling Grange?"

"That, I believe, is the name. The Merridews had been there for a long time, and it seems a pity. Marian is now a childless widow, and I think it is a relief to her to have a small manageable house and fewer responsibilities."

"Could you go and stay with her?"

"She has invited me to do so."

"Then listen."

As he unfolded the tale of Maggie Bell, with its possible ramifications into the experiments now being carried on at Dalling Grange and the Air Ministry's perturbation on the score of possible leakages of information, Miss Silver continued to knit. When he had finished she said gravely, "There seems to be very little to go upon."

Frank threw out a hand.

"Practically nothing. They appear to think there has been some leakage, but I don't believe they are sure. It's not unknown for two people to hit on the same idea in different countries and at about the same time, and if there is, or has been, a leakage, what is there to connect it with the disappearance of Maggie Bell? I don't quite see what we are expected to do about it anyhow. The disappearance took place a year ago. We haven't been told very much about the leakage, but I gather it is a good deal more recent. The fact remains that there is a pretty considerable flap going on, and it wouldn't do any particular harm if you were to pay this visit to your friend Mrs Merridew."

She knitted in silence for some moments, and then began to ask questions.

"Maggie worked for this Miss Cunningham?"

"For four hours every morning — eight to twelve."

"And the nephew, Nicholas Cunningham, is employed on research work at Dalling Grange?"

"Exactly."

"And the other inmate of the house, Mr Henry Cunningham — what does he do?"

"He is engaged upon a book dealing with the local moths and butterflies."

"Has he ever published anything?"

"Not that I know of. One of these dawdling dilettante kind of chaps, I should think, with enough of a hobby to give him an excuse for being idle."

"He has been living there with his sister for how long?"

"For the last three years. The Security people have been over his whole dossier, and it all sounds harmless enough. A bit of a rolling stone, but nothing against him. During the war he was in a Japanese prison camp, and his family had given him up for dead. Then one day he walked in, and has been there ever since. Naturally he has been suspect number one, but none of the ends tie up. On the face of it he is just an elderly drifter, not in very good health and glad to come home and slip back into his place in the family. Well, what am I to say to the Chief? I'm being sent down myself to stay with a cousin. He's got a job as architect on the new Melbury housing estate. Are you going to come down and hold my hand?"

Miss Silver knitted to the end of her row. Then she said, "I will write to Marian Merridew tonight."

CHAPTER
SEVEN

After twenty-four hours of the Holly Tree, Craig Lester made up his mind to go no farther. The ostensible reason for his journey into these parts being a dutiful visit to a nonagenarian great-uncle, he felt that Uncle Rudd could be duly and daily inspected just as well from Hazel Green as from a hotel in Melbury. For a good many years now it had not been practicable to stay in the house, where everything went like clockwork and an elderly housekeeper and an elderly nurse united in a benevolent despotism. Uncle Rudd was beautifully looked after, and his visits were a matter of form, yet he paid them with regularity, and would do so to the end. They had not always been convenient, but at the moment they provided an admirable reason for his remaining in the neighbourhood.

On the third day of his visit he encountered Henry Cunningham in the bar, a tall stooping figure with a beard and an untidy head of greying hair. Remembering Jenny's story of a romantic attachment in the Romeo and Juliet manner, he reflected that no one could possibly have looked less like Romeo. But then, in spite of all his other misfortunes, that young gentleman had been spared the detractions of middle age. Looked at dispassionately, it was possible to conceive that Henry might have had his points before he let his shoulders sag, grew a beard, and stopped incurring the expense of a haircut. The current growth had every appearance of being botched at home with the nail scissors. He strolled over with his own glass and made a few observations on the weather. They were received in a limp but perfectly amiable fashion, and some desultory conversation followed, in the course of which names were exchanged.

"I have to come down to these parts every now and then to see an old uncle of mine, and this time I thought I would stay here instead of in Melbury."

In a quite detached manner Henry Cunningham echoed the words.

"An uncle . . . "

Craig Lester said, "Retired doctor. Used to have quite a practice in these parts — Dr Rudd Lester. He's in his nineties now, but quite spry."

Henry Cunningham said, "Ah, yes — Dr Lester —" He might or might not have said any more. From his general habit of letting a subject drop it could have been deduced that he had no more to say, but at this moment a man who had just come in crossed over and hailed him.

"Well, well, well — always merry and bright! A pint of mild and bitter, Mr Stubbs, if you please. How's bugs, Mr Cunningham?"

The hearty voice, the rubicund appearance, were in the strongest contrast to Henry Cunningham's lack of vigour. He lost no time in naming himself to Craig.

56

"Newcomer here, aren't you? . . . Oh, staying for a day or two? Well, nobody could make you more comfortable than Mrs Stubbs — I'll guarantee that. My name's Selby — Fred Selby at your service. Hit on this cosy little village when I was looking for somewhere to retire to, and I've never regretted it. Nicest place you could find anywhere, and the nicest people. Used to be in business in London, and everyone said I'd find it too dull in the country — never stick it." He laughed heartily, took a pull at his beer, and went on. "Well, I don't say I don't take a run up to town now and again, because I do. But as to going back there to live — no, thank you, sir! Not if you were to offer me a fortune! Why, I used to have nerves, and where are they now? Suffered from insomnia — I give you my word I did. And now — well as often as not I don't so much as turn over before the alarm goes off in my ear."

"Early to bed and early to rise?"

"That's the ticket! I've got a few dozen hens — just for a hobby, you know — and it makes all the difference if they get their hot mash in the morning. I tell you, three years ago I didn't think I'd be getting up at half past six to cook breakfast for a lot of hens! I tell my wife she ought to take a hand, but she says she's got enough to do without, and I suppose she has, though we've a girl comes in mornings and gives a hand, which is more than she had in town." He went on talking.

Presently Henry Cunningham drifted away.

Next morning in his uncle's bright, hot room Craig brought up the name.

"I met a chap called Cunningham last night. Henry Cunningham — Hazel Green. Do you remember the family?"

Old Dr Lester was a good deal like a monkey. The neat black skull-cap which he wore added somehow to the resemblance, so did the red flannel dressing-gown. An organ-grinder's monkey, looking about him sharply to see what was coming along, only instead of the brown eyes being sad they were still capable of a lively spark of mischief. At the moment they were a little vague. He said, "Cunningham?" And then, "Sister called Lucy?"

"I believe so."

The eyes brightened.

"Yes . . . yes — oh, dear me, yes! Henry Cunningham — lord, what a hoo-ha there was!"

"What about, sir?"

"Hazel Green you said. Come across any of the Crewes?"

"I've met Miss Lydia Crewe."

"Then you've met the whole lot of 'em rolled into one. Know what I used to call her? Only to myself, you know — a doctor can't afford to be witty about his patients. 'Pride and Prejudice', and it hit her off to a T!" He chuckled to himself and went on. "Lydia Crewe — and Crewe House — and no money. And her father sold the Dower House to the Cunninghams. She put herself in such a state I had him in bed for a month with a hospital nurse to keep her out of his room. Well, he had to have the money. And after all the fuss, she made friends with the Cunninghams and fell in love

58

with Henry. Silly affair — very silly, and a good thing it didn't come to anything, because she'd have swallowed him whole. Dominant personality, quite ruthless, and ten years older than he was — he'd have been swallowed. So it was all just as well, but there was a lot of talk at the time." He gave a half chuckle and rubbed his hands together, lacing and interlacing the fingers.

When Craig said, "What kind of talk?" he said in a falling voice,

"God bless my soul — I don't know — it's all too long ago . . . What were we talking about?"

"Henry Cunningham and Lydia Crewe."

Dr Lester brightened.

"Made a lot of talk — a lot of talk. But there wasn't any proof. Mrs Maberly was a very careless woman — couldn't go into a shop without leaving a bag or an umbrella — she probably left the ring somewhere when she went to wash her hands, and forgot all about it. I don't suppose she had it on at all the day she said she missed it, and of course nothing was proved. But there was a great deal of talk — a great deal of talk — and when Henry went off like that, of course everyone believed the worst. Did you say he was back again now?"

"Yes, sir, he's back."

Dr Lester nodded.

"Well, well, it's a long time ago — quite a long time ago."

CHAPTER
EIGHT

That same afternoon, coming out of the Holly Tree, Craig Lester observed a tall figure making a leisurely approach from the direction of Crewe House. No one had ever told him that Miss Crewe was a secluded invalid, but he had somehow received that impression. His visit to her room had not been repeated, though upon one pretext and another he had managed to see Rosamond and Jenny every day, but the picture of her sitting there in her velvet wrap with the blazing chandelier throwing its unsparing light upon all those crowding relics of the past had remained with him, and he had thought of her as fixed in that place and unable to leave it. Jenny had said things about Aunt Lydia's bell ringing all the time and Rosamond having to run because she didn't like to be kept waiting. He had heard the bell himself time and again and seen Rosamond start up and hurry away, yet here was Miss Crewe in the flesh coming towards him and walking without so much as a stick. Seen on her feet, she was even taller than he had supposed — and more formidable. She carried herself as if her spine were a steel rod with no joints in it. Her eyes under a rather battered felt hat stared at him first blankly and then with haughty recognition. She wore dark grey tweeds with a skirt nearly down to her ankles and a shabby black fur coat. No one could have taken her for anything except what she was — autocrat and aristocrat to the tips of her rubbed kid gloves. She gave Craig the slightest of bows and passed on, her destination being the white house set back from the street on the opposite side from the Holly Tree and some twenty yards farther on. It had a small garden in front of it gay with crocuses, and a pair of yews cut into an archway over the gate and continued in a low hedge on either side of it.

After three days in Hazel Green Craig was aware that Mrs Merridew, the late owner of Dalling Grange, resided there. "A very nice lady," as Mrs Stubbs informed him. "And a deal more comfortable at the White Cottage than she'd be at the Grange, which wants a regular staff to run it, and cold and draughty past belief. I worked there as a kitchenmaid when I first went out — all stone passages and great big rooms that hadn't been used for years, enough to break your heart. But she's very comfortable here with Florrie going in to do for her every day."

In the true spirit of village gossip Craig inquired, "And who is Florrie?" and received quite a flood of information about Florrie Hunt herself, her parents, now both deceased, and her other relations, of whom there appeared to be several in the neighbourhood.

"Mr Hunt, he was second gardener at Dalling Grange. No ambition, that was what was wrong with him. All he wanted was to go on growing the vegetables same as he'd always done, and Florrie's a chip off the same block. She's a real good cook, and she could do a lot better for herself than going in daily like she does to Mrs Merridew. But there, it takes all sorts to make a world, and the Hunts are all the same. Poor Maggie Bell now — her mother was a Hunt, and she was just such another. And then in the end off she goes and never a word out of her, which is a thing you couldn't credit, not when you knew her. And if you ask me, she must have met with an accident or something, and nothing to tell anyone who she was."

There was a lot more about Maggie Bell, and how the police had come into it but nothing found out. And then back to Mrs Merridew again, and how nice for her to have an old schoolfellow to stay.

With this in the back of his mind, Craig Lester watched Miss Crewe go by. He had arrived at a rear view of her uncomfortably straight back, when Henry Cunningham emerged from the narrow lane between the White Cottage and the Vicarage wall. It was obvious that he and Miss Crewe would meet. Craig found himself a little curious as to their present relationship. So far no talk on this point had come his way. It was not so much that there had been any avoidance of the subject as that Mrs Stubbs, his main source of information, had been much too busy telling him all about Dalling Grange and how it was to be hoped that they wouldn't all be blown up in their beds some night, and the haunted house at Hazel Lea where, according to local repute, a clock struck twelve at the half hour past midnight every Michaelmas Eve and you could

62

hear the splash of something falling into the well that was filled in fifty years ago. Mrs Stubbs had a stirring repertory of ghost stories, and as one put her in mind of another, she had not so far got round to the Cunninghams and the Crewes. It might be that discretion as well as charity began at home. Whatever the cause of her silence, he felt enough curiosity to make him stand where he was and watch to see how these two people met.

He saw what everyone in the village had seen during the last three years — what anyone in the village might see on any day of the week. He saw Henry Cunningham put up a nervous hand to his hat, and he saw Miss Lydia Crewe look him full in the face and cut him dead. Craig Lester could not see that bleak stare, since he had only a sideways view, but he could imagine it well enough. There was a slight glacial pause. Henry Cunningham's hand dropped to his side, and Miss Lydia Crewe turned in between the arching yews and walked up the flagged path to the White Cottage.

CHAPTER
NINE

Mrs Merridew turned from the window with a sound of dismay.

"Oh, dear!" she said. "She has done it again! I can't think how she can — so dreadfully awkward!" Then, as she encountered Miss Silver's inquiring glance and heard Miss Crewe's deep voice at the front door, she added hastily, "I will tell you afterwards, my dear," and assumed the posture of one who has just risen from her chair to receive a guest.

The door was opened by Florrie, who herself remained unseen. Lydia Crewe came into the room. She had discarded her coat and appeared immensely tall and thin in the straight dark tweeds. There was a double string of pearls about her neck, and a valuable diamond brooch on the lapel. She did not exactly smile, but her face relaxed to a quite noticeable extent as she greeted her hostess and acknowledged the introduction which Mrs Merridew at once proceeded to make.

"My old schoolfellow, Miss Silver. We only met again the other day after — well, we won't say how many years. So pleasant, so very pleasant, to meet an old friend again, isn't it?"

64

There was a slight pause before Miss Crewe said, "Not always." It was borne in on Mrs Merridew that a fatal propensity for saying the wrong thing had once more asserted itself. She hoped that Miss Crewe would not think she had meant in any way to refer to Henry Cunningham, and began in a hurry to speak about something else, only to realize that she had embarked upon a topic which she certainly would not have chosen.

"No, no — it all depends, doesn't it? Especially when it is a case of relations. Poor Muriel now —" She turned in explanation to Miss Silver " — Lady Muriel Street — an old friend and near neighbour. Mr Street owns that big place Hoys just outside the village. I'm sure I sympathize very much with her. I met her yesterday, and she was telling me that she had relations of Mr Street's to stay, and they seemed to find the country so dull. They have been accustomed to go abroad in the winter, and now that they can no longer afford it they find the English spring so very trying — the cold winds, and so much rain. And then, of course, they are not gardeners, which provides one with a constant interest, and they do not care for walking. And with petrol the price it is! Muriel is afraid they have been finding their stay very monotonous, and as she says, she would really rather not have had the house so full at the moment."

Miss Silver remarked that entertaining was now by no means easy, to which Miss Crewe replied with the one word, "Impossible". After which she directed her cold glance upon Mrs Merridew.

"Since there are twenty bedrooms at Hoys, I can hardly believe that the house has been full."

Mrs Merridew was a large fair lady. In her youth she had had an apple-blossom prettiness. She still had the blue eyes and the rather appealing manner which had made up the youthful picture, but now everything was on a much more ample scale. The once fair hair was an untidy pepper and salt. It strayed in wisps about the neck of a faded mauve jumper and continually shed the hairpins with which she made a harassed attempt to control it. Over the jumper she wore an old black cardigan, now much too tight. At the moment she was quite flushed, since the agonized thought had presented itself that dear Maud whose companionship she was enjoying so much might think that any of the foregoing remarks, hastily thrown up as a smokescreen, could possibly refer to her delightful visit. She took up the teapot and began to pour with rather an unsteady hand as she said, "Yes, yes — all those rooms, and hardly any staff — so difficult. I cannot say how thankful I am to have this dear little house, and my good Florrie to look after it so beautifully and to make it so easy for me to see my friends."

She turned her large, kind smile upon Miss Silver, who returned it in a way that quite allayed her fears. The flush faded, and she was able while putting in the milk, proffering sugar, and handing the green Rockingham cups, to pursue the theme of how thankful she had been to hand over Dalling Grange and retire to the modest comfort of the White Cottage. It was only when Miss Crewe accepted one of Florrie's scones in an affronted manner that she realized that the diversion was not a happy one, since everyone knew that whatever happened to the country, to herself, or to her nieces, Lydia always had been and always would be determined to hold on to Crewe House. The flush mounted, and once more she said what she had not intended to say.

"Poor Muriel — I really did feel sorry for her — such a disappointment. But I expect she has told you all about it."

Lydia Crewe held out her cup.

"I have no doubt she would have done if I had happened to see her. She never could keep anything to herself, and I don't suppose she ever will. You have quite drowned me with milk — I only like a few drops . . . Yes, tea right up to the brim — I have a perfectly steady hand. Well, what is Muriel disappointed about now?"

"Her brooch," said Mrs Merridew, "the one with the large diamonds which was left her by the godmother who died a year or two ago. Quite handsome, you know, but rather heavy. You remember, she showed it to us. And it wasn't the sort of thing you could wear very much, but she said she always looked upon it as a nest egg. Not being one of the family things and coming to her like that, she said she wouldn't mind selling it if she ever wanted the money. Well, the other day she took it up to town to have it valued, and, do you know, the stones are not diamonds at all — they are only paste."

Miss Silver said, "Dear me!"

No one took any notice. She therefore continued to sip her tea from the cup with the apple-green border and to listen to the conversation of the other two ladies.

Miss Crewe, it appeared, had no sympathy for the disappointed Lady Muriel.

"People should not sell their family jewels. I consider it a breach of trust."

"But this was not —"

Lydia Crewe broke in with impatience.

"Of course it was! Muriel's godmother was Harriet Hornby, no more than a second cousin twice removed. She had no business to try and sell the brooch. If she had not done so, nobody would ever have known that it was paste." She gave a short grim laugh. "If the truth were told, I fancy a good many people's family jewels would turn out to be paste nowadays. They can't afford to insure them, and they can't afford the death duties. And as long as nobody knows, they can pocket the value and keep up appearances just as well on a sham. But as a rule they have enough sense to hold their tongues. Muriel Street can't even do that — she didn't get called the Babbling Brook for nothing when she was a girl. And you needn't sit there wondering if you ought to have told me, Marian, for I dare say half the county knows by now." She took another scone and continued with a wintry smile. "Felicia Melbury had better sense. I don't suppose any of us ever guessed that her necklace with the big square rubies was just a copy, but that's all it turned out to be. I must say it amuses me to look back and remember the nerve with which she used to display it and tell us that her grandmother wore it at

68

Queen Victoria's coronation. And no one would know anything about it to this day if Freddy Melbury hadn't gone round confiding in all and sundry and saying he couldn't imagine what she had done with the money."

Mrs Merridew, who was doing her best to turn the conversation in some direction which would include Miss Silver, found herself unable to stem the steady flow of Miss Crewe's strictures upon the behaviour of most of their mutual friends. She seemed to know everyone in the county, and to have very little that was good to say about any of them. Mrs Merridew need not really have troubled herself, since her old schoolfellow was able to listen with some interest, and had no disposition to feel slighted. The tea was of the strength she preferred, Florrie's scones were almost equal to those of her own devoted Emma, and there was a kind of tea biscuit just touched with a meringue mixture which was new to her and most agreeable to the taste. Really good recipes were not easy to come by. The fortunate owner cherished them and was not always willing to part, but in this case dear Marian was so perfectly amiable. She allowed herself to entertain the modest hope of being able to present Emma with what would be a decided addition to her repertory.

Tea being over and the tray removed by Florrie, she produced a flowered chintz bag and took out of it a pair of grey needles from which depended about two inches of knitting in a cheerful shade of cherry red. When presently Miss Crewe, fastening a derogatory look upon this employment, inquired what she was making, Miss

Silver proceeded to furnish her with quite a detailed account of her niece Ethel Burkett and her family.

"She has three boys of school age, and they grow so quickly that it is almost impossible to keep them in clothes. A good deal of my time is necessarily taken up with their stockings and socks, so it is a pleasant change to be able to turn to something pretty for the only girl, little Josephine — and I suppose I shall have to stop calling her that soon, for she will be six next birthday. I have just made her a twin set, and I thought this bright wool would make her a really charming hood and scarf. The spring winds are so treacherous. Do you knit, may I ask?"

Miss Crewe's "No" did not trouble itself to be polite, and Mrs Merridew, colouring, interposed with the first thing that came into her head.

"That nice-looking man who is staying at the Holly Tree, Mr Lester — is he an old friend of yours, Lydia?"

Miss Crewe's eyebrows had a natural arch. Thirty years ago they had been very effective in conjunction with a pair of fine grey eyes. The lids were puckered now, and the eyes had sunk. They looked coldly as she said, "My dear Marian!"

"Oh, isn't he?"

In her most disdainful voice Miss Crewe said, "Is he giving out that he is? If so —"

"Oh, no — of course not! I haven't really had any talk with him, but he was most polite when I dropped one of my parcels yesterday getting off the Melbury bus — such nice manners, and such a pleasant voice. And after hearing from Mrs Stubbs that he was a nephew of old Dr Lester's and seeing him about with Rosamond —"

She had blundered on, but at this point she could no longer be unaware that she was saying quite the wrong thing. It was not really possible for Lydia Crewe to draw herself up — her back was already as straight as a ramrod — but she did manage somehow to produce an effect of added rigidity.

"What do you mean by 'about with Rosamond'? Rather an odd expression, it seems to me. She has had one or two business conversations with him on Jenny's behalf, I believe. The silly child scribbles. A lot of nonsense, I dare say, but it has helped to keep her amused. Mr Lester belongs to a publishing firm, and it seems Jenny sent him some of her rubbish. I am told it has become the fashion to publish the writings of children and of uneducated persons. Another symptom of modern decadence!"

Mrs Merridew beamed.

"Is Jenny really going to have something published? How exciting for her!"

Miss Crewe had removed her gloves before partaking of Florrie's scones. Her impatient gesture set the colour flashing in the crowded rings. Miss Silver reflected that it could not be good for the settings to be worn really jostling one another in such a manner. Such fine stones too — diamond, emerald, sapphire, ruby. And very much better kept than was often the case with the rings which elderly ladies wore.

The impatience was not in gesture alone. It was in Miss Crewe's voice as she said,

"Certainly not! Even if it were proposed, I shouldn't allow it! Mr Lester appears to have enough sense to agree that she is too young, but he seems to think that there might be a prospect later on, and he has been advising her as to what she should read. She should, of course, be at school. Her education has been disastrously interrupted, and Rosamond spoils her in a ridiculous manner, but the very first moment she can be packed off I shall certainly see that it is done."

Mrs Merridew gave a little gasp of dismay.

"Rosamond won't like that at all!" she said with more truth than tact.

Miss Crewe began to put on her gloves — black kid, very old and rubbed. The flashing rings were swallowed up, the fingers stroked down over them.

"Rosamond will do as she is told," said Lydia Crewe.

Mrs Merridew evaded the issue. It was sometimes exceedingly difficult not to quarrel with Lydia, and it wasn't any good, besides being so awkward in a village. She pulled down the old grey and black skirt which was rather too tight and had an embarrassing tendency to ride up, and said, "Dr Lester was always so kind, and very clever too. I was so glad to hear that he keeps well."

Lydia Crewe gave a short unpleasant laugh.

"I thought you said you had no conversation with the nephew." Tone and phrasing removed Craig to a distance quite beyond her own circle.

"Well, it was really Mrs Stubbs —"

Miss Crewe's eyebrows rose.

"Village gossip? My dear Marian!"

72

Mrs Merridew flushed.

"I was so glad to have news of him. Mr Lester is most attentive to his uncle. It is not every young man who would take so much trouble. He tells Mrs Stubbs that Dr Lester is really wonderful — asking after everyone at Hazel Green and most interested."

Miss Crewe pushed back her chair with a jerk and got up.

"I always thought him a very disagreeable and sarcastic old man," she said, and made her farewells.

When she had gone out under the arching yews, Mrs Merridew told Miss Silver all about the engagement to Henry Cunningham and the breach which now existed.

"Nobody really does know quite what happened, but he went away in a hurry and poor Lydia changed very much. There is no doubt that she was very fond of him, but I have always wondered how it would have turned out — if they hadn't quarrelled, I mean, or whatever it was that happened. Because he was really very young. She must have been quite ten years older than he was, and not at all an adaptable person, if you know what I mean."

Miss Silver said that she knew perfectly.

Mrs Merridew gave a reminiscent sigh.

"Well, there it was. She was quite handsome in those days, but never what you would call attractive to men — too much inclined to lay down the law, and always wanting her own way, and of course they don't like that, do they? But she and Lucy Cunningham were the greatest friends, and she saw a lot of Henry. I don't want to say anything unkind, but it always seemed to me that he didn't have much chance. He was only just down from Cambridge and rather at a loose end — and then there was this silly scandal —"

Miss Silver was brightly attentive.

"I don't think you told me about that, Marian."

Mrs Merridew hesitated.

"No-no — I don't suppose I did. It was a very stupid affair. The Maberlys have left the neighbourhood, and it's better forgotten — only of course these things never are — not really."

Miss Silver had added several inches to little Josephine's hood. She looked across the bright wool with her head very slightly on one side and said, "You interest me extremely."

After being snubbed by Lydia Crewe this was balm to the feelings. Mrs Merridew relaxed and gave herself up to what a rather startling poet has described as "the rapture of the tongue's prolonged employ".

"Well, it doesn't matter with you, for you don't know any of the people. The Maberlys were immensely rich. He was a company promoter or something like that, and they rather threw their money about. It was all a little ostentatious, but I think they meant to be kind. She certainly did, but you know how it is? Her clothes were much too new and too expensive, and she wore too much jewellery. And then she lost a very valuable diamond ring, and somehow it began to be put about that Henry Cunningham had taken it. I can't remember all the ins and outs, and one never does know how that kind of rumour starts, but there it was. I didn't believe it myself, because — well, one doesn't,

74

not about people you know, and Mrs Maberly was the sort of woman who couldn't even go out to tea without leaving her bag or scarf, and she might have taken off the ring and left it simply anywhere. I remember they dined with us at the Grange, and she was showing us a very handsome bracelet which her husband had given her for Christmas. Well, after they had gone the butler found it behind the cushion in her chair. It had slipped down where the loose cover was tucked in, and really it might not have been found for a day or two, because we were short-handed even then — and as Lucas said at the time, it wouldn't have been at all pleasant. So you see, Mrs Maberly might have done anything with that ring."

"It was never found?"

"I really don't know. The Maberlys went away. He had business interests in the States, and they went over there for a time — I don't think they stayed anywhere for very long. So she might have found the ring and never troubled to let us know — she was one of those good-natured, casual women. And meanwhile Henry Cunningham went away and never came back. Nobody knows whether it was the talk, or whether he just got into a panic about marrying Lydia. His sister Lucy did nothing but cry, and poor Lydia just turned to stone. Nobody dared ask her what had happened, and it wasn't any good asking Lucy, because she obviously didn't know. Oh, well, it's all a long time ago."

Miss Silver pulled on her cherry-coloured ball.

"But Mr Cunningham came back in the end?"

Mrs Merridew nodded.

"About three years ago. Such a surprise — and of course he was very much changed. But Lucy was so pleased. She went about telling everyone what an interesting life he had had, but I think he had really been one of those rolling stones, and I don't believe she knows a great deal about it."

"And Miss Crewe?"

"Oh, my dear, that is the embarrassing part of it. As far as Lydia is concerned, he hasn't come back at all. Of course in a village they are bound to meet, and she just cuts him dead — stares straight at him and walks past as if he wasn't there. Why, only this afternoon —"

She went on talking about Lydia Crewe.

CHAPTER
TEN

Having seen miss Crewe enter the White Cottage, Craig Lester walked briskly up the road and turned in at the gates of Crewe House. He was expected, for the door opened as he came up the steps. Rosamond stood back and shut it behind him. She had a little colour in her cheeks and her eyes were bright. There was no formal greeting. Her breath came rather quickly as she said.

"Did you meet Aunt Lydia? She has only just gone."

"I didn't expect to see her walking."

"Didn't you?"

"I did not. The time I saw her she looked as if she had been sitting in that chair of hers for the last fifty years or so."

She tried for a reproving look, but it turned into an appealing one.

"Oh, yes, she walks when she wants to. She has only gone as far as Mrs Merridew's today — just opposite the Holly Tree."

"I know — I saw her go in. The wretched Cunningham came round the corner, and she cut him dead."

"She does," said Rosamond in a distressed voice. "I don't know how she can. Everybody else minds dreadfully. She just looks right through him and walks on."

"A very fine dead cut. He's been back how long — three years? He must be getting used to it by now. By the way, what about Miss Cunningham — does she cut her too?"

"Oh, no. They go on being friends, only Aunt Lydia won't go to the house, because of meeting Henry. Lucy comes here, and so does Nicholas."

"So Jenny informed me. She said Nicholas was in love with you."

Her colour rose faintly.

"Jenny talks too much."

"And it's all nonsense — I know, I know. Are you in love with him?"

"Craig!"

He laughed.

"Outrageous, isn't it? Don't hold it up against me. Everything in this house is either dead or half asleep, and I've got an idea that I'd like to wake things up. Don't let's talk about Nicholas any more. When am I going to see you alone?"

The corners of her mouth tilted.

"Well, you are seeing me alone, aren't you?"

He laughed derisively.

"Not by a long chalk I'm not! Ancestors to the left of us, ancestors to the right! You have really some of the gloomiest family portraits I've ever seen in my life!"

"They want cleaning."

"They might be worse if you could really see them. By the way, isn't there one of Miss Crewe? I'd rather like to see it."

"Would you? It's in the drawing room. We can go there if you like."

They went. Rosamond was wondering. Perhaps he really wanted to see the portrait. It was by Amory, and considered to be very fine. Perhaps he wanted to spin out this time with her. Her colour brightened as she opened the door and took him into a well-proportioned room with windows to a terrace and all the furniture done up in dustsheets. Craig was instantly and disagreeably reminded of a mortuary. The air was heavy and cold, the room full of dead things in their shrouds. There was a gilt clock on the mantelpiece, and some china figures. Above them the portrait of Lydia Crewe in a white satin dress. She held a black feather fan, and she looked out across the sheeted room. Her face was colourless, dominant. It had a kind of stiff beauty like a conventionalized flower — one of the heavy hot-house type, camellia or magnolia, carved in stone. There was a black velvet curtain behind her, and a diamond star at her breast. The shadows in the painted dress were a curious greenish grey.

Craig looked, frowning.

"How old was she when this was done?"

"I don't know — about thirty, I suppose. Not much more, because her father was ill after that, and there wasn't any more money."

"You mean, she found out that there wasn't. It must have been a shock."

He thought Lydia Crewe would have taken it hard. He said abruptly, "I suppose you have to dust this damned room too."

"A lot of the things in here have been put away."

He dropped his hands on her shoulders.

"Do you want to stay here till you freeze to death like she did?"

She let her eyes meet his, but only for a moment. There was trouble in them.

"There's Jenny. I'm not trained for anything. I've got to think of Jenny."

He said, "Think about me for a change. Start now and keep right on. I'm thirty-two and sound in wind and limb. I'm not rolling in money, but I've got a decent job, and my last book did quite well."

"Craig —" Her voice shook.

"You'd better listen to what I've got to say. I've got a temper, and I can be a brute when it's roused, but I don't suppose I should beat you. You might do a lot better, but you might do a lot worse too. I wouldn't actually knock you about, and I'd be good for Jenny. I've got a house — an old cousin left it to me last year. It's not at all bad. In fact I think you'd like it. My old nurse keeps house for me. She's a comfortable person. I don't want you to say anything now — I'm not such a fool as to expect you to make up your mind before you've known me a week."

Rosamond had a quite extraordinary feeling that they had somehow got into one of those dreams in which you just say anything that comes into your head and it doesn't matter. She said, "You've only known me for a week too."

His hands were warm and very strong. He laughed and said, "That's where you're wrong, my sweet. I've known you much longer than that. I don't know whether Jenny did it on purpose or not, but there was a photograph of you with the manuscripts she sent us. It was a snapshot. You had on a white dress, and you were carrying a tray. Even in the photograph I could see it was too heavy for you."

"Nicholas said so too — he took the photograph. It was all nonsense really."

"And what was Nicholas doing that he was letting you carry trays like that?"

His voice was too harsh for a dream. Something in her began to shake.

"Craig, let me go!"

"In a minute, when you've promised to think about what I've been saying."

"What am I to think about? It doesn't seem real."

"Oh, it's real enough. I'm not asking you to marry me, because it's too soon. I'm just telling you that that is what I'm going to do as soon as you know me better. I don't want to rush you. Just think it out. I don't see that I could possibly be worse to live with than Aunt Lydia, and I might be quite a lot better. I'd take care of you, my dear. It seems to me you want someone who will do that. And now I'm going to make you angry."

Before she had any idea what he was going to do he put a hand under her chin and kissed her. It was over before she realized that it was going to happen. And she wasn't angry. There was nothing to be angry about. He had kissed her because he loved her. She felt quite sure about that, and it made her feel safe.

He let go of her at once and walked to the door.

CHAPTER
ELEVEN

They went down the passage towards Jenny's room. Craig was aware of a release from tension. Imagination played its tricks, and he thought he would have known that Lydia Crewe was no longer behind that closed door on the left, even if he had not seen her turn in at the White Cottage. There was, of course, the fact Rosamond knew the room was empty. He became aware of how continually she was on the stretch, waiting for an imperious bell to summon her. With Miss Crewe out of the house, she was different — less at the mercy of a rigid code, less shut away from him. And as far as he could judge she wasn't angry. He had kissed her, and she wasn't angry.

She walked beside him in a silence which seemed natural to both of them. There was so much between them that was unsaid because the time had not come to say it, but both of them knew that the time would come when it would be said. Just short of Jenny's door the sound of voices came to them. She was a step ahead. Without turning she said,

"Oh, I didn't tell you, did I? Nicholas is here. I've wanted you to meet him."

Something in him was angry, and something laughed. She would, would she? Of course it was Sunday and the fellow wouldn't be working. What a nice interesting tea party they were going to have!

He followed Rosamond into the room, and saw Jenny laughing with a young man who looked like a film star. The comparison was there in his mind, and then he wondered why. Nicholas Cunningham was good-looking, but so are a lot of other people who are not film stars. His fair hair had a wave in it, but to do him justice, it looked as if he had tried to brush it out. It wasn't his fault that his eyes were almost as blue as Jenny's. For the rest, he had a slight active figure, a ready smile, a pleasant voice, and an air of being very much at home. Upon which of these counts was he to be indicted? Craig didn't know, but the indictment was there. It seemed that any peg would do to hang it on.

It was Jenny who performed the introduction.

"Craig — Nicholas. Now you know each other, and we can have a party. The cakes are all here. And you're not going down for the tray, Rosamond, because Miss Holiday is still here, and she said she would bring it up as soon as we rang."

Rosamond said, "Oh, but she never does."

Jenny forgot to be grown-up. She giggled.

"She's making a simply dreadful favour of it. And she wouldn't if she wasn't dying to have a good look at Craig. She has always just missed him, and she had pretty well got to the point where she was going to demean herself and answer the front door bell, only Rosamond always beat her to it."

"Jenny!"

"Well, you did. And when I suggested she might bring up the tea she made a favour of it like I told you, but she was really as pleased as Punch."

Craig said, "Who is Miss Holiday, and why does she want to look at me?"

It appeared that of the two girls who came in by the day only Ivy really answered to that description. The other was Miss Holiday, a person of uncertain age and some pretensions. She was also unfortunately a good deal less competent than the bouncing Ivy, who was not yet seventeen. With all her rough and ready ways and the scrambling hurry with which she plunged china into boiling water and whisked it out again, Ivy according to Mrs Bolder didn't break above half what Miss Holiday did. "And how she does it, Miss Rosamond, I couldn't say. Not that she hurries herself, for she's the slowest ever I watched. She just doesn't seem to have any grip in her fingers. So if you did feel you could take on the china for Miss Crewe's trays there'd be more of it left, if you see what I mean."

Jenny mimicked all this with a will. She looked down her nose and said, "Another of the Minton plates!" in Aunt Lydia's harshest voice, and had got to Miss Holiday explaining limply that of course a thing like washing-up wasn't what she had been accustomed to, when there was a bump against the door and Nicholas sprang to open it. Miss Holiday stood there with a small tray upon which were five odd cups, a brown earthenware milk jug, and a large flowered teapot with a broken spout. She was a thin person with a poke, and she appeared to sustain the tray with difficulty. It tilted, and Nicholas took it from her and set it down in front of Rosamond.

Miss Holiday had a good sideways stare at Craig Lester. She thought he was a fine-looking gentleman. She liked a big man herself, and he would make two of Nicholas Cunningham. Not but what the girls thought a lot of Mr Nicholas. Enough to make anyone ashamed the way they ran after him. And all very well for him to come here smiling at Miss Rosamond the way he did, but she had seen him with her own eyes no later than last Wednesday night at the Odeon in Melbury with that flashy girl from the tobacconist's in Cross Street. Painted up to the nines and the best part of her salary on her back, if it wasn't the best part of *his*. And her head on his shoulder half the time — at least it was there when she came in and there when she went out, and nothing to say but what it had been there all the time. She did not sniff out loud, because she prided herself upon her manners, but she sniffed inwardly and mentally as Nicholas took the tray from her and set it down.

She took another look at Mr Lester. Since he was a man, he wouldn't be what you could really approve of, but for the moment she preferred him to Nicholas Cunningham. Of course it went without saying that there would be something wrong somewhere. Her own sense of superiority was largely maintained by the contemplation of other people's faults.

She was so much interested in her own thoughts that it simply did not occur to her to retreat. She stood where she was, just inside the door, in the limp faded overall which rather failed to cover a green stuff dress, a row of bright blue beads about her stringy neck, her mouth a little open and her light eyes goggling at Craig. She was imagining him in a Western, galloping down on one of those horses they had in the films and snatching you up just before the Indians got you, when Rosamond's voice broke in upon the pleasant dream.

"Thank you very much, Miss Holiday."

She went away with regret, and forgot to shut the door.

When Nicholas had rectified the omission he said in an exasperated voice, "That woman is barmy. She'll burn you all in your beds one of these days."

Jenny laughed pertly.

"She isn't here when we're in our beds — at least I might be in mine. And I don't know about Aunt Lydia, but Rosamond wouldn't be in hers. She doesn't get a chance, poor lamb. The girls" — she went off into a fresh peal — "fancy calling Miss Holiday a girl! Anyhow they go off at eight sharp, and Ivy doesn't come on Sundays at all, but Miss Holiday rather likes to because of getting lunch and tea." She mimicked again, and had the dragging voice to the life. "As long as it is quite understood that there is no *obligation*, Miss Maxwell."

Craig handed her a cup of tea. Rosamond said, "Jenny darling!" But Nicholas laughed and put a plateful of Mrs Bolder's sugar buns down on her lap.

"Eat, my child, and give your elders a chance to talk," he said, and had the satisfaction of seeing the angry colour run up to the roots of her hair.

Miss Holiday did not immediately return to the housekeeper's room. Mrs Bolder would not make the tea until she returned, and since she was in a pleased frame of mind, it occurred to her to make up Miss Crewe's fire before she went downstairs. She would not have admitted that there was some curiosity mixed up with the goodwill, but it is a fact that she had never yet been alone in the room. She had, in fact, hardly ever been into it at all. It was Miss Maxwell who hoovered the carpet and dusted all those innumerable ornaments. If there was one thing more than another for which Miss Holiday was thankful, it was that she didn't have to handle that china and Miss Crewe watching her all the time like a cat with a mouse. She wasn't often sorry for other people — she'd had her own troubles, hadn't she? — but there were times when she could find it in her heart to be sorry for Rosamond Maxwell.

She came into the room, leaving the door ajar behind her. It was still daylight, but the corners were full of shadows. She switched on the light in the chandelier and almost cried out at the sudden brightness. It made her blink and look over her shoulder. Suppose anyone was to come in! Well, she had to have a light, hadn't she, if she was going to see to the fire? She went over to it and knelt down. It didn't really need anything doing to it, but she wasn't to know that. There was a silly little set of andirons hanging on a stand to the right of the hearth. Just one more thing to clean. Nobody had them nowadays — only Miss Crewe. If there was anything in the world that made work, it was brass. And look what it did to your hands!

One of the things on the stand was an ornamental brush. You could tell it wasn't meant to be used. Miss Holiday gave her head a toss. Whether it was, or whether it wasn't, she was going to use it, and no one was going to stop her. She whisked away a cinder and flicked at some imaginary dust. This gave her a feeling of superiority. Her nervousness at being alone in Miss Crewe's room had gone as she hung the brush up in its place and got to her feet. Now that she was here, she wasn't in any hurry to go. She walked all round the room, looking at the china and being glad all over again that she didn't have to dust it. She thought most of it very ugly, but there was a plate with birds on it that took her fancy. She was partial to birds. There was a row of them in a cabinet which she wouldn't have minded having if they had been going cheap in a sale. She'd have gone up to a pound if they had gone for that. There were six of them, in pairs like ornaments ought to be — two green, two yellow, and two with brown feathers and rosy breasts. She made the circuit of the room and went over to straighten the cushions in Miss Crewe's chair.

She didn't think she had ever got such a start in her life as when she heard the footsteps. Her hand went to her overall pocket and her mouth dropped open on a suppressed scream. And after all it was only Mrs Bolder come to see why in the world she hadn't come down to her tea. Not that she would have wanted to put Mrs

Bolder about like that, because she wouldn't, but who'd have thought of her coming through into the front like? Once a day to see Miss Crewe about the orders, but that was the beginning and end of it. To say that Mrs Bolder was put about was to draw it very mild indeed. She was a little woman with a high colour and a lot of grey hair, and everyone in Hazel Green knew about her temper. She stood in the doorway and looked at Miss Holiday as if she could do her a mischief.

"And what are you doing here?" she said. "Oh, you come in to see to the fire, did you? And Miss Crewe only gone out a half an hour! Coal burns quick enough, we all know that, but it don't burn as quick as that would come to. And you've no business in this room, as well you know, or you wouldn't have jumped like you did when I come in. And I'll thank you, Miss Holiday, to mind your own business and to let me get on with mine which was making the tea, and the kettle boiling over this quarter of an hour, and me wondering whether you'd been took with a stroke or fallen down somewhere in a fit."

Miss Holiday was moved to feeble protest.

"Fits *nor* strokes is not what we've ever had, not in our family," she said.

Her hands had gone into her overall pockets, but she could feel them trembling there. She went past Mrs Bolder, standing to see her out of the room, and heard the clap of the door as she followed her. She had been looking forward to her tea, because there was always a nice cake Sundays, but she wasn't

90

going to be able to enjoy it, not if she had to eat it with temper sauce. She went meekly down the passage, and across the hall, and through the baize door with Mrs Bolder's tongue driving her.

CHAPTER
TWELVE

It was about half an hour later that Miss Lucy Cunningham joined the tea party in Jenny's room, coming in by the side door without troubling anyone to answer it, as she had done for the last thirty years. Since she never left the house without preparing for rain, she wore a man's waterproof over her winter coat and carried a stout umbrella.

"Well, here I am," she said, "and better late than never, but I do like to give Henry his tea. And then I thought I would just drop in and have a word with Mrs Stubbs about the broody hen she has promised me. My crossed birds won't sit. But I won't have that light Sussex she lent me last year — a most contrary bird, and I lost half the chicks. I thought I'd just make sure I didn't get her again, so I went down to the Holly Tree and came along by the road. How do you do, Mr Lester? You are at the Holly Tree, are you not? I think my brother met you there. I hope Mrs Stubbs makes you comfortable — but I needn't ask, she always does." She dropped the hand which she had been shaking and addressed the room in general. "Now don't let me go away without my umbrella. Perhaps I had better keep it by me. But you can take my waterproof, Nicholas. And yes, perhaps the coat too. It's really quite dreadfully hot in here. Much better for Jenny to have the windows open. There isn't any tonic like fresh air. How are you Rosamond? You look peaky. You should take yoghourt three times a day — there's nothing like it. And no trouble at all — you just set the milk and let it turn sour . . . Yes, you can take this scarf — I shan't want it in here."

Divested of successive layers of clothing, she appeared a good deal less bulky, though still more than comfortably plump. Yoghourt or no yoghourt, she made an excellent tea, and continued to talk in a rapid discursive manner whilst partaking of buttered scone, fruit cake, and Mrs Bolder's own particular tea biscuits, which were the subject of a keen rivalry with Florrie Hunt. Lucy Cunningham had been trying to get the recipe for thirty years, and if she tried for another thirty she would still be wasting her time. Mrs Bolder was one that kept herself to herself, and the recipe for her biscuits would go to no one but her own flesh and blood, and not to them whilst there was breath in her body. For the moment Miss Cunningham left well alone. She continued to press the claims of sour milk upon Rosamond and Jenny, together with black treacle and a horrible mixture of milk and brewer's yeast.

Nicholas burst out laughing.

"I should have thought dieting would begin at home. You don't take any of these things yourself, and thank heaven you know better than to inflict them on your family."

Miss Lucy's round blue eyes had quite a hurt expression.

"But, my dear, I don't need them. I dare say I might become slimmer, but if you feel well you feel well, and what do a few pounds matter when all is said and done?"

Jenny giggled.

"But Rosamond and I don't want to lose any pounds. We're always being told we ought to put them on."

"Oh, but you would, my dear, I'm sure. You wouldn't be *slimming*, and you could have cream and butter and eggs, and even suet pudding if you wanted to."

"I shouldn't want to if I had black treacle and that sour milk stuff," said Jenny. "I shouldn't want anything for hours and hours and hours. I expect that's why you get slim."

Rosamond moved across until she was between Jenny and Lucy Cunningham. That was the worst of parties, Jenny got all worked up and began to show off. She did not know that the look she sent to Craig Lester was one of appeal, but as she began to talk to Lucy about hens she could hear him asking Nicholas whether he had seen a play which had set everyone laughing in town. He embarked on an amusing description of it for what was obviously Jenny's benefit, and soon had her laughing too.

The hens petered out after a little. Miss Cunningham looked at her watch.

"I would have liked to see Lydia. I suppose she won't be late?"

"Oh, no."

"It is not as if she has any distance to go. Henry saw her turn in at the White Cottage."

"So did I," said Craig Lester, and then felt that perhaps he had better have held his tongue.

Miss Lucy said, "Oh, dear!" in a tone which made it plain that she knew all about the meeting with Henry Cunningham. She made a little vexed sound, and began to praise Mrs Bolder's biscuits and to sound Rosamond as to the likelihood of her being persuaded to part with the recipe.

"I wouldn't dare ask her — I really wouldn't."

"Faint heart never won fair biscuit!" said Nicholas, laughing. "You all tremble before her, and she knows it. Rosamond is the worst of the lot."

Rosamond laughed too, but on a rueful note.

"Well, she's got a very daunting piece about being only a poor widow so of course anyone can trample on her, and once she has got started on it you simply can't stop her and every relation she has ever lost comes into it. It goes on for about half an hour and by the time it's over you feel as if it was all your fault."

Nicholas threw her a kiss.

"My sweet, you're a spineless worm! And she tramples accordingly!"

Lucy Cunningham shook her head.

"It doesn't do to have rows, and she's a very good cook."

"Aunt Lucy's a peace-at-any-pricer! She'd give in to anything rather than have a row — wouldn't you, Lu?"

"Nicholas, how often am I to tell you —"

"That you won't have that silly, undignified nickname? Well, I don't know, darling — it just depends. We might go into a huddle and arrive at a compromise — say once a day as a rule, and twice on high days and holidays."

She broke into an unwilling smile. Jenny said in a considering voice, "People don't call you silly names unless they are fond of you, and if you managed to stop them, perhaps they wouldn't be fond of you any more, so I suppose it's really better to put up with it. I'd much, much rather be called Jennifer, only nobody will."

"Well, I should go the whole hog and stick out for Guinevere," said Nicholas. "It's the same name and much more high-sounding."

Jenny was obviously taken with the idea.

"Yes, it is, isn't it!"

"Of course you would have to braid your hair into two long plaits and wear a wimple."

Her colour flamed.

"You're just laughing at me!"

"I wouldn't dare."

The angry tears were in her eyes. Her voice rose high.

"You're doing it — you're doing it all the time!"

Rosamond's soft "Jenny!" and Miss Lucy's "Nicholas, dear, don't tease her!" were lost in the sudden opening of the door. Craig Lester looked across at it and saw Lydia Crewe standing there, very tall and black. She waited for the hush that fell upon the room, and said in a most forbidding voice, "You were all making a great

96

deal of noise. Especially Jenny. Were you engaged in some game? How do you do, Lucy? How do you do, Mr Lester. Nicholas?" Her eyebrows rose. "Quite a party! I hope I am not intruding."

The two men were on their feet, Nicholas with his agreeable smile unchanged. But it was Rosamond who spoke.

"Can I get you some tea, Aunt Lydia?"

Miss Crewe surveyed the old papier mâché tray, the teapot with its broken spout, the odd cups and saucers.

"Your tea equipage is hardly worthy of the occasion, Rosamond. Am I to suppose that we no longer have five cups which match one another? And I seem to remember a silver teapot. It had at least the virtue of being unbreakable, and on that score alone I should like to commend it. Appearances naturally do not matter any longer, but from the most utilitarian standpoint that broken spout must waste a good deal of tea."

Jenny had a bright spot of colour on either cheek. She said in a high childish voice, "It hadn't anything to do with Rosamond. Miss Holiday brought up the tray."

Miss Crewe addressed Craig Lester in a condescending manner.

"One of our kitchen helps, and as you see, a very inefficient one. She had, of course, no business to leave the back premises. Rosamond will see that it does not occur again." She was aware of Miss Cunningham getting to her feet, a performance accompanied by some effort. "You are not going, Lucy?"

Lucy Cunningham flushed. She did not like rows, but Lydia being sarcastic was even worse. She said, "Well, I think I'd better. I really didn't come to tea — I just looked in to have a word with you. If you can spare the time. But I had better collect all my things first. Now let me see — what did I have? A scarf — no, two, because you can't tell what the wind is like until you are out in it, can you?"

Lydia Crewe said scornfully, "You coddle yourself, Lucy. The more clothes you wear, the more you will feel the cold. I've been telling you that for years."

Miss Cunningham arranged the two scarves carefully about her neck, assumed her thick tweed coat, and thrust her arms into the sleeves of the voluminous waterproof.

"I like to be warm," she said briefly. And then, "Thank you, Mr Lester. Now is that all? No, no, my umbrella — I mustn't forget my umbrella!"

As Craig handed it to her on one side, Nicholas retrieved a bulging handbag and offered it on the other.

"There you are — all complete! At least I hope so. No other unconsidered trifles? All right, I'll be seeing you."

"If you are quite ready, Lucy —" said Lydia Crewe.

CHAPTER
THIRTEEN

The hours of Sunday passed. The church bells rang. Miss Silver and Mrs Merridew attended the evening service. There were very few people there. The Vicar's wife played the organ, a memorial to the fallen in the first world war. The Vicar raised a robust baritone in the psalms and canticles, the District Nurse sustained a rather uncertain soprano. The old, beautiful words hung in the cold, close air. The church had been old when the Wars of the Roses were fought. There were the tombs of two Crusaders, one with his legs crossed at the knees to show that he had ridden out on his pious errand twice. There were worn brasses and a clutter of monuments. It came into Miss Silver's mind that the dead were better represented than the living. When they had prayed that the darkness might be lightened, and to be defended from the perils and dangers of the night, the Vicar went up into the pulpit and preached for five minutes on the duty of loving one's neighbour as oneself. He had a vigorous, resonant voice, and he said that the world would be a much nicer place to live in if we all took a little more trouble about being kind. After which they sang *Sun of my Soul*, and came out into the windy dark.

Florrie Hunt had Sunday afternoon and evening off, so the two ladies prepared their own supper and washed up after it. Peaceful hours slipping by with nothing to mark them, a peaceful village setting to its Sunday rest, church bells and evensong, Sunday supper, a quiet hour or two by the fireside, a little talk, a pleasant book, music to be summoned with the turning of a knob, and then goodnights exchanged and a leisurely preparation for bed.

But within a stone's throw of the White Cottage there was a bed that was not slept in that Sunday night.

Florrie came in with the news at eight o'clock on Monday morning. She set a tray down on the table by Mrs Merridew's bed and said in her gloomiest tones, "Miss Holiday never come home last night, *nor* her bed wasn't slept in."

Mrs Merridew blinked.

"Florrie, what do you mean?"

Florrie swished the curtains back, and Mrs Merridew blinked again, at the light this time. Very cold and grey, and not at all the sort of thing you wanted to look at if something unpleasant had happened. That cold light showed Florrie in a flowered overall, very clean but a good deal faded. Even though the colours were not as bright as they had been, they did not go at all well with what was by no means a shining morning face. Lank black hair drawn back above sallow bony features, pale thin lips, and a set expression, were not flattered by the pinks and blues and greens of what had once been a gay summery pattern. There were four curtains, and it wasn't till they had all been drawn that Florrie repeated what she had said.

"She didn't come home, and she didn't sleep in her bed. Mrs Maple is in a terrible taking. Says she's never known her to be out of her usual before — and that would be nine o'clock if it wasn't for the evenings she'd go over to Melbury for the pictures and come back on that last bus, and then she'd always let her know beforehand and Mrs Maple would let her have the key so as not to be kept about."

There was at this juncture a slight tap upon the half open door. It was followed by the entrance of Miss Silver in the warm blue dressing-gown which had replaced the crimson one long worn and only parted with when it had begun to show serious signs of dilapidation. The hand-made crochet trimming with which it had been adorned had been very successfully transferred to the new gown, and her niece Dorothy's gift of a pair of black felt slippers trimmed with blue pompoms completed a most comfortable outfit. Her hair, neatly coiled, was confined by a strong silk net. Her expression was one of concern.

"My dear Marian — has anything happened? I was on my way to the bathroom, and I could not help hearing . . ."

Florrie's usual reserve had been shaken. She repeated her story for the third time, and with some added details.

"Mrs Maple — she thought she was in," she addressed herself to Miss Silver. "She's that deaf she wouldn't hear, and it being gone half past nine, she never thought anything but that Miss Holiday had come in and gone up without speaking, which is what she's done time and again, it being a job to make Mrs Maple hear and nothing particular to say except goodnight. Anyway, it's all of ten years Miss Holiday has been lodging there, and that's how it's been. But come this morning when Mrs Maple gets up and there isn't any sign of her she goes knocking on her door, and when that doesn't fetch her out she turns the handle and goes in, and there's the bed not slept in, and not a sign of Miss Holiday having been near it."

Mrs Merridew said, "Oh dear!" And then, "Oh, Florrie — she can't just have disappeared!"

Florrie said what she wouldn't have dreamed of saying if she hadn't been shaken out of her usual discretion.

"That's what everyone said about Maggie, isn't it? And where is she? Walked out of the house no later than eight o'clock in the evening a year ago and never come back."

Mrs Merridew found herself explaining to Miss Silver.

"She was Florrie's cousin, Maggie Bell, and it was just as she says. She lived with her parents in the cottage with the rose arch over the gate, and she worked by the day for Lucy Cunningham. And she went out one evening and never came back. She had been ironing, and she said she wanted a breath of air."

Florrie tossed her head.

"And that was just a manner of speaking! The old people were that jealous of her going anywhere, she'd

102

be obliged to have something to say like that. And she'd run in to me and get a bit of a change without having words about it."

Mrs Merridew reached behind her for the shawl which she wore when she sat up in bed.

"I didn't know she was coming round to you, Florrie."

Florrie looked angry.

"I didn't know it myself! She'd come when she wanted to and welcome!"

"Did you ever tell the police about this?"

"They didn't ask me. Made up their minds she'd gone off to London. I could have told them better than that, but they had their own ideas. The old people were tiresome enough — I'm not saying they weren't — but Maggie wasn't the one to run off and leave them. I'd say that, no matter who said different. And as to that postcard that come down from London, well, I can tell you right away, Maggie never wrote it."

Miss Silver had been listening with the deepest interest. It was not necessary for her to speak, since without any prompting on her part Marian Merridew was asking all the right questions, and how much better that she herself should not appear to be too much concerned.

Florrie's last statement produced a cry of surprise from Mrs Merridew.

"Oh, Florrie, you've never said that before!"

Florrie's left shoulder jerked.

"Least said, soonest mended," she said. And then, in an accusing voice, "And what good will it do my saying anything? They didn't ask me for one thing, and I didn't want to get mixed up with the police for another. Nor I don't know, so we won't go on talking about it!"

"But, Florrie, you must have had some reason."

"Reason enough and to spare, but none for talking about!"

Mrs Merridew's large fair face fell into lines of indecision. Even the pressure of Miss Silver's hand upon her arm failed to produce a further question.

Florrie had turned to leave the room, when a slight cough stopped her. It was immediately followed by the sound of her name.

"I mustn't take up your time, and I can quite understand that the subject is a painful one, but if as you say, there has been a second disappearance, then the trouble may not even stop there. There may be others who are in danger."

Florrie stared, and said in an obstinate voice,

"I've said enough. Maybe I've said too much."

Miss Silver said gently, "You have said that your cousin Maggie did not write the postcard which came from London. You saw it of course?"

"Yes, I saw it."

"It said, did it not, that she would come back as soon as she could, and that you would come in and help her parents?"

Florrie's face darkened.

"Who told you that?"

There was something in Miss Silver's look which was asking her to speak. She resisted it. There was something in her voice which put her in mind of not knowing her answer in school and the teacher making it easy for her. She resisted this too, but with a lessening force. Before the encouraging smile which followed she no longer wanted to resist at all. She felt instead the impulse to clear her mind of the thoughts which had burdened it for so long. It became easier to speak than to hold back. When Miss Silver said, "What made you think the card was not from Maggie?" she said in a different voice, "It was because of the way the names were spelt. Maggie wasn't any scholar, but we went to school together, and what she would always put on her exercise-book was Maggy — written with a Y. And the same with my name too. She hadn't much call to write it, but if she did she'd spell it with a Y like she did her own. And the names on the card was both spelt out long with an IE at the end of them and not a Y, so I knew it wasn't Maggie that wrote them."

Mrs Merridew looked shocked. This time the pressure on her arm counselled silence. Miss Silver said quietly, "Maggie's parents showed you the card. Did you point out to them that the names were not spelled as she would have spelled them?"

Florrie said, "No." She was twisting her hands together, and they were shaking.

"Why did you not do so?"

Florrie caught her breath.

"They were taking on — bad enough — without. As it was, I could see they wouldn't get over it — Maggie being all they had, and never away from them except just to go up the road to Miss Cunningham's. So I thought — so I thought —" She broke into a hard sob.

"They'd enough, hadn't they — and the card was a bit of comfort — I hadn't the heart to go taking it away —"

Mrs Merridew said, "Oh dear! But you should have told the police — you really should."

Florrie flung up her head.

"And how long would it have been before they came worrying my aunt and uncle? I kept it, and I wouldn't forgive myself if I hadn't! And I don't know what made me speak of it, but they're both gone now, and I suppose it don't matter. All I know is, Maggie wouldn't have gone off like that, and no more would Miss Holiday. They hadn't got a boyfriend, neither of them, and that's gospel. Maggie was two years older than what I am, and Miss Holiday isn't ever going to see fifty again. And not the dressy sort, nor the sort that's out to get a man, no matter how. Maggie couldn't be bothered with them what with the dirt they bring into the house and the work they make. And her father the old bully he was — well, the way she saw it, you can't get away from the relations you're born with, but to go and tie yourself up with a husband is clean flying in the face of Providence. And as for Miss Holiday, men just scared her stiff. Why, she wouldn't go to work in a house where there was a gentleman. Wouldn't go down the lane to see Mrs Selby that she'd taken a fancy to and that was always asking her in — wouldn't even go down to her except when she knew Mr Selby would be out of the way. Not quite the gentleman of course, no more than Mrs Selby is what you'd call a lady, but not the

106

kind anyone would be afraid of if it wasn't Miss Holiday."

Mrs Merridew said, "The Selbys live down at the end of the Vicarage lane. He is a retired businessman. They have a great many hens, and he goes and plays darts at the Holly Tree every night. He is a very sociable, friendly kind of person, but I think she finds it lonely in the evenings when he is out. I didn't know that Miss Holiday went there so much."

Florrie had come back to her usual manner. She said briskly, "Well, I don't know about so much. She'd go in there now and again when he was at the Holly Tree, but go before he went or stay after he came back was what she wouldn't do and nothing would make her. And if she'd feel like that about Mr Selby she wouldn't be likely to pick up with any strange man, nor he wouldn't be likely to want to pick up with her, for if anyone was the moral of an old maid, it was her, poor thing."

Mrs Merridew pulled her shawl closer about her and began to pour out. Births, and deaths, and disappearances were things that happened, but it didn't help anyone to let a good pot of tea get stewed. She filled two cups and said in a determinedly cheerful voice,

"Well, Florrie, we must hope for the best."

CHAPTER
FOURTEEN

Miss Holiday had no relations — at least there were none that anyone had ever heard of. She had been personal maid to old Lady Rowena Thorne, who had allowed her, so everyone declared, to get into dreadfully muddly ways. But then Lady Rowena was a dreadfully muddly old thing who looked like a ragbag and lived in a cottage full of clutter and cats. There was very little money, and out of what there was she left Miss Holiday an annuity of fifty pounds a year, since when she had lodged with Mrs Maple and gone out to work by the day but never staying anywhere for long. She was, in fact, too incompetent to be tolerated except in a case where there was no one else to be had. All this, which was common knowledge, Mrs Merridew imparted to her guest.

Having become aware of Miss Silver's professional activities through the mutual friend in whose house they had met after so many years, she readily acceded to a request that she should not speak of them. Since she had from the time of her marriage been a person of some consequence in the county, she was in fact rather more than willing to give the desired pledge. Detection did not appear to her to be at all a suitable career for a gentlewoman, and she had no wish that it should be obtruded. At the same time, with poor Miss Holiday disappearing like this, she found herself discussing the affair in a very interested manner, deferring to Miss Silver's opinion as to an expert, and very ready to communicate any particulars which might prove helpful.

Florrie went grimly about her work and contributed nothing more, except to remark in tones of gloom that those that hadn't turned up by now wasn't going to, and no use saying any different. Mrs Maple was understood to be of the same opinion, and was already beginning to turn over in her mind the rival merits of two prospective lodgers.

The Melbury police, to whom the disappearance had been reported, had sent over a constable to make inquiries, but rumour had it that he had found it quite impossible to induce Mrs Maple to hear his questions. It being well known in the village that she didn't hold with the police and could at any time be as deaf as she chose, nobody was surprised. It was, in fact, considered that Constable Denning had taken an unfair advantage by submitting a set of questions in writing and Mrs Maple's defensive action in mislaying her glasses and declaring that she couldn't read a word without them was warmly approved.

Meanwhile there was quite a lot going on behind the scenes. There were consultations on a gradually ascending scale, arriving ultimately at what are termed higher levels. Never could Miss Holiday have supposed that she would be the subject of so much speculation and interest. Hazel Green communicated with Melbury, and Melbury with the Chief Constable of Melshire, who got busy with Scotland Yard and with the Security people. The affair might be negligible or it might not — it might be of the utmost importance. But there must be no publicity, no headlines in the press. The greatest discretion must be observed. Hazel Green might buzz with gossip and come to its own gloomy conclusions, but, at any rate for the present, the official attitude must be that it was a purely local matter, and that Miss Holiday had probably taken it into her head to go off and visit a friend.

The village did not take kindly to this theory. Mrs Stubbs spoke for everyone when she inquired with a toss of the head, "And what friends has she got, poor thing? None that ever I heard tell about, nor anyone else either! In to Melbury for the pictures and back again, that's all the outings she ever had — and she wouldn't go there of a Sunday. And if she went anywhere by bus, someone would have seen her, wouldn't they? As to getting a lift in a car, well, anyone that knew her wouldn't talk so silly — she'd have been frightened to death!"

Craig Lester had got a little tired of the subject by the time he set out for Crewe House. With the church clock striking four as he went up the road, he could make sure of being on hand to walk back again with Rosamond, who like himself had been bidden to tea at the White Cottage.

Since none of the windows commanded the drive, which, to tell the truth, was a good deal overgrown, it

110

was his intention to remain in its shelter until Rosamond appeared. As he waited he thought how badly the whole place needed attention. Trees and shrubs crowded one another in a struggle for light and air. The undergrowth was a mere tangle. The leaves of many seasons lay rotting where they had fallen. Moisture dripped upon them from above, though there had been no rain since lunch. A grey sky and more rain to come. Damp air moving overhead.

Rosamond came into view, hurrying a little because Lydia Crewe had rung her bell just as she was starting. She wore an old tweed coat and a blue scarf over the dark clusters of her hair. It brought up the blue in her eyes. She was almost running, but when she saw him she slowed to a walk.

"Oh — I'm going out!"

"To tea with Mrs Merridew? So am I. I thought I would walk down with you. If you hadn't any real objection."

She gave him a wide friendly smile.

"How nice of you. But we ought to hurry, because I think I'm late. Aunt Lydia wanted me."

"What for?"

"Oh, just — something she wanted. It didn't take long, but I had run it rather fine talking to Jenny."

He said deliberately, "They are both quite good at seeing you don't get too much time off, aren't they? If one of them isn't holding on to you, the other is. You know, you're going to make Jenny just as selfish and exigeante as Miss Crewe if you're not careful."

"Craig!"

"Well, it's true, isn't it?"

She said in a protesting voice, "She has been so ill. They thought she was going to die."

"Well, they don't think so any longer. Wake up, Rosamond, and use your common sense! You know as well as I do that Jenny isn't leading a normal life, and she could —" He paused and added, "*now*."

He saw the startled colour rise as she turned towards him.

"What do you mean?"

"You know very well. She is too much with grown-ups and with books. She ought to be learning and playing with children of her own age."

She opened her lips to speak, but the words didn't come. He slipped a hand inside her arm.

"All right — go on and say it. It's not so easy to think of Jenny as a child — that's what you were going to say, wasn't it? And you stopped yourself because it gave your case away. As a matter of fact, my sweet, you haven't got a case, and it's no use your trying to cook one up. Neither you nor Jenny has any business to be at Crewe House, and you know it."

She still had that startled look, but there was anger as well.

"You want to send Jenny to school, and you want to get me away from here!"

"I certainly do. And I certainly think that Jenny would be better at school."

"She isn't nearly strong enough."

Another turn of the drive and they would be within sight of the road. Instinctively she stopped.

112

"Craig, you mustn't — you mustn't really! Don't you know it's what Aunt Lydia wants — to get rid of Jenny, so that I can do more, and more, and more for her and for the house?"

He said coolly, "It may be what she means, but it isn't what is going to happen. You give her a month to find someone else, and then you marry me, and you take Jenny away. After which we decide what is the best kind of school for her."

"She isn't fit for it."

At least she hadn't said that she would not marry him. Perhaps she had merely overlooked his assumption that she would. He left the point to be settled later.

He said, "Has it occurred to you that Jenny can walk a great deal better than she makes out?"

She pulled away from him.

"No, of course it hasn't!"

"Well, it has to me. As a plain matter of fact she limps when you are there, and she doesn't when you are out of the room."

Her eyes were bright and angry.

"She is proud and sensitive. She doesn't like to let a stranger see her limp."

"Rubbish! She puts on an act for you, and she doesn't bother about it for me."

"Why should she?"

"Oh, she has to outbid Aunt Lydia."

"Craig!"

"When did the specialist see her last?"

"Two months ago."

"Did he say she could walk?"

"Well —"

"I see — he did. Did he want to see her again?"

"He said —" The words broke off.

"He didn't!"

She took a step away from him.

"It isn't only the limp. If she does too much — it hurts."

"Not very seriously, I think."

All her colour was gone. She said in a stranger's voice, "I think we had better stop talking about it. Mrs Merridew won't like it if we're late."

"I suppose not. Why don't you ask me why I've been saying all this?"

Something in his tone arrested her. The startled look returned. She said in a voice like an echo, "Why . . ."

Craig Lester said, "I think we must keep Mrs Merridew waiting whilst I tell you. I couldn't sleep last night — it's always fatal to start thinking after midnight. In the end I dressed, got out of one of the back windows, and went for a stroll. It was about a quarter past one. I walked up in this direction, and someone was getting over the stile just across the road from where the drive comes out. There was a car coming, and whoever it was stood still and waited for it to pass. As it came round that little bit of a bend, the lights picked up the hedge and the person standing there. Well, it was Jenny."

"Jenny? Oh, no!"

"Oh, yes, it was Jenny all right. There's no mistaking that hair. Besides I saw her face."

They both had the same picture — Jenny in the beam of the headlights, her bright hair glowing. Rosamond said on a gasp, "Craig, she looked — there was something different about her this morning. I couldn't think what it was — as if . . . as if . . . oh, I don't know. She must have been walking in her sleep."

He shook his head.

"Oh, no, she wasn't! Anything but! As soon as the car had gone by she laughed and came skipping across the road. Then she ran off up the drive. I followed at a discreet distance and saw her go in at the side door. When I heard her lock it I went back to the Holly Tree. But I thought you had better know."

"But why — why?"

"I imagine she slips out because she wants to walk and skip, and she doesn't want anyone to see her because she doesn't want to be packed off to school. I think it's quite simple. And there's no need for you to look as if the roof had just fallen in. It can be dealt with all right. And now perhaps we had better put our best foot forward and save our faces with Mrs Merridew."

CHAPTER
FIFTEEN

Mrs Merridew's drawing room suffered from the fault of all rooms which have been furnished with the treasures of a much larger one. There were a number of fine pieces, but no space to display them. There were too many pictures on the walls, a sizable antique mirror on the chimney breast, and a great deal too much china everywhere. The chairs and a very deep sofa, though much too large, were extremely comfortable, and the loose chintz covers, in spite of being a good deal faded, went very well with a worn but valuable Persian rug and the curtains which had once adorned the morning room at Dalling Grange.

Miss Silver considered the whole effect to be pleasing, and was particularly appreciative of the fact that the windows fitted extremely well. Old houses were often so sadly draughty, but in this case there was nothing to complain about. A pleasant fire burned on the hearth, and the room was so comfortably warm that she was able to wear the dress which she had bought at Clifton at the end of the previous summer. She had hesitated a little over the price, but her niece Ethel Burkett had persuaded her. "Such a good style, Auntie. I am sure you would never regret it." She wore it now with a large mosaic brooch representing an Italian scene — cupolas against a very bright blue sky. The material, being dark, threw up the vivid colouring of the brooch in a decidedly pleasing manner. She felt modestly satisfied with her own appearance, and wished that dear Marian would take more trouble. So much hair and so badly controlled, and her figure really too large for that tight mauve jumper. The colour too, not at all becoming, but Marian had always been fond of it, even at school.

Mrs Merridew who, having once acquired a garment, never thought about it again but continued to wear it until either Florrie or some candid friend intervened, was now discoursing placidly about the friends she was expecting to tea.

"Lucy Cunningham I feel sure you will like. She has had a difficult life, but she is wonderfully cheerful as a rule — devoted to her nephew and to poor Henry, and a good deal taken up with her hens. As I told you, she and Lydia Crewe are great friends, but I purposely didn't ask her yesterday, because Lydia does ride roughshod over everyone, and when she is there she doesn't give Lucy a chance. I asked Henry too. I always do, but he never comes. Such a pity to shut himself away like that — don't you think so?"

Miss Silver opined that men very often seemed not to care about tea parties.

"I know — but such a pity. There are so few ways left in which one can entertain. I really hesitated to ask Mr Lester, but he seemed quite pleased to come. As I told him, we knew his uncle very well indeed. And then, I'm afraid, I did just drop a hint that I had asked Rosamond Maxwell. They are certainly on very friendly terms, and Lydia may say what she likes, but when young people are on friendly terms they like to be asked to meet one another. It's really shocking how Lydia keeps that girl mewed up. I used to think that perhaps she and Nicholas — but of course there isn't any money there and Jenny needs so much care —" She broke off as the sound of footsteps and a murmur of conversation announced that two of the guests were coming up the flagged path to the front door. She had just time to say, "That will be Rosamond and Mr Lester. Lucy is always late," when Florrie opened the door and showed them in.

Rosamond had left her coat in the hall and taken off the scarf which had been tied over her hair. Her blue jumper threw up the colour of her eyes. Miss Silver thought her a most attractive girl. She also thought that she had something on her mind. It was, of course, quite obvious that Mr Lester was in love with her. He made no attempt to hide the fact. But in Miss Silver's opinion it was not the pleasing disturbance of a love affair which had brought that anxious look to Rosamond Maxwell's face.

Lucy Cunningham walked in without ringing the bell, a habit to which Florrie ought to have been accustomed, but which never failed to annoy her. She followed with an air of protest and set the tray down in front of Mrs Merridew with what was almost a clatter.

Miss Cunningham, having hung her largest coat on a peg in the hall, was now divesting herself of a voluminous cardigan and three scarves.

"I'm sure I don't know how you can sit in such a hot room, Marian, but I shall be all right when I get some of these things off. The temperature must be at least sixty-five. There — I'm down to my jumper! I made it myself, and Nicholas is very rude about it, but I like the colour — it reminds me of moss. Of course Henry never notices what one has on. Well, my dear Marian, I'm sorry if I am late, but just as I was putting on my hat I saw that dreadful cat of Mrs Parsons's sharpening its claws on the standard Alberic Barbier which Nicholas gave me for Christmas — one of those weeping ones, you know. So of course I had to go out and shoo him away! . . . Oh, yes, I've met Miss Silver. Don't you remember, you introduced us at the bus stop. How do you do? You and Marian were at school together, weren't you? So nice to meet one's old friends."

It was clear that when not held in check by Miss Crewe, Lucy Cunningham could be depended upon to keep any conversation from flagging. The broody hen which she had borrowed from Mrs Stubbs was settling down nicely with her clutch of eggs — "My own cross, Rhode Island Red and White Leghorn. Nothing like it!" And she actually discoursed for at least ten minutes upon its virtues whilst at the same time disposing of three scones and a slice of cake before Miss Holiday's name cropped up.

Rosamond was talking to Mrs Merridew, and Craig Lester was joining in, when Miss Lucy interrupted her own remarks about the very unsatisfactory eggs she had procured for setting last year — "Only three hatched out of the dozen, and I told her quite plainly that they were stale," to say with a sudden change of voice, "Oh dear, hasn't Miss Holiday turned up yet?"

Mrs Merridew shook her head. Rosamond said, "No, she hasn't. It's the most extraordinary thing. We can't think what has happened."

"Lydia must be dreadfully put out," said Lucy Cunningham.

It became clear that it was from this angle that she viewed the disappearance, the burden of her remarks being that of course Miss Holiday would turn up, but that meanwhile Lydia was being inconvenienced, and that if you had to go away in a hurry, the least you could do was to let your employer know.

"Only that's the last thing they ever think about. I suppose she didn't have words with Mrs Bolder? A wonderful cook, but oh, my dear, what a temper! It couldn't have been that, could it?"

Rosamond said reluctantly,

"I don't know — there may have been something. Mrs Bolder didn't seem so very much surprised when she didn't turn up this morning — just tossed her head and said something like 'Oh, she'll get over it'. So I thought perhaps — but that was before we knew about her not having been home all night."

Miss Cunningham nodded vigorously.

120

"Well, I dare say they'd had a tiff, but I don't suppose it amounted to anything. And she's been coming to you for some time — she ought to be used to Mrs Bolder by now. It can't be the first time she's had the rough side of her tongue. I can't imagine — I really can't — what could possibly have taken her away. When there's a family, of course, you never know, but she hasn't got a relation in the world — she often said so. And she was quite all right when I met her."

"Oh, when was that?" Rosamond and Mrs Merridew spoke together.

Miss Lucy beamed.

"When I was on my way up to you, my dear. You know I couldn't come to tea, and then I was later than I meant to be because of going in to see Mrs Stubbs about the broody hen, so it must have been all of half past five if not more — but I don't suppose that matters. She was just coming out of the drive as I turned in, and she seemed perfectly all right then."

Miss Silver regarded her with interest.

"Did you speak to her?" she inquired.

Miss Cunningham had a full cup in her hand. She had been about to drink from it when Miss Silver spoke. Somehow the cup slipped and some of the tea splashed down upon the moss-green jumper. Miss Lucy exclaimed, produced a large clean but extremely crumpled handkerchief, and proceeded to dab at the stain. Recourse was had to the hot water jug. Rosamond ran and fetched a tea-cloth. The overflowing saucer was emptied, the cup replaced, and the opinion expressed that no mark would be left on the bright green wool.

"A most unfortunate accident," said Miss Silver, "but I believe there will be no ill effects. Now, what were we talking about? Oh, yes that poor Miss Holiday. You had met her coming away from her work, and you said she seemed quite as usual. You spoke to her, then?"

"Oh, just a few words," said Lucy Cunningham.

CHAPTER
SIXTEEN

The tea party broke up rather early. Rosamond was uneasy about Jenny, and Lucy Cunningham about Mrs Parsons's cat.

"I did ask Henry to keep an eye on the garden, but you know what men are, they become immersed. And cats are so determined. If it wants to sharpen its claws on that particular tree it will persevere."

"Well, I don't see how you are going to stop it, my dear."

"A squirtful of water," said Miss Cunningham firmly. "If I get back now there will be just enough light."

When they had gone Mrs Merridew allowed herself a little indignation.

"I can't imagine why Lucy should expect the Parsons's cat to be sitting there waiting for her to come home and fill a squirt. It seems ridiculous to me, and I very nearly told her so. Dear me — who on earth can this be?"

She had been looking in the direction of the window to watch Miss Lucy go. She now saw a tall, elegant young man come up the flagged path and disappear behind the jasmine on the porch. Miss Silver had a premonition. She was therefore not really surprised when Florrie looked round the edge of the door, a habit of which Mrs Merridew had tried in vain to break her, and announced that Mr Abbott had called to see Miss Silver — "and I put him in the dining room." Had Frank but known it, this was an almost unexampled tribute. If Florrie knew anyone she showed him in. If she didn't she left him standing in the hall, or in an extreme case upon the doorstep. Mrs Merridew had laboured in vain. In this, as in a good many other directions, Florrie took her own way.

Miss Silver picked up her knitting-bag and made haste to forestall the invitation which she saw rising to Mrs Merridew's lips.

"An old friend who, I believe, may have called on a matter of business. You will not mind if I see him in the dining room, Marian?"

Mrs Merridew was disappointed. She would have liked to meet her schoolfellow's old friend. She said so as Miss Silver withdrew, but she was not at all sure that her remark had been heard. The door closed, and she was left to wonder what the old friend's business could be.

In the dining room Miss Silver took a chair. When Frank Abbott had also seated himself she said, "I must not stay too long, or my kind hostess will feel hurt. If you can spare the time before you go, I should like to introduce you. I did not really like to neglect her offer to bring you into the drawing room, but in the light of recent developments it occurred to me that you might wish to see me privately."

He nodded.

"Yes, of course. I take it you are well up to date in the matter of this latest disappearance. Well, it is fairly fluttering the official dovecotes. You see, it may be important, or it may be nothing at all. They don't like to neglect the first possibility, but they don't want to make fools of themselves by treating it as a matter of urgency, and then find out that the lady has just gone off on a jaunt."

"No one in Hazel Green believes in that as a possibility."

He laughed.

"Of course they don't! Trust a village to make up its mind to the worst! No one will actually say so, but there will be the deepest disappointment if it turns out that she has been weekending with the odd friend or relation."

Miss Silver looked grave.

"She has lived here for a good many years, and no one knows of any such relation or friend. But you were saying?"

"So I was. Delicate situation of the high-ups. And when the high-ups are in a delicate situation the low-downs don't always know exactly where they are. And that goes for you and me. In the upshot, I continue my visit, and you continue yours. You, in fact, are just where you were, and you keep your eyes and ears open and pass on anything that comes your way. I am rather more complicated than that. Scotland Yard has been asked to allow me to remain, but I've been given a strong hint to be as unobtrusive as I can. Just in case it all turns out to be nothing, when nobody will want to look as if they had picked up a sledgehammer to take a swipe at a midge."

Miss Silver had opened her knitting-bag. She produced little Josephine's cherry-coloured hood, now more than half completed. The bright wool made a pleasant contrast with the dark blue of her dress. She said, "I understand perfectly. The whole affair calls for discretion."

"You've said it! And that being that, what have you got to tell me?"

The grey needles clicked.

"Not very much, I am afraid, and probably nothing that you do not already know. I am, of course, fortunately placed here, as Mrs Merridew knows everyone in the neighbourhood and her daily maid is a cousin of Maggie Bell who disappeared from Hazel Green a year ago. She is, in fact, the Florrie mentioned on the card received by Mr and Mrs Bell after Maggie's disappearance and supposed to have been written by her."

"Supposed?"

"Florrie says that Maggie always wrote both their names with a Y, whereas on the card the spelling is IE."

"I thought there were no specimens of Maggie's handwriting."

"Maggie and Florrie were at school together. She is quite positive that Maggie did not write that card."

"Then why didn't she say so? She didn't — did she?"

"Oh, no. She is the type who would never tell anything to the police. And she said the card was being a comfort to Maggie's parents and she couldn't take it

126

from them. They are dead now, but she only burst out about it in the shock of Miss Holiday's disappearance."

"It was a shock to her?"

"A very considerable one."

"Well, that's that. What else?"

She was knitting rapidly, her expression serious and intent. It was a moment before she said, "There are two households here intimately connected with one another and with the two women who have disappeared. The Cunninghams live in the Dower House, just out of the village, and next door to them in Crewe House there is Miss Lydia Crewe. Both these ladies are old friends of Mrs Merridew's, and I have met them here at tea. Maggie Bell worked for the Cunninghams. The household consists of Miss Lucy, who is in her middle fifties, a brother Henry, and her nephew Nicholas, employed as a draughtsman at the Dalling Grange experimental station. Miss Crewe is, or was, Miss Holiday's employer. She is on terms of old and intimate friendship with Miss Cunningham, whom she is said to dominate. More than twenty years ago there was an engagement between her and Miss Cunningham's brother Henry. Following on the unsubstantiated suspicion that he had been concerned in the disappearance of a valuable diamond ring, Henry Cunningham left the country. I have not been able to discover what foundation there was for this rumour. The lady who owned the ring has long since left the neighbourhood. She was a Mrs Maberly, the wife of a rich self-made man, and notoriously careless about her belongings, but Henry Cunningham seems to have

127

taken the gossip very much to heart. In fact, my dear Frank, he ran away from it, and from his engagement to Lydia Crewe. He returned about three years ago, and lives in a very retired manner, occupying himself with birdwatching and nature study. Most of this you will know already, but you may not be aware of the persistent and painful breach between him and Miss Crewe. Only yesterday they met just outside this house as she arrived to have tea with Mrs Merridew, and according to what I am told is her invariable practice she cut him dead. In spite of which her intimate friendship with his sister continues. Nicholas Cunningham is also a constant visitor at Crewe House, and she is said to be devoted to him. Her household consists of herself, her nieces Rosamond and Jenny Maxwell, the latter a child of twelve and recovering from a serious motor accident sustained a couple of years ago, and the cook, Mrs Bolder, an old and trusted servant with a rather celebrated temper. Miss Holiday and a girl called Ivy Blane are daily helps, but Ivy does not go there on Sundays."

"Do you mean that Miss Holiday does?"

"Yes. As I told you, she has neither friends nor relations, and I gather that the midday meal is an attraction. She had just the one room at Mrs Maple's, and she is no cook."

Frank laughed.

"I've been hearing about Mrs Maple. I gather she routed Denning horse and foot. I want you to come round there with me if you will by and by. At present all we know is that the cook at Crewe House says Miss

Holiday left at about half past five and we don't know whether she ever got home or not, because Mrs Maple can't be induced to tell us. Which leaves Mrs Bolder the last person to see her. In other words, we don't know for certain that she ever left Crewe House."

Miss Silver stopped him.

"Oh, yes," she said, "Miss Cunningham met her."

"And how do you know that?"

"Because she mentioned it when she was here at tea this afternoon. Mrs Merridew was wondering whether there had been any quarrel between Miss Holiday and the cook; and Miss Cunningham said, 'Oh, she looked all right when I met her'. She was apparently on her way up to Crewe House, when she encountered Miss Holiday coming away. They met at the foot of the drive. I asked Miss Cunningham whether she had spoken to her, and she spilt her tea. I do not wish to stress this incident, because I believe it may have been quite accidental. Miss Cunningham is a large, untidy person. Her movements are very often jerky. She appears to be very good-natured."

"But she spilt her tea."

"Yes, she spilt her tea. And when I recurred to the subject of Miss Holiday and again asked whether she had spoken to her, she looked vague and said in an absent-minded sort of way, 'Oh, just a few words'."

CHAPTER
SEVENTEEN

Mrs Maple sat and looked at her visitor. Naturally, she knew Miss Silver by sight — visiting Mrs Merridew at the White Cottage, and an old school friend. Florrie Hunt spoke well of her, and it wasn't everybody that got the soft side of Florrie's tongue. But the gentleman with her — well, he was a bit of a puzzler. A gentleman he was and you couldn't get from it, and none of those nasty uniforms. But if he hadn't got something to do with the police, why was he here and wanting to know about Miss Holiday? For the matter of that, why was Mrs Merridew's friend here either? Questions they wanted answered. Nice clear voices they'd got — took the trouble to open their mouths and speak plain so that you could hear what they said. But she hadn't properly made up her mind whether she'd let on that she'd heard them or not. Perhaps she would, and perhaps she wouldn't — she was in two minds about it. She was getting a little tired of being out of whatever it was that was going on, but on the other hand she wasn't going to make herself cheap by talking to constables and such.

She was a very clean, tidy old woman with a round face, blue eyes, and an obstinate chin. Her white hair was done up in a great many tight plaits at the back of her head, and she wore a black stuff dress and a hand-knitted purple cardigan. No one could have found a speck of dust anywhere in the house. She gazed mildly at Miss Silver and said, "I'm hard of hearing."

Miss Silver made the comment that it was a sad affliction, and Mrs Maple found that she could hear her comfortably. Approving the sentiment, she made up her mind to oblige. She folded her hands in her lap and said graciously, "I don't rightly know what it's all about. There's people that come in and you can't hear a word they say — nothing but mumble, mumble, mumble. And most upsetting it is, for what you don't hear you can't answer, but so far as I can I'm sure I'm more than willing if there's anything the gentleman wants to ask me — or you, ma'am."

Frank leaned towards her.

"That is very good of you, Mrs Maple. We just want to know whether Miss Holiday came home at all last night."

Mrs Maple shook her head.

"Seven o'clock I woke up same as I always do, and went downstairs to get myself a cup of tea. There was a lady I lived with put me in the way of it, and Miss Holiday she likes one too, so I come down, and as a rule she won't be long. As soon as she hears me she'll slip into her dressing-gown and be after me for her cup of tea. Then back she'll go upstairs and into her clothes and off up to Crewe House where she gets her breakfast. Mrs Bolder's a good hand with hens, and there'll be an egg most days this time of the year. I'll say that for Mrs Bolder, a temper she may have and there's no denying it, but she don't grudge anyone their food. Very good meals they have up at Crewe House and Miss Holiday couldn't say different."

"But this morning she did not come down for her cup of tea?" said Miss Silver.

Mrs Maple shook her head.

"Not a sign of her. So I called up the stairs, and when I'd called three times I went up, and there was her room with nobody in it and the bed not slept in."

Frank Abbott said, "You don't think she could have got up and gone out early? If she had done that she would have made her bed before she went, wouldn't she? Are you quite sure she didn't go out?"

Mrs Maple produced a slight air of triumph.

"With both of the doors locked and all the windows latched!" she said.

"I see. Then it comes to this — the last you saw of Miss Holiday was when she went off to Crewe House yesterday morning?"

Mrs Maple tossed her head.

"Time enough to say what it comes to when you've heard me say it!"

Frank smiled in an agreeable manner.

"Well, when did you see her last?"

Mrs Maple was enjoying herself. There wasn't anyone could tell them what they wanted to know except her, and she wasn't going to be in too much of a hurry. If you made things too easy for people they didn't think any the better of you for it. She retreated into being rather deafer than she need have been.

132

"Ten years past she's been lodging here," she said, "and never gone over her time."

"Yes, but when did you see her last, Mrs Maple?"

She decided that perhaps she had better hear him. She shook her head in a melancholy way.

"Ah, now, if you'd said that to start with. I'm sure I'm not one to keep anything back — far from it. Now let me see — she came in at a quarter to six by the church clock, but I didn't speak to her then — not to say speak."

"That is what we wanted to know — whether she came back here after leaving Crewe House."

"Oh, yes, she came back all right."

"You are sure about that?"

Mrs Maple drew herself up in an offended manner.

"I may be hard of hearing, but I've the use of my eyes, sir."

Miss Silver judged it prudent to interpose.

"And you saw Miss Holiday come into the house at a quarter to six?"

"With my own eyes," said Mrs Maple. "And up the stairs to her room."

"Would there be anything out of the usual about that?"

Mrs Maple couldn't say that there would, adding that Miss Holiday wasn't the chattering kind, which she didn't hold with herself and wouldn't have kept her ten years if she had been.

"And when did she go out again?" said Frank Abbott.

"Well now . . ." She considered, her plump form upright, her head a little on one side. "Just after seven it would have been, because I'd heard the church clock strike the hour."

"Then you can hear the clock strike all right?"

"Seeing it's just about overhead, so I ought! Deaf as a post I'd have to be before I couldn't hear that! When she first came here Miss Holiday used to complain about it, but I told her she'd get used to it, and she did."

Frank maintained his agreeable smile. If he tried to push her he would get nothing.

"So she went out again at seven. Did she say where she was going?"

It is possible that Mrs Maple discerned the impatience which he was at so much pains to hide. She produced a clean pocket handkerchief and leaned her nose against it in a meditative manner.

"She wouldn't go out without letting me know," she said.

"Where was she going, Mrs Maple?"

This time she gave him his answer.

"Oh, just down the road to see Mrs Selby."

Miss Silver said in her ordinary voice, "They live just at the end of the lane. He is a retired businessman, and they keep hens. Florrie tells me that Miss Holiday would sometimes go in to keep Mrs Selby company in the evening while Mr Selby was at the Holly Tree."

It appeared that Mrs Maple had been perfectly able to follow this speech. She said, "That's right. Miss Holiday's a bit soft about men — don't hold with them

134

and wouldn't go down to the Selbys only when Mr Selby was out of the way."

"She was afraid of him?"

Mrs Maple looked superior.

"Not of him special — it was just men she didn't hold with. Nobody couldn't be afraid of Mr Selby. Sweets for the children and a laugh and a joke for everyone. Why, in most houses where there was a gentleman Miss Holiday wouldn't go into them at all, but she'd go down to Mrs Selby's when she knew Mr Selby would be out."

"And she could count on that — Sundays and all?"

Mrs Maple nodded.

"Till closing time — regular as clockwork."

Frank Abbott took up his questioning again.

"So Miss Holiday went out to see Mrs Selby soon after seven o'clock. What time would you ordinarily expect her back?"

"Nine o'clock. Not often she'd be later than that. Come nine o'clock I'm in my bed, and she knows it."

"And if she should be any later, would you sit up for her?"

"Not for her nor for no one," said Mrs Maple in an obstinate voice. "I've got to have my rest. Nine o'clock I'm in my bed and I won't go from it."

"Then if she came back after nine?"

"She'd find the key under the mat same as I put it when she goes in to Melbury for the pictures."

"And where was the key this morning, Mrs Maple?"

She said in a voice with a sudden quaver in it, "Under the mat — same as I put it when I went upstairs."

"So she didn't come in?"

Mrs Maple had recovered herself. She didn't know why she had had that moment when everything seemed to shake. She was all right again now. She said, "Stands to reason she didn't — not if the key was under the mat."

CHAPTER
EIGHTEEN

The church clock struck again. It certainly sounded as if it was right overhead. Frank looked at his watch. A quarter to seven. Mr Selby would doubtless be at the Holly Tree indulging in darts and the social glass. Mrs Selby would, however, be at home.

He walked down the lane with Miss Silver. The house, when they arrived at it, could be discerned as a bungalow, and he could definitely smell the hens. There being no barking dog to announce their arrival, he used a knocker with a modern gimcrack feel about it. There was a pattering of footsteps and one of the casement windows on the right was pushed open a little way. A nervous voice said, "Is there anyone there? Who is it?"

It was Miss Silver who answered.

"Mrs Selby? May we come in? I think you may know me by sight. My name is Silver, and I am staying with Mrs Merridew."

Mrs Selby sounded relieved.

"Oh, yes — of course — I've seen you with her. Oh, yes — Miss Silver."

She came pattering round to the door and opened it. There was no light in the passage behind her, but at the far end a door stood open to a lighted room.

"You will excuse me for keeping you waiting, Miss Silver . . . and . . . and . . ."

"Mr Abbott," said Miss Silver in her most reassuring voice.

Mrs Selby caught her breath in a nervous manner.

"Miss Silver and Mr Abbott — you must excuse me — but when Mr Selby is out I just like to see who is at the door before I open it."

Miss Silver said, "A most prudent step," and they all went down the passage to the lighted room.

Everything in it was new. The fact struck upon the eye and made rather the same effect as a painting without light or shade. There was a crimson carpet with a striking and quite hideous pattern resembling green and yellow tadpoles, now thinly scattered, now densely clustered. There was a suite covered in green plushette, curtains of crimson chenille, and two very large blue vases on the mantelpiece. The overhead light streamed down through an inverted bowl of pink glass.

As she closed the door and turned to her visitors Mrs Selby wore an air of modest pride. She did not share Mr Selby's delight in a country life, but this room was a quite undoubted solace. There wasn't a thing in it that hadn't been bought new when they came here — nothing old, nothing shabby, nothing used until you were sick and tired of the sight of it. She came forward, a small woman rather bent and looking older than the jovial Mr Selby, but then she had a worrying

138

disposition and the delicate skin which takes on lines before it need. She had on a bright blue skirt and an equally bright pink jumper. Her hair showed hardly any grey.

Miss Silver said in her pleasant voice, "This is very kind of you, Mrs Selby. Mr Abbott and I are making some inquiries with regard to Miss Holiday. I am sure you must be most concerned on her behalf."

The tears sprang into Mrs Selby's faded eyes. She produced a handkerchief with a bunch of flowers embroidered across the corner and dabbed.

"Oh, yes, I am. We can't think what has happened to her, Mr Selby and I. We are most distressed. You see, he is out a good deal. Gentlemen do like a bit of society, and he goes up to the Holly Tree for his game of darts most evenings. So then he has always said to me, 'You have in anyone you like — there's no need to be moping alone', and Miss Holiday being so near, only a step up the lane — well, I asked her in, and after a bit she'd come once or twice in the week, and nice for both of us."

Miss Silver sat primly upright in one corner of the crimson settee. She wore her black cloth coat, but had loosened the warm fur tippet which made it so cosy in a wind. Her hands were encased in black woollen gloves, and her neat pale features shaded by the black felt hat which had now been her second-best for a couple of years. A small bunch of purple stock and mignonette nestled among the loops of ribbon with which it was trimmed.

Frank Abbott had seated himself in a chair on the left of the fire. He spoke now for the first time.

"Did Miss Holiday come and see you last night?"

Mrs Selby turned her eyes on him. They must have been pretty eyes once, but the colour had gone out of them, and even the few tears she had just shed had reddened the lids.

"Oh, yes," she said, "she came in about seven and we had a cup of tea together."

"And did she seem just as usual?"

"Oh, yes, she did — except that —" She broke off, the handkerchief at her eyes again.

"Except what?"

"It wasn't anything — only . . ."

He said with quiet pertinacity, "Only . . ."

"Well, it wasn't anything at all, only there had been a few words with Mrs Bolder up at Crewe House where she goes to oblige."

"Do you know what the words were about?"

Mrs Selby became more animated than he had seen her.

"They don't need to be about anything when it's Mrs Bolder," she said. "Dreadful to have a temper like she has, and all for nothing."

"Do you know what it was about this time?"

Mrs Selby shook her head.

"Something to do with making up a fire as far as I could tell, but I tried to turn her thoughts from it."

"Was she upset?"

"Well, not to say *upset* — you really couldn't say as much as that. Just talking about Mrs Bolder having such a temper and never knowing what would set it off. And then we had our cup of tea and she started telling me all about that Lady Rowena she used to be companion to, and how she never thought she'd come down to going out to oblige."

"She was depressed, then?"

Mrs Selby looked surprised.

"Well, no, not *depressed*. It always cheers her up talking about Lady Rowena. She likes talking about her."

Miss Silver said, "Was she quite cheerful when she went away?"

"Oh, yes, Miss Silver."

"Mrs Selby, at what time did she leave you?"

"It would be just before nine o'clock. Oh, Miss Silver — you don't think anything has happened to her, do you? She was quite pleased, and she thought she must be going because of Mrs Maple not liking her to be out after nine — only the night she'd go into Melbury to the pictures, and rather a fuss about that. It's nothing but a step up the lane — oh, I don't see how anything could have happened to her when it's such a little way."

Frank Abbott said cheerfully, "Well, we don't know that anything has happened to her, Mrs Selby, but we must just go on making inquiries. Now, as you were the last person to see her, perhaps you can tell us how she was dressed."

"Oh, she had on her blue."

"That wouldn't be what she was working in up at Crewe House."

Mrs Selby looked shocked.

"Oh, no — she wouldn't come down here in *that!* This was her blue that she got last year — a very nice shade that went well with her beads."

"She was wearing a string of beads?"

"Well, yes — she wore them always. Such a pretty blue, with bits of gold and silver in them. They came from Venice or somewhere. That Lady Rowena she lived with gave them to her. She thought a lot of them."

"I suppose she had a coat?"

"Oh, yes — a black one."

"Any hat?"

"Oh, no — not to come that little way."

"But if she had been going any distance, to Melbury or anywhere like that, would she have worn one then?"

"Why, yes, Mr Abbott. She didn't hold with all this going about with nothing on your head."

There did not seem to be anything much more to say, but as they made their way to the front door, Miss Silver remarked on the convenience of living in a bungalow.

"I expect you are glad to be saved the stairs. In an old house they are often so steep. Have you water laid on?"

"Well, not company's water, Miss Silver. Mr Selby says we couldn't expect that really. There's a very convenient pumping arrangement with a cistern in the roof. It just has to be pumped every so often, and it runs from the taps just the same as if we were on the main."

"Then you haven't a well?"

Mrs Selby said, "Oh, no! I shouldn't fancy drinking water out of a well — oh, not at all!"

They said goodnight and walked away.

When they were at a safe distance Frank Abbott said, "Did you think they might have a well?"

"It was a possibility. Mrs Maple has one at the bottom of her garden."

"How do you know that?"

"Florrie Hunt told me."

He said, "Do you really think —"

"I do not know. By all accounts Miss Holiday is, or was, a person of very few ideas, extremely nervous in some directions — she could hardly enter a house where there was a man — and a good deal taken up with her own superiority and the fact that she had come down in the world. The quarrel with the cook at Crewe House may have been more important than has been admitted. Or, without being of any importance in itself, it may have weighed on Miss Holiday's mind. Whilst she was with Mrs Selby this weight might have been lifted, only to return more heavily when she came out by herself into the dark. There could have been an impulse towards self-destruction. I do not say that there was. It is just one of several possibilities."

Frank Abbott said, "I'll get the Melbury people on to Mrs Maple's well tomorrow."

CHAPTER
NINETEEN

Rosamond was not at all happy about Jenny. She had it on her mind to speak to her about Craig Lester's extraordinary story. He said that he had seen Jenny out of her bed and getting over a stile across the road at well after midnight. If he said that, it was true. One part of her mind believed what he said, but the other part just couldn't. And every time she thought about saying to Jenny, "Craig saw you out in the road last night," she felt as if she couldn't bring herself to do it. If Jenny denied the whole thing point-blank, where did they go from there? Jenny lying — hardening herself with lie upon lie — and a wall growing up which neither of them could pass. She had an instinct that it would be like that, and that nothing would ever be quite the same again. If she pushed Jenny too far, Jenny would lie. She mustn't push Jenny into lying. What she must do was to watch and make sure that it didn't happen again.

At first when they had come to Crewe House she had slept in Jenny's room. Jenny needed attention in the night. But as soon as she could manage for herself she had pushed Rosamond out. The room wasn't really big enough for two beds. She liked having her own room where she could put on the light if she wanted to read. She didn't like anyone else's dreams getting all cluttered up with hers. Rosamond began to wonder now how much of all this nonsense was Jenny wanting to get out of bed and try her walking all on her own and with no one there to see. One thing was certain, she couldn't move back into Jenny's room now, and she couldn't lock her in. She must just make sure that Jenny was asleep before she put her own light out and be ready to wake at the slightest sound. When you are anxious you never go right down into the depths. She must just take care not to go far enough to miss the least, faintest sound from Jenny's room next door.

Jenny had a new Gloria Gilmore to read, and remained lost in it all the evening. It was like being in another world where none of the things that happened to Jenny Maxwell were real. There was a girl called Colleen O'Hara, and she was having a series of the most thrilling love affairs with one young man after another, but you knew that in her heart of hearts she really loved her guardian, who was much too noble to ask her to be his wife, so he just went about being broken-hearted and stern, and too marvellously handsome for anything — only of course with a few grey hairs on his temples because of his secret sorrow. In this enthralling society Jenny could forget just what she wanted to. The trouble was that as soon as you came back into your own world it was all there waiting for you, and no matter how much you kept on saying to yourself that it was just a dream and none of it had ever happened, you didn't really believe it.

Jenny put off saying good night as long as she could, but in the end Rosamond stood over her with a cup of hot milk and tucked her up. She didn't mind hot milk as a rule, but tonight she put up a fight over it and drove a bargain. If Rosamond would have some too, then she would drink hers, but not unless.

"And that's flat!"

It wasn't worth struggling about, and Rosamond gave way. She did not see Jenny slip something into the cup she gave her. She had turned to take up her own cup, when a plaintive voice from the bed stopped her.

"This cup's got all the skin on it."

"Jenny — it's only cream!"

Jenny sat up in bed, her nose wrinkled with disgust.

"It's horrible crawling, slimy skin, and I'll be sick if I drink it! You give it me on purpose because you think it's fattening!"

"Oh, Jenny, I don't!"

"Oh, yes, you do! Change cups with me! I won't drink this one!"

The exchange made, Jenny drank without further protest. She even flung her arms round Rosamond's neck and hugged her when she said good night.

A quarter of an hour later when Rosamond opened the door and stood on the threshold listening, nothing could have been more satisfactory than the sound of Jenny's gentle, regular breathing. She herself felt drowsy beyond anything she could remember. It was all she could do to keep her attention on shutting the door noiselessly, opening her window, and putting out the light. As soon as her head touched the pillow she went down into depths of sleep.

Jenny had not meant to go to sleep at all. It was Rosamond who was to sleep while she herself remained awake to carry out her plan. The gentle, regular breathing to which Rosamond had listened with so much satisfaction was just an act, and she had very nearly spoilt it by laughing in the middle. It had been fun to slip one of her sleeping-tablets into the milk and then get Rosamond to change cups. The tablet was one which had been left from some that Mr Graham had prescribed when she was having all that pain last year and couldn't sleep. Rosamond didn't know that there were any of them left, but she had come across the box the other day, and there were two of them rattling about inside. Rosamond was going to sleep soundly and she was going to sleep all night.

But Jenny didn't mean to go to sleep at all. She was going to stay awake, and when everyone else was asleep she was going to go out. Because no matter how often she told herself that what had happened last night was a dream, she couldn't quite believe it unless she went to the place again and saw the thing which had frightened her wasn't there.

A thing which had been taken away wouldn't be there any longer. Not seeing it tonight wouldn't mean that it hadn't been there the night before. She began to think how funny it was that you should argue one way and something inside your mind should answer you back. It gave her the kind of feeling you have when you get out of bed in the dark and you don't know where the door is, or the window, or how to get back into bed again and put your head under the clothes. Everything in her mind began to drift, until it carried her into a frightening dark place where somebody said, "Well, nobody's going to miss her," and somebody shone a torch upon wet trodden ground. There was an old sack lying there, and a hand that it didn't quite cover. She couldn't see the whole of the hand, only the three middle fingers, and they were bone-white under the beam of the torch. She took a gasping breath and cried out, "It's a dream — it's a dream — it's a dream!" If you say that, you always wake up. No matter how strong the dream is, it's bound to let go of you if you know it is only a dream.

Jenny woke with her heart beating hard and her hands thrown out. It was a dream — a dream — a dream! And dreams came out of nowhere. She put on the bedside light and looked at her own little clock which Rosamond had given her for Christmas. So she must have been asleep for quite a long time. The curtains were drawn back from the half-open window. She went over to it and looked out. If there wasn't a light in the room, it wouldn't seem so dark outside. A feeling of adventure came up in her. She wasn't sleepy any more. She wanted to be out in the dark, running down the drive, crossing the road, getting over the stile, right away from everyone, where she could dance and nobody could see her.

She dressed quickly — a warm skirt, a thick pullover, and the shoes which she had hardly walked in yet. Rosamond had been afraid that she would find it difficult to get used to them at first, but she didn't — not a bit. Her feet tingled with liking them — they tingled, and wanted to dance. She opened the door and slipped down the dark passage without a sound. She had Rosamond's torch, but she didn't need to switch it on. She let herself out of the side door and turned her face to the wind. It moved softly, and it was full of the smell of growing things. There was no moon, but it wasn't dark. She could see the black shapes of the trees against a luminous sky.

She walked slowly down the drive lest she should displace a stone or break a dry branch under her feet and be heard by Rosamond or — a much more dreadful thought — Aunt Lydia. She went slowly. There was no sound, and no one waked.

Going over the road was like crossing a river. She waded into it and swam, and climbed out over the stile on the other side and into Mr Johnson's field. There was a footpath close along under the hedge, and if everyone was asleep, there wouldn't be anyone to see her if she made patterns on the ground with the torch and danced to keep them company.

At the corner of the field the path turned away from the road, and two fields farther on there was another stile coming out upon Vicarage Lane. Jenny switched off her torch, crouched down by the hedge, and listened. There wasn't a sound of anything at all except that soft air moving overhead. This was where she had had her dream last night. She had crawled right up to the stile and looked through. And there had been sounds in the dream — people moving — and the

149

brightness of a torch upon the sack. She hadn't really seen what was under the sack. She *hadn't* seen the fingers of a hand. Not last night — oh, no, not last night. It was only tonight when — she was asleep in her bed that the hand had come into the dream.

And now there wasn't anything at all. That was what she had come here for — to know for certain — to see for herself with her very own eyes that there wasn't anything here. There hadn't ever been anything. It had all been nothing but a dream. That was the worst of having a lot of imagination. You had to have it, or you couldn't make up stories that anyone would want to read. But sometimes the stories made themselves up and came banging into your mind whether you wanted them there or not. This had been a horrid one and she hadn't wanted it at all. She wanted to push it out and lock the door so that it couldn't come back. Something lying on the grass at the edge of Vicarage Lane — something that was covered with a sack, and a torch shining down on it. It wasn't her torch. Two people there in the lane, whispering together. One of them had a torch, and the beam shone down on the sack —

She made herself get up and put on her torch and look over the stile. There wasn't anybody there. There hadn't ever been anybody there. She made herself get over the stile and walk along the grass edge. Mrs Maple's cottage was behind her on the other side of the lane. It looked like a dark hump breaking the line of the hedge. The Selbys' bungalow was before her at the end

150

of the lane. After that there was only a footpath. She sent the beam of the torch along the grass to make a little light path for her feet. She walked on this path right up to the Selbys' gate, and then she turned and went back. There wasn't anything lying at the edge of the lane. There wasn't anything to dream about any more. She could go home and get into bed and sleep. She sent the round light at the end of the beam skipping and dancing. Everything inside her felt light and happy.

She had almost reached the stile when the dancing light picked up a golden spark. It was like a little gold point pricking up through the pale moony beam. It was there, and it was gone again. She flicked the light to and fro, but she couldn't find it. She tried again, and she saw part of a little round thing like the half of an orange, or an apple, or the moon before it is full. Only much, much smaller. Just a little round thing pushed down into the grass and the mud at the side of the lane — a little thing no bigger than her thumbnail. She wanted to leave it lying there and over the stile and run all the way home, but something wouldn't let her.

She stooped down and picked it up. There was mud on it, but it wasn't broken. It was a round glass bead, the colour dim in the light of the torch, but she knew very well that it was a bright sky blue and that there were little flecks of gold and silver mixed with the glass. It was one of the gold flecks which had been caught in the beam like a spark. It was dull and dirty now in the palm of her hand, but she had seen it too often not to know what it would look like if it was clean. She had been seeing it for more than two years, day in, day out, with a lot more like it on a string round Miss Holiday's neck.

CHAPTER
TWENTY

Florrie was a quarter of an hour late with the early morning tea next day. She brought it in with the air of one who serves a funeral feast and said, "If it's Mrs Maple's well, she never done it herself."

Mrs Merridew was awake, but not so much awake as not to find this both startling and enigmatical. As the curtains went rattling back, she blinked at the light and said, "Mrs Maple's well? What do you mean, Florrie?"

It was at this point that Miss Silver came in through the door which Florrie had left open behind her. She wore her blue dressing-gown and the black slippers with the blue pompoms, and, as always, she was immaculately neat. Her slight murmur of apology was lost in Florrie's loud repetition.

"If it's Mrs Maple's well, she never done it. That's what I've said, and that's what I'll hold to, Melbury police, or London police, or anyone. She'd as soon have flown over the moon, and you can't get me from it."

Miss Silver had the advantage of Mrs Merridew. In the light of last night's conversation with Frank Abbott, she was able to clarify Florrie's remark.

"Mrs Maple's well is being investigated by the police?"

Florrie gave a jerky nod.

"That's what I said. And she never done it."

Mrs Merridew was sitting up in bed. She reached under her pillow for the old fleecy shawl which had served her for so many years and survived so many washings that it was now the colour of old ivory. She said in a horrified voice,

"Oh, surely no one could suspect Mrs Maple!"

Florrie said angrily, "There's no knowing what the police will say! But it was Miss Holiday I had in my mind. If she went down that well, it wouldn't be because she threw herself in — no one's going to make me believe that! She may be there, or she may not, poor thing, but she won't be there without someone put her there — and I'm not saying who that someone might be. And I'd like to know what good the police are! They didn't find poor Maggie, did they? All they could say was she's run off to London — and anyone that knew her could tell them different to that! And as likely as not, they'll be saying the same about poor Miss Holiday. What would Maggie go to London for? I say she never, nor Miss Holiday neither! And when they find her murdered somewhere, maybe they'll believe me!" She marched out of the room and shut the door with something that was very nearly a bang.

Mrs Merridew was arranging the shawl about her shoulders. When she had finished doing this she picked up her cup of tea and said in an agitated manner, "You don't really think that poor thing — oh dear, I never did like wells! Maud, you don't suppose . . ."

Miss Silver said with composure, "We have no grounds for supposition at present. If there is a well in Mrs Maple's garden, the police would, I think, feel obliged to investigate it."

Mrs Merridew sipped from her cup. There were tears in her eyes, and the tea was certainly not hot enough to account for them. She said, "Oh dear!"

The two ladies were both dressed and downstairs, when Frank Abbott walked up the path to the front door and used the knocker. Miss Silver, meeting him on the threshold, took it upon herself to conduct him into the drawing room, Mrs Merridew being already in the dining room and about to make the tea. As he shut the door behind them Frank said, "Well, she was there all right."

Miss Silver made no comment. She looked gravely at him and waited for more. He continued.

"There is an injury to the head, but it could have been done as she fell. The post-mortem will show whether she went into the water alive. On the face of it, I should say she did, because either it was suicide, or if it was murder the only point in putting her there would be to make it look as if it was suicide. I don't know how it seems to you, and we should not, of course, be too much prejudiced by the fact that we were sent down here to look out for anything fishy that was going on, but I do get the impression that there is a whole lot more in this than meets the eye. Two women of no importance disappear — dull elderly people without sentimental entanglements. Nobody could possibly be supposed to want either of them out of the way. Yet

Maggie Bell has never been traced, and Miss Holiday turns up at the bottom of a well. I don't know about you, but I get the feeling that what we're looking at is just a few of the bits out of a jigsaw puzzle. They don't make sense on their own, but if we had the rest of the pieces they might add up to quite a picture."

Still with that grave look fixed upon her face, Miss Silver said, "Not a very pretty one, I am afraid."

He went away, and Miss Silver joined Mrs Merridew at the breakfast table.

Later on when the meal was over and Florrie had cleared it away Miss Silver followed her to the kitchen. She had been waiting for just such an opportunity, and it seemed to her that the time for it had now arrived. Mrs Merridew had settled down to write a letter, and Florrie would be occupied in washing up the breakfast things.

It cannot be said that she was in an approachable mood. After her outburst of the early morning she had retreated into rather more than her customary reserve. To Miss Silver's offer of drying whilst she washed there was a very cold response. She could do her work, she was glad to say, and no one had ever said she couldn't. Whether it was the sincerity of Miss Silver's "But I should like to help you, Florrie," or the smile that went with it, there is no means of knowing, but she made no further protest when a wet cup and saucer were lifted from the draining-board, meticulously dried, and set aside for her to put away. Both the smile and the desire to help were completely genuine, and had won more confidences than can be counted.

It was not until Miss Silver was drying the last plate that she said, "I wonder, Florrie, whether you would tell me a little more about your cousin Maggie Bell."

Florrie jerked a shoulder.

"There's nothing more to tell."

She met a grave, steady look and turned from it.

"I don't know what you think there is to tell."

Miss Silver said, "I am not asking from curiosity — I think you know that. But I would be glad to check over one or two points with you. Maggie went every day to the Cunninghams?"

Florrie looked sideways. No harm in answering that. She said, "Yes."

"What time did she leave?"

"That would depend. Mostly she would get away by half past two."

"Do you know what time she got away on the day she disappeared?"

There was rather a noticeable pause before the answer came.

"It would be the same as usual."

"Did she go straight home?"

"Mrs Bell said she was in before three."

"What did she do after she came in?"

Florrie emptied the washing-up bowl with a swish.

"How do I know what she did? There was always plenty to do — her mother saw to that. Maggie hadn't any time to have idle hands. There'd be the tea to get, and after she'd washed up she would get on with her ironing."

157

"You say that she would sometimes come down to you in the evening. Was that one of the evenings you were expecting her?"

"What if it was?"

Miss Silver's look was kind but searching.

"Was it?"

"It might have been."

Rightly interpreting this as an affirmative, Miss Silver repeated it in a more definite form.

"You were expecting her. But she did not come."

Florrie's face twitched painfully.

"No, she never."

"What time did you expect her?"

She turned the washing-up bowl over and spread the dishcloth on it to dry.

"Eight o'clock it would be, unless she was kept."

"Do you know when she actually left her parents' house?"

"Eight o'clock was what my aunt said."

Miss Silver said in a meditative tone,

"She left at eight to come to you. It would be quite dark. Can you remember at all what sort of a night it was — whether there was a moon?"

Florrie shook her head.

"It was a dark night and a drizzle of rain."

Miss Silver said, "Florrie, was there anyone who knew that Maggie would be coming in to see you that evening?"

Florrie turned from the sink with an abrupt movement.

"She'd come when she could."

158

"I asked you if anyone knew that Maggie would be coming to see you."

"Most things get known in a village. Maggie's father and mother would know, but they wouldn't talk about it. They didn't like her to come and see me — she'd have to pretend she was slipping out for a breath of air. But they'd know all right."

"Florrie, did anyone else know?"

She turned a haggard face.

"I'm not saying who knew, or who didn't know. There's been too much said already, and I'm not putting anything to it. And that's my last word."

Miss Silver said, "Thank you, Florrie," in a very thoughtful voice.

CHAPTER
TWENTY-ONE

Walking with Mrs Merridew that afternoon, Miss Silver saw Miss Cunningham turn out of the drive of Crewe House. She was swathed in her usual quota of scarves, one of which she held closely muffled up about her in a manner to suggest that she might be suffering from toothache. To Mrs Merridew's solicitous inquiries, however, she replied that there was nothing the matter, thank you — oh, no, nothing at all — it was just that the wind was chilly, and that a warm scarf was always comfortable. As she went on her way, Mrs Merridew said in a mildly indignant tone, "I suppose Lydia has been bullying her again. Poor Lucy, I can't think why she puts up with it."

Lucy Cunningham sometimes wondered herself. But it isn't easy to break an old yoke. Lydia Crewe had dominated her for thirty years, and when you have put up with something for thirty years, it isn't easy to rebel. She went home and occupied herself with her usual tasks. There were the hens to be fed, and since Mrs Hubbard who had succeeded Maggie Bell was gone by half past two, there was Henry's tea to get and the things to be washed up afterwards.

Henry was late. He was very often late, but of course, with his tastes, that was to be expected. You can't tramp about looking for things like chrysalises and hibernating dormice and get home punctually for your meals, and it was no good anyone expecting it. If she sometimes felt a little rufflet, she had only to remind herself of the years when she hadn't known whether Henry was alive or dead to feel an instant remorse. Of course, after such a long time you couldn't expect things to be just the same as they used to be. To be sure, Lydia wasn't so young even then, and she herself was rising thirty, but when you looked back on it across all those years thirty did seem quite young. And Henry had been only twenty-five. Rather sweet too, with that sudden smile he had when things went right, and the way he turned to you for help when they went wrong. He had changed a lot — people did in twenty-five years. Henry Cunningham had come back, but not the boy that he had been. He had lost the quick bright smile and the habit of turning to her for help. He wasn't interested in people any more. A new kind of spider or a moth with different markings, a butterfly that was common in Belgium but which hadn't been seen over here for fifteen years — these were the things which brought some of the old light to his eyes, the old zest to his manner. But as far as human beings were concerned, he lived in the house with them, or he met them when he went out, but they didn't matter any more.

Even Nicholas didn't matter. And in some ways Nicholas was so like what Henry had been. He was lighter-hearted, and he had more to say for himself, but there were ways of moving, speaking, looking, that brought Henry back again as he used to be before that dreadful wicked rumour drove him away.

She got the tea, and Henry was later than usual. He was in one of his most abstracted moods too, and hardly spoke except to ask her to pass the scones or to fill his cup again.

When the meal was over and cleared away she put on the wireless and sat down to darn the socks which both he and Nicholas continually wore into holes. There was quite a pile of them, and the old tweed jacket which Nicholas would go on wearing though it was getting quite past it. However, this time the hole was only in the lining of the pocket. She would have to put in a good strong patch. As she moved the coat, something rustled under her hand. No, that was too strong a word. There really wasn't any sound, but she could just feel something down by the hem between the cloth and the lining. Well, with a hole like that in the pocket —

She fished out a crumpled piece of paper. There was writing on one side of it, but she didn't look at it — she wouldn't do a thing like that. She folded it over so that the writing didn't show and put it aside to give to Nicholas when he came home.

He rushed in at something after six, very gay, very lively and in his usual hurry. He didn't want anything to eat or drink, and he wouldn't be back until late because he had a date in Melbury and no more than just enough time to change and make it. He threw her a kiss as he went out, and the front door slammed on him. She wondered who he was going to meet. Not

Rosamond, or he wouldn't have said he had got a date in Melbury. Or would he? If it was Rosamond, they would be meeting at the bus and going out together. She hoped very much that it was Rosamond, but she didn't think it could be. Rosamond wouldn't like to leave Jenny for so long. And that meant it might be simply anyone, because any girl would be only too glad to go out with Nicholas. Her thoughts dwelt on him fondly.

He hadn't come in when she went up to bed at half past ten, but then she didn't expect him as early as that. He had a key, and she had reminded Henry not to bolt the door. She was tired and quite ready for her bed. It occurred to her in rather a vague, wandering manner that you wouldn't really be able to bear it if you had just to go on all the time. There was a hymn they used to sing when she was a child about "those endless Sabbaths the blessed ones see". The idea of any day, let alone a Sunday, going on for ever and ever appalled her. Even in early youth she had found it very depressing, and now it simply didn't bear thinking about. She felt a sincere gratitude for the fact that she could still sleep.

But on this particular night she woke, coming up out of the pit of sleep with a ringing sound in her ears and blinking at the dark. After a moment she could see the window. The ringing was still going on, and this time she knew that it was the telephone down in the hall. When Papa had bought the Dower House and they had moved in all those years ago he had had the telephone put in the hall, and there it had remained ever since. It was, of course, the most inconvenient of all possible places. You stood in an icy draught, and everyone could hear what you said.

Lucy Cunningham blinked the sleep from her eyes and switched on the light beside her bed. The clock that ticked there informed her that it was three o'clock in the morning. A sense of calamity swept over her. No one would ring you up at such an hour unless something dreadful had happened — no one. Without waiting to put anything on she ran out as she was, barefoot and in her nightdress. The bell was ringing down in the hall, unnaturally loud, unnaturally insistent. There was enough light from her open door to mark the top of the stair. Without waiting for anything more she began to run down the long steep flight.

If her hand had not been tense on the balustrade, she couldn't have saved herself. Everything about her was tense. Her hand closed spasmodically. The cord which left a raw mark four inches above her right ankle tripped her with so much violence that but for that unnatural grip she must have pitched down on to the old flagstone of the hall below. The cord cut her, her body took a sickening lurch forward, but the right hand held and the left hand joined it. She found herself standing about six steps down and shaking from head to foot. The telephone bell was ringing.

The noise made it difficult to think. She groped, and got hold of a word — light. As soon as she was able she turned herself, still holding to the baluster. She went up step by step to the landing and put on the light. Then she went back to the head of the stair and looked down.

164

She had been right about the number of the steps — she had gone down six of them. From the balustrade by that sixth step on the one side to the balustrade on the other a taut line of cord spanned the stair. As soon as she saw it she knew what it was, a length of the garden twine she used for tying her roses. It was the strong tarred kind. It hardly showed at all against the dark carpet and the dark polished treads. If it had been new, she would have smelt the tar, but it was all of two years since she had bought any.

The telephone had stopped ringing. She went back into her room, fetched a pair of scissors, and descended the stair as far as the sixth step. She was shaking all over, but she made herself do it. The twine was very securely fastened. When she had cut it through she gathered up the bits and took them into her own room to burn them. She cleaned the scissors carefully and put them away. Then, and not until then, she went across the landing and opened Henry's door. The room was dark and the window wide. There was the smell of a man's room — tobacco and boot polish. There was the sound of Henry Cunningham's deep and regular breathing. She stood and listened to it for a while. Then she stepped back and shut the door again.

Nicholas had the room beyond, at the back of the house. She stood in front of it, her mind full of dreadful irrational prayers — "Don't let it be Nicholas! Oh, God, don't let it be Nicholas! He couldn't! He *couldn't!* If he was in Melbury, it couldn't be Nicholas! Let him be in Melbury! Don't let him be here!" She put her hand on the door knob and turned it. The room

165

was dark, the window stood wide. There was the sound of deep quiet breathing.

Lucy Cunningham shut the door and went back to her room. Her mind was dreadfully clear. She had come up to bed at half past ten. The stairs were safe then. At some later time Henry had come up. Nicholas had come up. One of them had stopped at the sixth step and stretched the cord above it. One of them? They might have come up separately, or they might have come up together. Or the one who had come up first might have gone down again to do what had to be done. Henry or Nicholas — Nicholas or Henry. There was no one else in the house. One of them had tied the cord which was to trip her to her death. The stair was steep, and the hall was paved with stone. She would be hurrying blindly, and she would fall to her death.

But who wanted her dead? Henry or Nicholas — Nicholas or Henry?

The words went round and round in her head until the morning.

CHAPTER
TWENTY-TWO

Mrs Hubbard would not arrive until eight o'clock, and since Nicholas must be got down to his breakfast by then, Miss Cunningham could not allow herself the indulgence of a cup of tea in bed. She had to wake Nicholas, hurry into her clothes, open the back door, and cook whatever they had been able to contrive for the meal — fish, or sausage, or the occasional egg. On this Tuesday morning Lucy Cunningham had plenty of time. It was a relief to leave the bed which had afforded her no rest. The water was still hot from the night before. She washed her face in it, and then sponged it repeatedly with cold water from her bedroom jug. The nights went near to frost, and the water was icy. When she came to do her hair, the image in the glass had a less ghastly look. She never had much colour, and a round face does not go haggard in a night. She put on the old grey tweed skirt and the grey jumper and cardigan and went across the landing to bang on Nicholas's door. He always took some waking, but the sleepy voice that answered her in the end was no different from what it had been for all the years she had come to his door and knocked like this.

She went to the head of the stairs and looked down. The cord had marked the balustrade, but no one else would notice a stray mark on the old paint. It had been tied very tightly, and it had had to take her weight when she stumbled. Oak would not have marked, but the balustrade was made of a softer wood. It had dented where the cord had pulled on it. She could see the dent every time she went up and down the stairs. She went down now to unlock the back door and get Nicholas's breakfast.

There was no need for her to go and wake Henry. He had views about sleep, and considered it injurious to interfere with what should be a natural process. If you had had enough sleep you woke up. If you had not had enough, it was harmful to be roused. It was, of course, extremely inconvenient never to know when he would want his breakfast, but when you had a man in the house you had to put up with things like that. Papa had had views about early rising, and as long as he lived they had breakfasted at seven. Lucy Cunningham had been brought up on the famous adage, "Early to bed and early to rise, Makes a man healthy, and wealthy, and wise". She had never been able to make up her mind which part of it she disliked most, getting up at half past six or going to bed at nine, at which hour the electric light had been turned off at the meter and the family restricted to candles in their bedrooms. Henry, of course, did not mind whether the lights were on all night or not — but then he did not pay the bill.

There were a couple of sausages left from supper. She heated them on the small oil stove, since the fire was out and would be left for Mrs Hubbard to see to. Meanwhile she took the milk and the butter out of the larder and across the hall to the dining room. Everything else was there already, since she always laid the table before going up to bed. She stood now and checked the things over just to make sure that nothing had been forgotten. Two packets of cereal — Henry sometimes liked the kind that always reminded her of little straw mattresses, but Nicholas wouldn't touch them. Brown sugar, marmalade, a fresh pot of mustard . . . Oh, the bread —

As she was bringing it through the hall, Nicholas came running down the stairs. Her heart jerked. He came running down without a glance at the sixth or any other step. She felt such a rush of relief that the bread board tilted and the loaf began to slide. The knife fell clattering.

Nicholas caught her about the shoulders.

"Hold up, Lu! What are you doing? Are you all right?"

"Oh, yes."

He laughed and bent to pick up the knife.

"Well, don't go throwing things about! Here, you'd better let me have that bread. I really like it better when it hasn't been on the floor."

She turned back to fetch his sausage, whilst he went on. When she came into the dining room he gave her a laughing, affectionate glance.

"You know, you do look a bit wonky. You weren't by any chance sitting up to watch for the wanderer's return, were you? I'm the one who ought to be looking pale, not you."

She had not meant to speak, but everything in her was shaking. The words came of themselves.

"Were you very late?"

He was tipping wheatflakes into a soup-plate and pouring milk on them.

"Oh, fairly. I got a lift, so I didn't have to depend on the bus. Did you hear me come in?"

"No."

"Well, I've got to hurry now — I was very nearly late yesterday. Old Burlington has got a complex about punctuality. And he doesn't care for me much. There's nothing he'd like better than to catch me out."

"Why doesn't he like you?"

"Odd, isn't it? Darling, pour me out a cup of tea. He thinks I'm frivolous. Not one of our blither spirits!"

When she had poured out his tea she went away and came back again. There was a crumpled piece of paper in her hand. He looked at it across his cup.

"Where did you get that?"

"There was a hole in the pocket of your brown tweed jacket. It had slipped down between the stuff and the lining. I found it last night when I was mending the pocket."

He put out his hand for it and took it.

"Thanks, Lu."

He was still smiling, but there was something — some change. It was as if the temperature had suddenly dropped whilst the sun was shining, a thing quite apt to happen in an English spring. Lucy Cunningham had a

170

bewildered sense of there being something wrong, but she had no idea what it might be.

Nicholas put the paper into an inner pocket, gulped down the rest of his tea, and was off in a hurry. But when she went out into the kitchen it was not quite half past eight. He really had plenty of time.

Mrs Hubbard was busy lighting the fire, which was being contrary. Presently she would help Miss Cunningham with the beds, but at the moment she wanted the kitchen to herself. Anyone would think something had got into the range this morning. Three times she had lighted the dratted thing and it had gone out. If Miss Cunningham would take and go away, there was a mite of paraffin in the scullery that nobody was going to miss.

There are ways of letting people know when they are not wanted. It came home to Lucy Cunningham that Mrs Hubbard would prefer her room to her company. She went through into the drawing room and began to straighten the chairs and tidy up, a thing she never could do the night before because of Henry sitting up late and not liking to be disturbed. She had just finished, when she heard him come out of his room. She had left the door open, and by moving a very little she could see as well as hear. He had a slow, heavy tread. It was no slower or heavier than usual. He came across the landing with an abstracted air and on down the stairs without looking to right or left. When she came out to meet him in the hall he took no other notice than to say, "I'm down," after which he proceeded into the dining room, leaving the door ajar behind him.

All the time she was getting his hot plate and the sausage which she had been keeping warm the thoughts in her head went round and round — Henry or Nicholas — Nicholas or Henry. She had watched them both come down the stairs, and neither of them had so much as glanced at the step where she had stumbled, or at the balustrade where the trip-cord had been stretched. Nicholas had come down in his usual rush, and Henry in his own deliberate way. Neither of them had done anything at all that was different from what she had seen them do year in, year out all the time that they had been together — Nicholas tearing down as a schoolboy, Henry, young and in love with Lydia Crewe, moving as if he had come only half-way out of a dream. It might have been any day as long ago as that, or in the years between.

But if either of them had fastened that cord to trip her to her death, he wouldn't have left it there to be found in the morning. There must have been some time in the night when one of them had come to the top of the stair and looked over. But the cord would not have been there for him to see, because she had taken it away and burned it in her bedroom grate. So then whoever it was would have turned round and gone back to his bed again.

She had not closed her bedroom door. She did not think that she had slept. Could a man move so silently that she would not hear him? She looked back over the hours of the night, and she wasn't sure. She didn't think that she had slept, but she wasn't sure. There were stretches of time which were like some dreadful dream. She couldn't be sure whether the dream had crossed the boundaries of sleep or only trembled on the edge.

She took Henry his sausage, and found him reading the paper and dawdling over a brown mess of cereal.

CHAPTER
TWENTY-THREE

Making the beds with Miss Cunningham, Mrs Hubbard was perfectly aware that she was not in her usual. Under an appearance of great neatness and restraint she herself was one of the most inquisitive women in Hazel Green. She had a nose for a secret comparable only to that of a ferret on the trail, but all very quietly, very decorously, and the prize when attained to be shared only with the chosen few and under pledge of secrecy. When Miss Cunningham took the side of the bed which enabled her to keep her back to the windows, she was at once aware that this had been done in order to conceal the fact that she had been crying and that she had passed a wakeful night.

When brushing down the stairs she did not fail to observe a slight flattening at the edges of two of the balusters. It was an old staircase, but at some time it had been painted. Where the flattening had occurred the paint on at least one edge had flaked away. It was perfectly plain to Mrs Hubbard that something tight had been tied round the baluster. Now what would anyone want to do that for? And blessed if there wasn't just such another mark on the far side of the step. The stairs ran down without a break, the balusters on either side. You couldn't get from it but that someone had stretched a cord across the stairs — as nasty and spiteful a trick as she had ever heard of. Must have been some boy. There were those she could name that wouldn't think twice of breaking anyone's leg if they were up to a lark, but how in the world would a boy get in to play off one of his jokes on Miss Cunningham, or why would he want to? There wasn't anyone with what you could call a spite against her, not that she knew about — and there wasn't much that she didn't know.

When she had finished the stairs she took her dustpan and brush round the hall, and right underneath where that mark was on the baluster the brush picked up a little curly piece of twine — some of that black garden stuff that gets used for tying up creepers and such. She put it in the pocket of her overall and went up to Miss Cunningham's bedroom. There had been no fire in the grate, but something had been burned there. When she picked up the piece of tarred twine it came to her that there had been ash in the bedroom grate, and she hadn't to look at it twice before she could see what it was before it come to that — twine, same as the piece she'd got in her pocket. There was a bit with the very shape of it in the grey ash, and when she raked the stuff over there was a knot that hadn't burned at all. Mrs Hubbard put it in her pocket with the bit she had picked up in the hall. It was altogether past her to think of any reason why Miss Cunningham should have cut the twine from the baluster and burned it, but that was what she had done. She had cut it — you could see the mark of the scissors

175

close up by the knot — and she had burned it in her bedroom grate.

All the time that she was doing her work, Mrs Hubbard kept on putting two and two together. The trouble was she couldn't get them to make anything, and it was pain and grief to her. It wasn't until she was going away at half past two that she noticed something which excited her curiosity to a really passionate degree. Miss Cunningham had come out on to the back door step to ask her whether they needed another packet of Vim. It had been a grey morning, but the sun was out now. It slanted in across the step and across Miss Cunningham's ankles. There hadn't been anything to notice in the house, which was dark enough like a lot of these old houses were, but out here with the sun right on it, you just couldn't help noticing the weal. Just about six inches up from the right ankle it was, and so red the stocking didn't hide it, not out here in the light. With the sideways look which took in a great deal more than it seemed to, Mrs Hubbard decided that there was quite a piece of swelling too. She didn't risk more than the one glance, and it was in her usual rather mousy little voice that she replied to the question about the Vim that they didn't really want it till next week, but no harm if Miss Cunningham was putting her order in.

Mr Hubbard worked in Melbury. He took a wrapped lunch with him which he supplemented at the canteen. It was therefore nothing to anyone if Mrs Hubbard liked to drop in on Florrie Hunt at the White Cottage. There was a faint faraway connexion between them, and Florrie would be pleased enough to give her a cup

176

of tea, and perhaps the latest about the finding of poor Miss Holiday's body. The White Cottage being right at the corner of Vicarage Lane, there couldn't be anything either coming or going but what Florrie would be bound to notice it.

She got her cup of tea, but she didn't get such a very warm welcome. Florrie was in one of her moods — she could see that at a glance. Put her in mind of a house with all the blinds down and the people away. Nothing but a yes or a no out of her, and not at all easy to get either. She handed up her cup to be filled a second time and began to tell Florrie about the marks on the balusters at the Dower House and the weal on Miss Cunningham's leg. By the time she had come to the end of her story Florrie was looking at her for the first time.

"Sounds like nonsense to me," she said.

Mrs Hubbard sipped her tea.

"Well, then, it wasn't," she said. "Plain as plain the marks were. And the bit of string in the hall — what would anyone be doing with that nasty tarred stuff indoors? And more of it burned in the bedroom grate. Just look here if you don't believe me!"

She had to put the cup down and slip a hand under her coat to bring out the little curl of twine and the knot which had survived the fire.

Florrie stared at them and said bluntly, "Seems to me you're hinting at something, Annie."

Mrs Hubbard lowered her eyes.

"I wouldn't be one to do that."

"Well, I don't know what else you'd call it. And if you're hinting that there was a string tied across those stairs to trip Miss Cunningham when she came down, well, who is supposed to have put it there?"

Mrs Hubbard sipped her tea.

"It's not for me to say. I'm not one to gossip, and that you know."

The conversation wasn't turning out at all as she had hoped. When Florrie was in that sort of mood she could be down right disagreeable, and no good trying to get anything out of her. She finished her cup and said she must be getting along.

It wasn't until she was half-way home that she remembered she had left the knot and the bit of twine behind her. Not worth going back for of course. She wouldn't have shown them to anyone except Florrie. The job at Miss Cunningham's suited her, and she wouldn't want it to get about that she'd been talking. Which she wouldn't do, only to Florrie. And Florrie was safe enough. Why, she could hardly get a word out of her herself.

Miss Silver came out to the kitchen with the coffee tray. Mrs Merridew had just dropped off behind the morning paper, an after-lunch practice in which Miss Silver had never allowed herself to indulge. A sad waste of time, and a habit which was apt to grow. She carried the tray down the passage, and as she approached the door she became aware of voices on the other side of it. She had no intention of listening, but they forced themselves upon her ear. It all happened quite naturally. She had paused when she realized that Florrie was not alone, and the door in front of her was ajar. She heard Florrie say in her deep, harsh voice, "If you're hinting there was a string tied across those stairs to trip Miss Cunningham when she came down, well, who is supposed to have put it there?"

Miss Silver stood where she was. As a private gentlewoman she would not have dreamed of listening to a conversation not intended for her ears. As a private detective she had not infrequently considered it her duty to do so. She stood quite still, holding the tray, and heard Mrs Hubbard turn the question aside and say that she must be getting along. When the back door had closed upon her, Miss Silver retired down the passage, and then returned, her footsteps rather more evident than usual. Arrived at the kitchen door, she said, "May I come in, Florrie?" and pushed it with the tray.

It was not until then that Florrie started and turned round. She had been standing at the kitchen table and staring down at it, too much immersed in her thoughts until the tray knocked against the door.

Miss Silver came into the room and set it down upon the table. As she did so she saw that what Florrie had been staring at was a little curl of tarred twine and a knot. The knot had been tightly tied and afterwards cut away. Across the coffee tray with its two empty cups Miss Silver looked at Florrie Hunt, and Florrie looked back. It was an angry, puzzled look, but behind the puzzle and the anger there was fear. When Miss Silver said, "What is it?" Florrie answered in a lost voice,

"I don't know —"

"It would be better if you would tell me."

There was a slow shake of the head. Miss Silver leaned across and touched the curl of twine. She said, "When I came down the passage the door was ajar, and I heard what you said. It was something about a string tied across the stairs to trip Miss Cunningham. You had a visitor, and you asked her who was supposed to have put it there."

Florrie spoke angrily.

"She hadn't got nothing to say!"

Miss Silver gave a slight corrective cough.

"I noticed that she did not say anything. May I ask who there was in the house who could have done such a thing?"

Florrie tossed her head.

"No one that I can see! There would be her, and Mr Henry, and Mr Nicholas. Well, it stands to reason she couldn't do it herself, and that leaves Mr Nicholas and Mr Henry. Well, I ask you! Annie Hubbard's got little enough to think of, coming round here with a story like that!"

She got a brightly interrogative glance.

"She works at the Dower House?"

"Took on the job after Maggie went."

"And what, do you suppose, put this story into her head?"

Mrs Hubbard's story about the marks on the balusters and finding the piece of twine just underneath in the hall and the knot upstairs in Miss Cunningham's grate along with what looked like the burnt remains of a longer piece, was retailed in what began by being a scornful voice. But somehow by the time Florrie had come to the weal on Miss Cunningham's leg the scorn had gone out of it and something like fear had taken its place. The last words dragged and were followed in a rush by a scared, "Who'd do a thing like that? I put it to Annie Hubbard, and you could hear for yourself she hadn't got nothing to say."

Miss Silver said in a meditative tone, "There was no one else in the house except the two Mr Cunninghams?"

"Not without someone come round visiting, and then one of the family would have had to let them in."

Miss Silver said, "Yes — I suppose so . . ."

She went through to the drawing room and sat down with her knitting. Little Josephine's cherry-coloured hood was now finished, and she had embarked upon leggings to match. She was not anxious to pursue the subject of the accident which Miss Cunningham had so narrowly escaped. She wished to be able to give it some quiet reflection. If anyone had intended to injure Lucy Cunningham by fastening a trip-cord across the stairs, what would be the most likely time to carry it out? It would surely only be attempted when the normal comings and goings had ceased and everyone had gone upstairs for the night. Lucy Cunningham — her brother Henry — her nephew Nicholas —

When the trip-cord had been fixed, there would have to be some device to bring the intended victim from her room, and in so much of a hurry that she would not notice the cord until too late. A black cord on a dark stair, and a woman hurrying down. Why? The thought of the telephone-bell presented itself in a very convincing manner. There is no sound more startling in the middle of the night. Yet how ensure that the telephone bell would ring? To employ an accomplice would be extremely dangerous. There came to her memory a sound very familiar in her own flat, the ringing of the bell on the alarm clock. Heard from any other room except her bedroom it was indistinguishable from the sound of the telephone bell. If anyone had wished to startle Miss Cunningham into running downstairs in the middle of the night, how easy to set the alarm at any of the hours past midnight and leave the clock in the hall, whence it could be retrieved before anyone observed it. It occurred to Miss Silver, and not for the first time, that all the things that had happened and were happening in Hazel Green had some association with Crewe House and the neighbouring Dower House, and that the occupants of these two houses were intimately connected. Furthermore, if two crimes had indeed been carried out and a third was being attempted, there was a certain economy of method calculated to arouse no suspicion and leave no trace. This would imply a criminal of no ordinary capacity, quick to decide upon a plan and ruthless in carrying it out.

When Mrs Merridew awoke from her nap Miss Silver was ready to suggest that it would be pleasant to take the air. A remark as to her interest in old houses, coupled with the mention of Miss Cunningham's name, produced some information with regard to the

Dower House, followed by the remark that, "Of course Lucy knows far more about it than I do. I am sure she would be only too pleased to show you the house. The Cunninghams are quite recent comers, but you know the saying about being more royalist than the king — well, it's like that with Lucy. She has all the stories by heart, and there's nothing she likes better than repeating them. We can call on her this afternoon if you would care to do so."

CHAPTER
TWENTY-FOUR

When Frank Abbott dropped in after supper that evening he was struck with the gravity of Miss Silver's expression. He had come to tell her the result of the post-mortem on Miss Holiday. They sat in the dining room, and she gave him her usual strict attention whilst her busy needles clicked and little Josephine's leggings lengthened.

"Well," he began, "she was alive when she got that bump on the head, and she was alive when she went into the water, but no one is going to swear that she didn't hit her head on the side of the well as she went down. It could have been that way, you know, though I'll give you this — the police surgeon doesn't think it was. He is inclined to believe that there may have been an earlier bruise."

"Were there any signs of a struggle?"

He paused for a moment before answering this.

"Not as far as any damage to her clothes went. But you will remember that Mrs Selby said she was wearing a string of blue beads —"

"Yes, Frank."

"Well, when we got her up out of the well it looked as if the string was missing, but afterwards at the mortuary it was discovered that two or three of the beads had run down inside her clothes and been caught there, which looks as if the string had broken when she was attacked."

"That could well have happened. And quite compatible with a theory that she may have been stunned by an initial blow but not put down the well until later. You seemed to suggest this as a possibility."

"Something like that."

She pulled on her ball of wool.

"It is what I would expect. She must have been attacked in the short distance between the Selbys' bungalow and the cottage. But it would be unlikely that the person or persons who attacked her would have taken the risk of carrying the body to the bottom of Mrs Maple's garden at an hour when she might still be supposed to be about. Florrie informs me that her bedroom looks to the back of the house, and though she is too deaf to have heard footsteps in the garden, she would certainly be able to perceive the transport of an inanimate body if she had happened to be looking out of her window at the time."

Frank nodded.

"People do look out of the window the last thing."

"It is an extremely common practice. I do not think that a murderer's guilty conscience would have allowed him to take the risk. He would, I am sure, decide to wait until there was no chance that anyone would be abroad. The question would then arise as to what was to be done with the body. We know now that she was not dead. For his purpose it was important that she

185

should go into the water alive. He could not, therefore, just finish her off and conceal the body in a ditch, and he must have been faced with a considerable problem. It is, of course, of the very highest importance to discover what his solution was. I need not ask you whether you have given particular attention to all this. The Selbys' premises constitute the nearest shelter. They comprise the bungalow, a garage, two sheds, and a number of hen houses. Mrs Selby was alone in the bungalow between seven o'clock and ten. Mr Selby is supposed to have been at the Holly Tree."

"He was there till closing time."

Miss Silver laid down her knitting for a moment, an occurrence so unusual as to direct particular attention to what she was about to say.

"I do not doubt that he was there at closing time. Is there, however, any evidence that he was there continuously between the hours of seven and ten, and particularly during the quarter of an hour just before and after nine o'clock? The distance from the Holly Tree to the bungalow is a very short one. If a game of darts was going on and Mr Selby did not happen to be playing at the time, would anyone have noticed if he had been absent for, say, fifteen minutes?"

"I don't know, but I'll do my best to find out. Fifteen minutes doesn't give him very long to come and go, hit Miss Holiday over the head, and get her out of the way."

"It would have had to be very carefully planned — but then careful planning is evident at every stage of this affair."

186

Frank said in a thoughtful tone, "Yes. But why Selby?"

"He is a stranger."

"My dear ma'am, the countryside is littered with strangers."

"There have been many changes since the war, but not so many in Hazel Green."

"There are a great many in and around Melbury, which is not so far away."

"But Mr Selby is here. And he was here a year ago when Maggie Bell disappeared. I am puzzled to account for it."

He sketched a shrug.

"Businessmen do retire. Quite a lot of them have an urge to settle down in the country and keep hens. A foul employment —" He gave a sudden laugh. "No, no, withhold your lightnings! I swear I didn't intend the pun — didn't even know it was there until I heard myself say it."

Rightly dismissing this as trivial, she said, "It is obvious that Mrs Selby has no leanings towards a country life. Mr Selby, whilst professing his enjoyment, is not infrequently away for several days at a time. He makes a joke of it and says the pavements call him. During his absence the care of the hens devolves upon Mrs Selby."

"All this from Florrie, who I suppose had it from Miss Holiday?"

"Yes, Frank. I gather that Mrs Selby not only dislikes the care of the hens, but that she is extremely nervous of being alone in the bungalow, especially as Mr Selby would not hear of their having a dog."

"Which might mean anything, or nothing at all — except that Mr Selby doesn't like dogs. You know, there really are people that don't."

Miss Silver herself had a preference for cats, but she did not consider this the moment to say so. She allowed him to proceed, which he did, and in a graver voice.

"You may care to know that Selby's antecedents are all on record. The Security lads thought of that over the question of leakages at Dalling Grange. As a newcomer, he was naturally suspect, but nothing emerged. He and his brother used to run a garage business in the Streatham Road. Perfectly decorous and respectable. Regular subscriber to the local Conservative Association. Life and soul of the party at local whist drives. In fact a perfectly blameless past."

Miss Silver inclined her head. It was in her mind that a perfectly blameless past would be essential if a man was to be either a catspaw or an active agent in some nefarious business. Not judging that this was the moment to say so, she observed that a careful examination of the garage and outhouses attached to the bungalow would, she supposed, be a part of the routine inquiries which the police would undertake. She was assured that this would be the case.

"They shall be gone over with a toothcomb. I suppose you don't include Mrs Selby in your suspicions?"

Miss Silver gave a slight hortatory cough.

188

"I do not suspect either Mr or Mrs Selby. There are not, as yet, any grounds for doing so. I merely suggest that their premises may have been used, and that in view of the fact that Miss Holiday's body must have been concealed somewhere, and that Mr Selby's garage or one of his outhouses stand out as the most likely if not the only possible places of concealment, there is an urgent necessity for a very careful and thorough investigation. As Lord Tennyson puts it — 'And in its season bring the law . . . Set in all lights by many minds. To close the interests of all'."

He took the impact of this with fortitude. After a slightly stunned silence he remarked, "As you say. Everything shall be gone through with the toothcomb. Well, I suppose I had better be getting along."

CHAPTER
TWENTY-FIVE

Miss Silver detained him with the slightest of gestures.

"If you can spare me a few moments . . ."

"Of course. What is it?"

"There are some inquiries which it would not be possible for me to attend to, but which I should be very glad if you could make."

He was able to recognize this mild and tentative approach and allow himself some irreverent amusement. There were chestnuts to be picked out of the fire, and he was for it. Recalling some other occasions, the amusement subsided and an alert attention took its place.

"Well, ma'am, what are they?"

"You will, perhaps, remember that I mentioned a Mrs Maberly to you."

"Did you? I believe you did — Henry Cunningham and the fatal diamond ring. She left it about, it vanished, and everyone made up their minds that Henry had taken it. After which he fled the country and didn't come back for twenty years. It's rather an old story, isn't it? Who am I supposed to interrogate — Mrs Maberly, or the submerged Henry?"

She looked some slight reproof and said, "Neither. Mrs Maberly left the neighbourhood and, I believe, the country not very long after the loss of the ring. I understand that she and her husband went to America. I merely wished to remind you of the occurrence."

There was a faint sardonic gleam in his eye.

"Synopsis of the story up to date. Now read on! What is the next instalment?"

She said soberly, "I have been struck by the fact that there seemed to have been quite a number of other incidents connected with the theft, or perhaps I should say the abstraction, of jewels. Mrs Merridew introduced the subject on Sunday when Miss Crewe was here at tea. A Lady Muriel Street was mentioned. She and her husband live at Hoys, a large place just beyond the village. I gather that she is one of those people who run round telling everyone their family affairs down to the last detail. It seems she has just discovered that a large and handsome diamond brooch left to her by her godmother is merely an imitation. The centre stone is of considerable size, and she had always supposed the ornament to be worth a very large sum, but on attempting to sell it she was informed that the stones were paste."

Frank said, "Well, well. I think she would have done better to hold her tongue."

Miss Silver turned the cherry-coloured leggings.

"That was Miss Crewe's remark. She then capped Mrs Merridew's story with one about Lady Melbury, who appears to have suddenly discovered that a necklace supposed to be extremely valuable and worn

191

by her great-grandmother at Queen Victoria's coronation was in reality a mere imitation. Miss Crewe commented very unfavourably upon Lord Melbury's folly in talking about the matter. Lady Melbury would, I gather, have remained silent, but her husband, who is one of those easy-going sociable men, went about telling everyone and rather openly wondering which of his ancestors had effected the substitution."

Frank said quickly, "The necklace would have had to be valued for probate. I'm afraid he can't put it on the ancestors."

Miss Silver coughed.

"That does not seem to have occurred to him. Lady Melbury is an extravagant woman, and has been a beauty. He is probably the only person in the county who does not believe that she disposed of the necklace herself. These grand jewels appear so seldom, and then only in circumstances where they are unlikely to be exposed to the eye of an expert, that a substitution could be made with very little risk of discovery."

He laughed.

"And by the time it came to valuation for probate Lady Melbury wouldn't have to worry! Just between you and me, I wonder how often it has been done. Most of the great families are broke, and why keep capital locked up in jewels which only the expert can tell from a copy? Well, all this is very interesting, but where does it get us?"

Miss Silver extracted a new ball from her knitting bag. The joining of the strands of wool took up her attention for a moment. Her reply when it came was in her most persuasive voice.

"If you could see your way to making some inquiries of Lady Melbury and Lady Muriel Street —"

"My dear ma'am — on what grounds!"

She said, "I supposed you would raise that point."

"What have you got at the back of your mind — a hunch?"

"My dear Frank!"

"It will do just as well by any other name. Shall we say a suspicion?"

"It is hardly that."

"What is it then?"

She stopped knitting and looked at him with a kind of earnest diffidence.

"I do not know quite how to put it. I have a feeling that when a number of curious things have been happening they may be connected with one another. I cannot at the moment bring any evidence to support this feeling, but I have wondered whether an interview with Lady Melbury and Lady Muriel might not produce some. The substitution of a copy for the original must have been made by someone able to obtain a drawing or photograph of sufficient accuracy to enable that copy to be made. There must also have been an opportunity of effecting the change. This opens up three possibilities. A member of the family. A confidential servant. A friend or relative with the requisite access. All these possibilities should be tested. The one which occurs to me is the last of them. I may be wrong — I do not know. There is a name that comes to my mind. I would like some inquiries to be made."

He said in a doubtful voice,

"What name?"

"I would rather not say. The person of whom I am thinking is related to many people in the county. As a young woman she amused herself with sketching. She worships her house and her ancestry, and has been put to it to maintain the family tradition. One of the missing women was in her employment."

Frank Abbott said, "Miss Cunningham? Miss Crewe? The official eye has been rather fixed upon the Dower House. Henry was off the map for more than twenty years, Nicholas works at Dalling Grange, and Miss Cunningham was the employer of Maggie Bell — whom I suppose we may now regard as the late Maggie Bell."

Miss Silver was knitting again, and quite briskly. She said in a decided tone, "Something of a very disturbing nature occurred here last night. I think I had better tell you about it."

"I think you had. When you say here —"

"I do not mean in this house."

He felt some relief, and showed it.

"Thank goodness for that! Who was disturbed, and in what way?"

She said, "Miss Cunningham," and proceeded to give him a very clear and succinct account of what Mrs Hubbard had observed and deduced. It raised a frown, and some scepticism.

194

"What it amounts to is that Miss Cunningham burned some string — probably after tripping over it somewhere — and that Mrs Hubbard found the bit that got away."

He was instantly aware of being a pupil who had not given the right answer. Her glance rested on him in mild rebuke.

"Not string, Frank — garden twine." She stopped knitting for long enough to produce a gummed-down envelope from her chintz bag and hand it over to him. "Here are the fragments found by Mrs Hubbard. You will observe that the twine has been treated with tar, doubtless as a preservative, and that this would make it unsuitable for normal use inside the house. If, however, it was to be used as a trip-cord on the stairs, the dark colour would render it extremely inconspicuous. In the second case, Mrs Hubbard reported that the balusters about six steps down from the landing were marked as if something had been tied tightly between them, and that some of the paint had flaked off."

He said more soberly, "This is third-hand evidence."

She was knitting with a certain briskness to which he was no stranger.

"Not quite, Frank. Mrs Merridew took me to call at the Dower House this afternoon, and Miss Cunningham was kind enough to take us over it. There are many points of historical interest, in addition to which I had the opportunity of checking Mrs Hubbard's story. The stair runs up to the bedroom floor, and there is a balustrade on either side. The woodwork has been painted a dark chocolate brown. Miss Cunningham

195

said what a pity it was, but it was like that when they came, and the stair being not oak but some much softer wood, they had never liked to risk injuring it by having it stripped. Whilst this conversation was going on I was able to observe the balusters, and to verify Mrs Hubbard's story. There had been a recent flaking of paint from the two balusters she had mentioned, and the square corners distinctly showed the marks of the twine. Furthermore, I could see for myself that there was some swelling above Miss Cunningham's right ankle, and a weal which could be plainly discerned through her rayon stocking. It was also quite obvious that she had had a shock of some kind. She had tea with Mrs Merridew yesterday, and there was no sign of it then. This afternoon she looked as if she had not slept all night, and it was plain that there was something on her mind. She was most kind in showing us over the house. I think she may even have been glad of something that would distract her thoughts, but she had difficulty in keeping them to the point, and on more than one occasion corrected herself in what she was saying."

"You think an attempt was made to injure her?"

"I believe it may have been more serious than that. The stair is a steep one, and the hall is paved with stone. If she had lost her balance on the sixth step she would have had another fourteen steps to fall, and she would have pitched down them headfirst on to stone flags."

"Who was in the house?"

"Her brother, Henry Cunningham, and her nephew Nicholas."

"No one else?"

"No one else."

After a pause he said, "What makes you think it was Miss Cunningham who was aimed at? What about Henry wanting to get rid of Nicholas, or Nicholas wanting to get rid of Henry? That sort of thing has been known to happen."

"Because I am convinced that Miss Cunningham herself believes it was she who was intended to fall, and her distress is occasioned by the conviction that either her brother or her nephew is attempting her life. There is the question of how she was to be induced to run down those stairs in such a hurry as to trip over the cord without noticing it. I do not think that a summons from below would have been risked. The next possibility which presents itself is a telephone call. The fixture is in the hall. Henry Cunningham will not speak on the telephone, so Mrs Merridew informs me, and Nicholas only when the call is for him. It is, therefore, always Miss Cunningham who hastens to it in the first place. But to suppose a prearranged telephone call would be to assume an outside accomplice, a thing which would greatly increase the risks. How much easier and safer to place an ordinary alarm clock in the hall. It could be set to any hour of the night, and the bell would be indistinguishable from that of the telephone."

He said with a faintly sardonic inflection, "You think of everything, don't you?" And then, "Perhaps you can tell me why anyone should want to disable or kill Miss Cunningham."

She said very gravely indeed, "What was the motive for the removal of Maggie Bell and of Miss Holiday? Miss Cunningham knows too much. I believe that to be the explanation in all these cases. Each of them had, or stumbled upon, a piece of knowledge which was dangerous to someone else. It is possible, perhaps even probable in the cases of Maggie Bell and Miss Holiday, that they were not aware, or at any rate not fully aware, of the implications of what they knew. In each case swift and ruthless action was taken to ensure silence. In the case of Miss Cunningham, she was one of the last people to see Miss Holiday alive. She met her coming away from Crewe House on Sunday evening, and she had a few words with her. She did not respond when I asked her what Miss Holiday had said, but passed the question off with a vague repetitive phrase. I did not say more at the time — she was having tea with Mrs Merridew — but I feel that she should be pressed upon the subject."

"But, my dear ma'am, she has been pressed. Didn't I tell you?"

"I think not, Frank."

He said in an apologetic tone, "I've been run off my feet. But here it is. Denning has been combing the place for anyone who might have met or seen Miss Holiday after she left Crewe House. Well, he turned up a girl called Mary Tufton who was bicycling back to Melbury after a visit to some people on a farm the other side of Hazel Green. She says that somewhere about half past five she saw Miss Cunningham near the drive of Crewe House. She knows her quite well by sight, because Mrs Tufton used to do a little odd dressmaking for her. Anyhow, she says a woman in a raincoat came out of the gate at Crewe House and Miss Cunningham stopped and spoke to her. One of them dropped what looked like a letter and Miss Cunningham picked it up. The other woman had her handkerchief out and was blowing her nose. She saw all this as she came up to them — there's a long straight piece of road there, as you know — and as she went by, Miss Cunningham turned in at the drive and the other woman went on in the direction of the village. Mary says it all passed in no time at all. They met, Miss Cunningham picked up the letter, and went on. Denning asked Miss Cunningham about it, and she said yes, that was just what happened. Miss Holiday dropped a letter when she used her handkerchief, and she picked it up again. She had just stopped to have a word with her. And as the letter was open and had been addressed to Miss Crewe, she offered to take it up to Crewe House."

"She did not say what the word was about?"

He laughed.

"I don't suppose it was about anything. Denning did his job all right, you know. He asked her if Miss Holiday seemed to be upset about anything, and she said oh no, she was just as usual. By the way, he went on and saw the cook at Crewe House — what's her name, Mrs Bolder — and she said the same. I gather he came away rather the worse for wear. She wanted to know what he thought she would be doing upsetting anyone. Umbrage was taken, and he wasn't sorry to get away from her. A lady with a tongue!"

Miss Silver was not knitting at quite her usual speed. After a moment she said, "Thank you, Frank. I cannot say that I am satisfied. If Miss Holiday was murdered, there must have been a motive for her murder. Someone who was in contact with her must have decided that she had become, or was becoming, dangerous and must be got rid of. It seems as if the danger may have arisen suddenly. In which case every contact with her during those last few hours of her life must be regarded as important and very carefully considered. Miss Cunningham may be aware of something which she has not seen fit to pass on to the police."

"You are suggesting that Miss Holiday had acquired some dangerous knowledge, and that she may have indicated as much to Miss Cunningham, or that she may have been thought to have done so. Well then, what about Mrs Maple and Mrs Selby? Don't forget they saw her too, and that in the case of Mrs Selby there was every opportunity for confidences."

Miss Silver inclined her head.

"Quite so. But I think Mrs Maple is negligible. The contact between her and Miss Holiday was brief and any confidence very unlikely when it would have to be shouted into the ear of so deaf a person."

"What about Mrs Selby — a very likely candidate? Nobody seems to have tried to get her out of the way."

200

Miss Silver put her head a little on one side in the manner which always reminded him of a bird and said, "I find the immunity of Mrs Selby very interesting, my dear Frank."

CHAPTER
TWENTY-SIX

Rosamond and Jenny had finished their tea. Jenny had already plunged back into her Gloria Gilmore, which was now at the very peak of sentiment and romance. Rosamond, for the moment unoccupied, lay back in her chair and considered with surprise her own reluctance to pick up the tray and get on with the business of taking it through to the pantry and washing up. After meaning to stay awake the night before, she had slept so deeply and heavily that it did not seem as if she was really awake even now. Her thoughts moved slowly and with an effort, and her body would not have moved at all if she had not pushed it.

The sound of Lydia Crewe's bell brought her to her feet with an effort. Jenny frowned, jerked impatiently, and said, "Blast!"

"Jenny!"

Jenny made an impish face.

"Wouldn't it be wonderful if it just happened when you said it? Ping — and no more bell! I think I'd blast Aunt Lydia too whilst I was about it."

"Jenny — please!"

Jenny giggled.

"Oh, go along! I'll say something much worse than that if it goes on ringing."

Rosamond went into the crowded room with an intensification of the feeling it always gave her. There were so many things — the air was so hot and heavy that it was like moving against a sluggish tide. Her limbs were heavy too, and for a moment her head swam.

Lydia Crewe sat in her upright chair. Her grey features were composed. An old purple wrap flowed round her to her feet. The stones in her rings glittered under the chandelier. Every light was on.

"What is it, Aunt Lydia?"

Lydia Crewe said in her harsh voice, "Come in and sit down. I want to talk to you."

Rosamond felt a stirring of alarm. You didn't talk to Aunt Lydia. She interrogated you, and she laid down the law. There was a cold remembrance of an interview when everyone thought that Jenny was going to die, and of another when the pattern of their life here was laid down and she had to receive it with what gratitude she could muster. She heard Lydia Crewe say, "I want to talk to you about Jenny," and the room was suddenly full of fear.

"Yes, Aunt Lydia?"

"She is a great deal better. In fact, to all intents and purposes I think we may say that she is well. We have now to consider what the next step should be."

"Yes —" The word came heavy and halting. She had not meant to let it stand alone, but Lydia Crewe did not wait for her to add anything to the one lame word. She went on in her decided way.

"It has been unavoidable, but no one can pretend that Jenny has been leading a normal life. A neglected education must have serious consequences in after years. She needs discipline, companionship, and a regular course of study. I do not think there can be any possible disagreement on these points. In fact, what she now needs is to go to school."

It was what Craig had said — it was what she herself believed. But coming from Lydia Crewe it struck like a blow. Before she could find the right words the dominant voice was saying, "I have therefore been instituting some inquiries. Miss Simmington's school at Brinton appears to me to be just what is required. It is neither too small nor too large, the air is bracing, and the pupils are equipped to earn their own living. Lady Westerham gives me a very good account of the school and of Miss Simmington. She was left with a cousin's children on her hands and has very kindly made herself responsible for their education, as I am prepared to do for Jenny's."

The deep-set eyes were fixed on Rosamond's face. They demanded gratitude. They compelled it. Rosamond did the best she could.

"It's very good of you, Aunt Lydia —"

The "but" which should have followed was never spoken. Miss Crewe had the word again.

"I am glad you should admit it. Young people are only too inclined to take everything for granted. I am prepared to pay Jenny's fees, and to supply the outfit which the school requires. In return I shall expect you to continue your present duties here, and since you will no longer have Jenny to care for, I shall expect those duties to be carried out rather more efficiently than they have been. I am sure you will agree that the sooner Jenny takes advantage of this arrangement the better. In the circumstances, Miss Simmington has agreed to receive her immediately. She tells me that the outfit can be supplied locally."

Rosamond was on her feet.

"Aunt Lydia, you don't mean — you can't mean that you have made all these arrangements without telling us!"

She met a formidable glance.

"You are taking a very strange tone, Rosamond. I have been put to considerable trouble, and I am prepared to undertake very considerable expense. I do not wish to remind you that you and Jenny are quite without resources of your own, but I feel obliged to do so. I have made these perfectly proper and suitable arrangements, and I expect you to fall in with them."

Rosamond's hands gripped one another.

"I know — Jenny will have — to go to school. I have been thinking about it — myself. I thought perhaps — next term — I thought perhaps — I could get a post — near her —"

Miss Crewe said harshly, "You have no qualifications for a post in a school. Your place is here where you can make some return, however inadequate, for what I am prepared to do for you." She lifted some papers and held them out. "Here is a prospectus of the school, and the last letter which I have received from Miss Simmington. You will see that she suggests your bringing Jenny down on Friday."

Rosamond made no attempt to take the papers.

"Oh, no — no!"

Miss Crewe said sharply, "Please control yourself! I am prepared to make some allowance for the fact that this seems to have come as a surprise to you, though after the specialist's last report you should have been prepared. You have, in fact, admitted as much."

Rosamond spoke with an effort.

"I know — she ought to go to school. But it's too soon. I must have time — to get her used to the idea. No one — no one would say it would be right to rush her like this. It would upset her — dreadfully."

Lydia Crewe gave an impatient sigh.

"Really, Rosamond, you will have to watch your tendency to hysteria. If you take this attitude with Jenny, she will naturally be upset. I expect you to dwell on the advantages I shall be giving her and the companionship she will have. This agitation is entirely out of place. Please sit down and control yourself. If you go near Jenny in your present frame of mind, she will certainly set herself against the plan. Now I want to ask you quite seriously whether you think that Jenny's present way of life should be prolonged."

Rosamond sat down again. She mustn't let Lydia Crewe shake her. The thing was unreasonable, and she must oppose it in a reasonable manner. She said, "No, of course not. She must go to school, but not at a moment's notice like this. And before she goes anywhere I should want to go down and see the head mistress, and the school, and the other girls. Jenny would feel quite differently about the whole thing if I could come back and tell her all about it."

Miss Crewe had been looking down at her rings. The colours moved under the light of the chandelier. There was a large square ruby jostled by a great half-hoop of diamonds. There was a sapphire which had been given to her great-grandmother by the Regent, and the emerald which had been brought back from the Indies by a Crewe who had sailed with Drake. She looked up now, her eyes colder than the jewels, and said in a new voice — quieter — slower — bleak, "So you are to call the tune? And take your time about it? Do you really know of no reason why time is just the one thing that neither you nor Jenny can be allowed to have?"

Rosamond felt cold at her heart.

"What do you mean?"

"You either know what I mean, or you are even stupider than I have thought you. Are you really ignorant of the fact that Jenny has been getting out of the house at night?"

The colour rushed into Rosamond's face, only to drain away again and leave her blanched.

Miss Crewe gave a short hard laugh.

"I see you do know. May I ask how long it has been going on?"

"Aunt Lydia, I didn't know. Someone told me — yesterday — that she had been seen —"

"Who told you?"

"Craig Lester."

"And who told him?"

"He saw her — himself."

"In the middle of the night?"

"He had gone for a walk — he couldn't sleep —"

"Where did he see her?"

Question and answer had come so fast that there had been no time to think. It wasn't thought that checked her now, it was the instinct to protect, to cover up, to make as little of Jenny's escapade as she could. She said,

"She was coming into the drive."

"And what was Mr Lester doing there?"

"He was passing by, but when he saw Jenny he followed her until he saw her go into the house again."

Lydia Crewe said grimly, "By the side door. I believe that is how she comes and goes. She was lucky not to find it locked against her. If I find it open again, that is what I shall do. Well, now that you have admitted this propensity, will you maintain that it can be allowed to continue? Do you think it is safe or suitable to have Jenny wandering heaven knows where in the middle of the night? You are not very sensible or very experienced, but I suppose you read the papers. You must have some idea of what might happen to a girl wandering about alone. She wasn't walking in her sleep, I suppose?"

Rosamond shook her head.

"Craig said not."

"Where had she been?"

"I don't know."

"What did she have to say for herself?"

208

"I haven't asked her anything — yet. It — it was a shock. I wanted time."

Miss Crewe looked at her with something like a smile.

"Oh, yes, of course — you must have plenty of time. And now that you have had it, are you still going to tell me that there is any to lose? This is Wednesday. If I could have had my way, I would have packed Jenny off today. As it is, you will lock her into her room the next two nights, and you will travel down to Brinton with her by the nine-thirty from Melbury on Friday morning."

Rosamond got up. She felt the pressure of a formidable will and she had nothing to set against it. It was Jenny herself who had plucked the weapon of reason out of her hand. Lydia Crewe had only to tell her story and everyone who heard it would say that she was doing the right thing. As she took a step towards the door, the harsh voice pursued her.

"You understand me, Rosamond — Jenny leaves this house on Friday morning."

She said, "Yes," and went out of the room. There was nothing else for her to say. It was an ultimatum, and they both knew it. Jenny was being turned out. If they had had any money or anywhere to go, it would have been an order of release. The plain fact was that they had nothing. When Jenny left Crewe House on Friday morning Rosamond would have no choice but to take her to the school which Lydia Crewe had chosen. She would have no choice at all.

CHAPTER
TWENTY-SEVEN

She turned away from Jenny's room and ran down the
passage into the hall. She had the feeling that she
couldn't run fast enough. Lydia Crewe and her harsh
dominant will reaching out to her, ruthless, compelling!
It was like knowing that there was a fierce animal shut
up in that oppressive room and that it might at any
moment be loosed and follow her. She snatched her old
coat from the cupboard under the stairs and ran out by
the side door and down the garden into the wood. To
be alone in the dusk had no terrors. It was the house
that frightened her — and Lydia Crewe. Out here in
the wood she would not hear, however stridently the
summoning bell might ring, however persistently Jenny
might call to her. She wasn't ready to face her yet. She
must have time to put herself out of the way, and to get
her to see the whole thing as an adventure. She must
keep Jenny from getting hurt, and that was the way that
would hurt her least.

It was very dark in the wood. There was still some
light outside, but here the trees moved with their
shadows and shut her in. They gave her a feeling of
safety. They were the walls of her house of defence. It
was her own place, where she could be quiet and steady

her thoughts. She walked to and fro in the little clearing at the heart of the wood. Presently she would have to think, but for the moment all she wanted was to stop thinking, to be quiet, and above all to be away from Crewe House.

She did not know how long it was before she heard the footstep. It was a man's step, quick and vigorous. She heard Craig calling her.

"Rosamond! Are you there?"

For a moment she was any wild wood creature. She had an instinct to stay quite still where she was and let the silence cover her, but when he said her name again, she was Rosamond and he was Craig. She moved and went to meet him.

"Jenny said you might be here."

There was a roughness in his voice. He had had the unreasoned thought that she might have just walked out of his world and been lost. His arm came round her.

"Why on earth do you go off by yourself like this? I don't like it."

She said, "I must — have somewhere —"

"That barrack of a house has rooms enough!"

She shook her head. He could see the movement, but not how she looked.

"I have to get — right away — sometimes —"

"And this was one of the times?"

"Yes."

"Rosamond, what has been happening?"

He was too close to her not to know when she was in trouble. He felt the trouble now, but he didn't know what it was. He had to know. He spoke her name again insistently, "*Rosamond* —"

She said on a quick uneven breath, "She's sending Jenny away —"

"Where?"

"A school at Brinton. She's got it all fixed up."

"Without telling you?"

"She never said a word. Craig, I knew she would have to go sometime. But not like this. Even if she hadn't been ill, I ought to see the place first. No one has seen it. A woman she knows sent some orphan cousins there — that's how she heard of it. It's just any place to send Jenny away to, and she has done it all behind my back."

He said in a controlled voice, "You must certainly see any place she suggests before Jenny goes there."

He felt the tremor that went over her.

"There isn't time — she's planned it so that there shouldn't be time. She says I'm to take her there on Friday — day after tomorrow! We're to take the nine-thirty from Melbury — it's all fixed up. And there's nothing I can do. She's got the whip hand and she knows it. She's always had the whip hand. We haven't got any money. There is no one else who would take us in, and she won't keep Jenny any longer. She is to go to school, and I am to stay here and do what I can to make up for the fees Aunt Lydia will have to pay."

He said in his strong voice, "Well, it's not going to work out that way, so don't worry. Even Miss Crewe can be made to see that she can't just bundle Jenny off like this at a moment's notice. Why don't you stand up to her?"

He felt her stiffen.

"You think I'm afraid. Well, I am, but I wouldn't let that stop me. If I were on my own I'd just walk out. I'd have done it long ago. In fact I wouldn't ever have come. It's like being in prison. But what can I do with Jenny? The specialist said she would need care for some time. I don't know what I could earn — not very much, because I'm not trained for anything. It would have to be housework, or a shop — and how could I leave Jenny alone all day? I did think if I could find a really nice school they might take Jenny for less and let me work there. I've heard of that sort of thing. But this doesn't give us any time. And, Craig, you say she can't do it all in a hurry like this — but she can, and everyone would back her up. You see, she knows about Jenny getting out of the house at night."

"How does she know?"

"She didn't tell me, but she does. And you see, it justifies her. She said how dangerous it was, and it couldn't possibly be allowed to go on. Everything she said was reasonable and just what anyone would say. But that wasn't why she said it. It was just something she'd got to make me come to heel and do what she wanted. Do you see now why I had to get out of the house? I couldn't see Jenny until I got hold of myself. I couldn't tell her she was going to be sent away — I don't know how to tell her now."

He had had his arm round her all this time, and she had let it stay. It crossed his mind to wonder if she so

213

much as knew that it was there. He put both hands on her shoulders now and let her feel their weight.

"Rosamond, stop talking! If you go on saying there isn't anything to be done, there won't be. It's quite futile. If you'll stop panicking and listen to me, there's a perfectly simple way out of all this. I should just like to feel that you are going to listen before I tell you about it."

"I'm listening."

"Well, to start with, I don't know whether you happen to remember that I've asked you to marry me. You didn't say yes, and you didn't say no, and I didn't want to rush you. I still don't want to — I'd like you to believe that. But events seem to be taking charge, and that would be one way of getting the better of them. If we were married there wouldn't be any problem to settle — we could just take Jenny and go. I've got a house, and I've got a job. It's all as simple as the ABC. But it depends on what you feel about it. I don't know whether I've mentioned that I love you, but I don't think you can have helped noticing it. I fell in love with your picture, and I fall farther and faster every time I see you. I know myself pretty well, and as far as I am concerned it will just go on like that. I'm not putting in any sob-stuff, because we've got to use our heads. Now what about your side of it? I think I gave you a brief catalogue of my faults. Anyhow you will have noticed them for yourself by now. All I can say is what I think I've said before, I'll look after you, and I'll look after Jenny. And I'll eat my hat if I'm not easier to live with than Lydia Crewe. What about it?"

Rosamond found it hard to believe that she could be shaking on the edge of laughter, but right from the beginning, even when he was saying the most outrageous things, even when he was making her angry, there had been a hidden spring of laughter bubbling up and threatening her self-control. If she let it have its way it would drown all the feeling of pride and self-respect to which she had been brought up. You can't laugh at someone and be proud at the same time. The two things just don't mix. When he said, "What about it?" it came over her how easy it would be just to say yes and let go of all her troubles.

He bent suddenly and laid his cheek against hers, not kissing her but just staying like that for a moment. When he said her name on a quick shaken breath, she pushed him away.

"You can't, you can't! It wouldn't be fair!"

"To me, or to you?"

"To you of course!"

"Thank you, I can look after myself. We're not driving a bargain, you know. We're talking about getting married — to have and to hold from this day forward, for better, for worse, for richer, for poorer, in sickness and in health, till death us do part. And that's quite a different sort of thing. It means there are two of you to take whatever comes along, and if they are bad times there are two of you to take them on, and if they are good times there are two of you to share them. It's not a matter of being fair or unfair. I'm in it up to my neck, and all you can do about it is to stay high and dry on the bank yourself. Only I warn you I shall never stop trying to pull you in."

She said with something between a sob and a laugh, "Oh, I'm in all right," and felt his arms close about her. There were no more words. She put up her face and they kissed, and it was the happiest, most natural thing in the world. It was like coming home after you have been out in the wind and the rain. It was like a fire-lit room when you have been cold for a long, long time. It was like food when you are hungry, and water to quench your thirst.

He became aware that his face was wet with her tears. He said, "Rosamond, why are you crying? It's all over — there's nothing to cry about now."

"That's why —"

"My darling idiot!"

"Yes — I am rather. There hasn't been anyone — for such a long time —" She was groping for a handkerchief and not being very successful.

"Here — have mine."

It was large and dry and clean. Tears were all very well in one of Gloria Gilmore's books, but in real life they made a sight of you and you had to blow your nose.

"Better now?"

She stuffed the handkerchief down into the pocket of the old tweed coat. He could just see the movement of her head which meant "Yes".

"Well, my sweet, that being that, suppose we get down to brass tacks. You're not the sort that faints when you have a shock, are you?"

"No, I'm not."

"Because it would be damned inconvenient, and the ground is sure to be wet."

"Craig — what is it?"

"Well, nothing much — nothing to get the jitters about anyway. It's just that I want you to marry me tomorrow."

It wasn't a shock at all — it just fitted in. But she heard herself say, "We couldn't!"

"Darling, that's where you make a mistake. I went to see my uncle's solicitor in Melbury yesterday morning and got all the low-down. I am of age, you are of age, and the registrar has to have one clear day's notice. I went on to see him, and we can get married tomorrow morning at half past ten. We can have a church wedding afterwards if you want to. It takes a bit longer, which is why I plumped for the registrar."

"Craig —"

"Darling, you had better let me do the talking. I've been getting steadily more enraged every day since I first came down here. You are not only being overworked and bullied, but there are all sorts of things going on in the background. Two people have disappeared in this village. One of them has certainly been murdered, and the other probably. Jenny gets out and wanders about in the middle of the night. And now Miss Crewe wants to pack her off to a school no one knows anything about. As things are, she would have public opinion on her side, and you can't fight her alone. I've got no standing and I couldn't do a thing, but once we were married it would be a very different

217

pair of shoes. Miss Crewe isn't Jenny's guardian or anything like that, I take it?"

"Oh, no."

"Then we can just take her and go, and nobody can say a word about it. But we can't do anything until I've got the legal right to take you away. I won't rush you afterwards, and I don't want to rush you now, but you must give me the right to look after you both. Once I've got that, it's all plain sailing. Rosamond, I've got to get you away!"

She had walked in the wood so many times and been solaced there. Now all at once it was a cold and desolate place. She wanted to be where there were lights and people. She wanted to be anywhere in the world away from Crewe House, and from Lydia Crewe. She couldn't look after Jenny by herself, but Craig would look after them both.

CHAPTER
TWENTY-EIGHT

At about half past two on that same afternoon Nicholas looked up from the plan he was drawing. Howard, who was Mr Burlington's secretary and whom he didn't much like, had come noiselessly between him and the light. As the scale to which he was working was a very small one and demanded absolute accuracy, he was annoyed, and showed it. Super secretaries who oiled around and suddenly sprang themselves upon you could hardly expect to be popular. Howard was not only not popular, he was detested. He looked down his long sallow nose and said, "Mr Burlington would like to see you, Cunningham," and stood waiting with rather the air of a warder for Nicholas to get to his feet. He did not, however, accompany him any farther than the door of Mr Burlington's private room, where he withdrew in a disapproving manner, leaving him to go in alone.

The room was a small and pleasant one. Successive mistresses of Dalling Grange had made music or sat to their embroidery where the light came slanting in through three tall windows. They had been hung with brocaded curtains then, now they were bare. The pale green panelling had a dusty look. Two serviceable rugs took the place of the delicate carpet which, with most of the furniture, had gone to the sale room, giving place to an office desk, bookcases, filing cabinets, and some rather utilitarian chairs.

Mr Burlington sat at the desk — a thin man with a quick frown and a sharp tongue. He had brains, or he wouldn't be sitting in that chair. That was about as far as Nicholas had ever felt inclined to go in his favour. He said abruptly, "Come in and shut the door!"

As Nicholas complied he was aware that there was a second person present. He had been looking out of the window. He turned round now and came forward. It had really been quite easy not to notice him. He was of medium height and medium build. He wore pale rimmed glasses, and his general colouring might have been described as protective — thin, fine hair of a mousy shade; the most ordinary of features; the least noticeable of clothes. Mr Burlington turned to him and said, "This is Nicholas Cunningham. I am going to ask him to give you his own account of the interview I had with him this morning."

Nicholas found this on the chilling side. He concluded that the indeterminate gentleman must be an Important Person. Even a Very Important Person. He felt that he had been named to him rather more as the accused is named in court than in the way of a social introduction.

Still shrouded in anonymity, the Important Person sat down. Nicholas was invited to sit down. He took a chair which had obviously been placed for him and faced the light from those long unshaded windows. Mr Burlington said, "Now, Cunningham —"

"I don't quite know where you want me to begin, sir."

Mr Burlington frowned.

"I want you to repeat what passed between us this morning from the moment that you came into this room and shut the door behind you. What did you say, and what did you do?"

This was an odd game. He supposed it to be some kind of test of his accuracy. He said, "You were sitting at your table writing, and I came up to it and said, 'It's happened again, sir'."

"And what did you mean by that?"

"Do you want me to go back over what had happened before?"

"Certainly."

"About a month ago I found an odd piece of paper in one of my pockets. It looked as if it had been there some time, but I don't see how it could have been. It was crumpled and rubbed. It had been written on in pencil, but the writing was very faint, and neither the words nor the lettering were English."

The Important Person with the extraordinarily unimportant air now spoke for the first time.

"What did you take them to be?"

"I thought they might be Russian, or one of the other Eastern European languages."

"What made you think so?"

"The letters were different."

"Do you know any Russian?"

"No, sir."

"What languages do you know?"

"French — a little German — the usual amount of school Latin —"

"You couldn't read the paper?"

"No, sir."

"What did you do with it?"

"I thought I had better show it to Mr Burlington."

"What made you think that?"

"I thought it might be Russian. I didn't like it being in my pocket. I thought he had better see it."

With the slightest of gestures he was handed back. Mr Burlington told him to go on.

"When it happened again, I liked it a whole lot less. I came down to breakfast this morning, and my aunt came in with another of those crumpled papers in her hand. She had been mending my jacket pocket the evening before. She said the paper must have worked down through the hole. She said it was caught between the lining and the stuff. She thought I might want it."

The quiet voice took up its questioning again.

"Had she read it?"

"She wouldn't read anything she thought was private."

"She might not have thought it was private. Did she read it?"

"I don't know."

"You didn't ask her?"

Some colour came up into Nicholas's face.

"No."

"Why not?"

222

"I didn't want her to think it was important."

"That might be quite a good reason if it wasn't a personal one. Was it?"

The last words were not loud, but they gave him the feeling that he had been flicked in the face. Quite unexpectedly. He said, "No, sir." He hoped he hadn't waited too long before saying it.

"Perhaps you will expand that a little."

"I didn't know what was on the paper. I remembered about the other one. I thought it was another of the same kind. Mr Burlington wouldn't want it to be talked about."

"You didn't read it immediately?"

"Not until I was alone. I just pushed it into my pocket and hoped my aunt would think it was of no importance."

"You had already made up your mind it was important?"

"I thought Mr Burlington ought to see it."

"When did you make up your mind to show it to him?"

"As soon as I read it."

Without any change the quiet voice said, "I am going to read it now."

The paper came out of a pocketbook. The glasses focused themselves upon it. The voice read:

"— you must see this for yourself. If you cannot get us any better material you are useless, and when anything is of no more use, it is better to scrap it."

"When you read these words, what was your reaction?"

"I thought someone was trying to frame me."

"And you decided to go to Mr Burlington. A very proper course, but one you might quite easily have taken if you had wished to safeguard yourself against some outside employer who had become dissatisfied, and who was prepared to scrap you."

Nicholas pushed back his chair and came to his feet with a jerk.

"Sir — I protest!"

The eyes behind the pale glasses rested upon him steadily.

"Yes. But then you would — wouldn't you? And all the more if it was true."

Nicholas Cunningham took a hold of himself. Easy enough to go off the deep end. And satisfying while it lasted. But there were always the bits to be picked up afterwards, and he didn't fancy the job. He looked across the table and said, "I can't prove anything. I can only tell you what's happened. I took both those papers to Mr Burlington as soon as I found them. I think someone is trying to frame me. If I knew who it was I shouldn't be here. I should be dealing with him."

Burlington looked at the other man, and back at Nicholas. He said, "Sit down, Cunningham."

CHAPTER
TWENTY-NINE

It was getting on for ten o'clock that night when Craig Lester came out of the Holly Tree and strolled across the road. As he came to the White Cottage he could see that the lights were on in both front rooms. With only the two ladies in the house, it occurred to him to wonder why two sitting rooms should be in use. But before he could reflect that he hadn't lost much time in acquiring the true village spirit the front door opened and Frank Abbott came out. During the moment in which he stood outlined against the glow from the dining room door Craig made up his mind. He was aware of the figure of Miss Maud Silver in the background, and as Frank turned to bid her good night he stepped between the overarching yews and walked quickly up the flagged path. Miss Silver, drawing back in order to shut the door, checked, looking into the darkness. Frank Abbott turned at the sound of his footsteps and almost bumped into him. Then, as recognition followed, he said, "Hullo, it's you! Which of us do you want? I was just off."

"I wonder if I could have a few words with Miss Silver? If it isn't too late."

"Well, if you don't want me I'll be going."

He went down the path. Craig said in an apologetic voice, "Is it too late, Miss Silver?"

The light was behind her, but he thought she smiled.

"By no means, Mr Lester. Pray come in."

She took him into the dining room and indicated the chair which Frank Abbott had occupied. When they were seated and she had resumed her knitting, he received an encouraging look.

"What can I do for you, Mr Lester?"

"A very great favour, if you will."

"Will you tell me what it is?"

"Well, before I do that, perhaps you ought to know that I have a pretty good idea of why you are here."

She said with a shade of rebuke, "I am paying a visit to my old school friend, Mrs Merridew."

"And Frank Abbott is paying a visit to one of his innumerable cousins! I suppose he has told you that we have known each other on and off for quite a time?"

"Yes, Mr Lester."

"Well, what I'm trying to get across is that I know a good deal about your particular activities. Frank gave me a hint not to do any broadcasting — I suppose he told you that too."

She smiled.

"These things make so much talk in a village."

He nodded.

"As far as I am concerned, you are Mrs Merridew's friend and nothing more."

Her needles clicked above the bright wool.

"It matters less than it would have done at first. Pray, what is it that you wish me to do for you?"

226

His face lit up with a smile that transformed it.

"You wouldn't feel inclined to come to my wedding, would you? Because that's what I came here to ask. And before you say no, will you be very kind indeed and let me tell you a little more about it all?"

"Certainly, Mr Lester."

He said in a quick boyish way which took ten years from his age, "You *are* kind! And that is what Rosamond wants. She has never had it, and just now she needs it badly."

Miss Silver looked at him in a most sympathetic manner.

"A most charming girl."

He said with complete simplicity, "I fell in love with her picture before I ever saw her — just an odd photograph slipped in with some manuscripts which Jenny sent my firm. Then when I saw her — well, it was all up. But of course I didn't expect it to be the same for her. I didn't want to rush her. I thought perhaps it would take a long time. And then I began to see that time was just the thing we hadn't got. Miss Crewe was working her to death, Jenny was all set to kick over the traces, and there was something pretty nasty going on in the background. This is all in confidence of course."

"Certainly, Mr Lester."

He could be sensitive to the finer shades.

"I needn't have said that — I *know*. You'll forgive me, won't you? Well, on Sunday I discovered that Jenny was getting out of the house at night. I couldn't sleep — I'd got a lot on my mind — and I went for a walk. When I was near the entrance to Crewe House a car came down the road. The headlights picked Jenny up. You know there's a stile there leading to a footpath over the fields — she had just come across from there. As soon as the car had gone she ran past me and went up the drive. I saw her let herself in by a side door. I told Rosamond, and she was very much upset. Now it seems that Miss Crewe either saw or heard her come in. She has been making arrangements behind Rosamond's back to send Jenny to school, and this afternoon she told her it was all fixed up and she was to take her down there on Friday morning. That just about put the lid on. I'd been taking precautions, you know. Those girls haven't a penny, or a soul in the world to take their part except me, and as things were I'd got just no standing at all. What I did was to give notice at the Registrar's in Melbury — you can get married after one clear day. We can get married tomorrow. I've fixed it for half past ten. Well, I want Rosamond to have someone with her. These things make talk — I want to stop as much of it as I can. I've come here to ask you whether you'll drive into Melbury with us and see us married. We can't ask anyone who lives here, because Miss Crewe would have their blood, and besides — I can't think of anyone I'd rather have."

He received a smile of great kindness and charm.

"You feel that this is really necessary, Mr Lester?"

"Yes, I do. If I'm Rosamond's husband and Jenny's brother-in-law, I can get them out of here. There are things going on — I don't like it. They're not safe."

She inclined her head.

"I will come to your wedding, Mr Lester."

CHAPTER
THIRTY

Lucy Cunningham had gone through the day, she hardly knew how. As long as Mrs Hubbard was there and she was doing things in and about the house she managed pretty well. Whilst she was making beds, dusting, emptying hot-water bottles — Henry liked one, and she wouldn't have done without hers for anything — mixing balancer meal with scraps, boiling up a mash and feeding it to the hens, the comfortable everydayness of these occupations stood like a wall between her and the events of the night. From the safe shelter of that wall it was possible to regard them as partaking of the unreal quality of any other dream. Looking back as far as her childhood, she could remember to have dreamed that she was being pursued by wolves or Red Indians, that she was trying to pack everything she possessed in one small handbag and catch a train for Australia, the missing of which would plunge her in unknown but quite irremediable disaster. She had also dreamed about falling over cliffs, a long, long swooping drop, and waking just in time to avoid being dashed to pieces at the bottom. All these were things which had happened in the night and had frightened her very much at the time, but in the comfortable daylight they thinned away and were gone.

She went busily from one task to another, and found that the weight upon her tended to lift. There were even times when she ceased to be aware of it for perhaps as long as several minutes on end. Mrs Parsons's cat was back on the wall again and she had to chase it away — a patchy tortoiseshell with a lot of white about it and really quite a malignant expression in its eyes. She would have to speak to Lydia about having down the tree between the hen-run and the wall, an old walnut that never bore, because the minute there were any young chickens that horrible cat would find it only too easy to climb down it and snatch them. Lydia wouldn't like the tree to be cut. She didn't like anything changed or altered. Of course she didn't *have* to ask her, because Papa had bought the Dower House and she had a legal right to cut down anything she wanted to. Only she couldn't stand on her legal rights — not with Lydia Crewe.

Henry was out for most of the morning, and they turned out his room. There was a dead frog in his collar drawer, and some rather slimy-looking plants in the bedroom basin. She was considering whether they could be thrown away, when she discovered that there were tadpoles hatching out amongst them. She desisted therefore, and laid the frog on the front of the washstand where he could hardly help seeing it. Mrs Hubbard, in the background, made small clicking sounds of disapproval punctuated by an occasional sniff. How Miss Cunningham could put up with it, she *didn't* know. Nobody could say he wasn't a quiet gentleman, but just as well he never got married, for there weren't many wives would put up with what his sister did.

By the time Henry's room had been left as clean and tidy as was compatible with not throwing anything away Lucy really felt a great deal better. All the years during which he had brought in eggs, and moths, and caterpillars, and practically every other mess you could think of, stood solidly between her and the horrid thought which had come to her in the night. Not Henry who mourned when so much as a beetle died — oh, no, not Henry!

She went into Nicholas's room to dust and tidy it, whilst Mrs Hubbard went downstairs. It was the room he had had since he was a little boy and George and Ethel had sent him home from India. They had both died out there, and she had been left to bring him up. There was still one bookcase full of books about submarines, and aeroplanes, and boy detectives. She picked up one or two and looked at them. There was a page all scribbled over with drawings of hens, very clever and funny. Nicholas could always draw. There was a caricature of Lydia, tall and black and severe, and one of herself, all round-about. She set the book back on the shelf and remembered Nicholas putting his arm round her and saying in his laughing voice, "But, Lu darling, what's the good of pretending — you *are* a roly-poly, and there's no getting away from it." Her heart softened. He had laughed at her, he had teased her, he had loved her.

It was after Mrs Hubbard had gone that the weight began to come down again. Henry had been in one of his most abstracted moods at lunch. He propped a book before him and only spoke to ask for a second helping of pudding, and when he had finished it he went away into the study and shut the door. There was nothing new about this, but Lucy Cunningham felt that it would have been pleasant to have had coffee together in the drawing room, and that it wouldn't have hurt him to tell her what he had been doing all the morning. She was therefore rather more than pleased to have a visit from Marian Merridew and the friend who was staying with her. She took them over the house, apologizing by the way for the tadpoles and the dead frog.

"My brother is writing a book, you know, and it upsets him very much if anything is thrown out or tidied away."

Miss Silver was all that was interested and sympathetic. She admired the needlework picture done by Georgiana Crewe in the year 1755. She admired the graceful portrait of her in the drawing room.

"Of course all the valuable portraits are at Crewe House, but this one, as you see, has been painted upon one of the panels, so Mr Crewe let it go with the house. My father bought most of the furniture as it stood. He and Mr Crewe thought it would be a pity to disturb it, and they had more than they wanted at Crewe House — but it upset Miss Crewe very much at the time."

She did not know what had made her say that about Lydia. She was just feeling that she wanted to talk, and it slipped out. It didn't really matter of course, because Marian Merridew knew, and this Miss Silver was just a passing guest. She went on telling her about the house.

But whether they went up or down, she found that her eyes went to the sixth baluster from the top of the stairs, where a trip-cord of garden twine had been tied so tightly that the edges had dented and some of the paint had flaked off.

She kept the two ladies as long as she could, but in the end they went away and she was left alone. Then, as the house darkened and silence filled it, her wall of defence came tumbling down and she was left face to face, not with a dream, but with stubborn inveterate fact. Someone had tried to kill her in this house last night. There were only the three of them there — all Cunninghams, all of one blood — Henry, and Nicholas, and herself —

One of them had tried to kill her. Would he leave it at that, or would he try again?

The evening closed down slowly. There was low cloud and a dampness in the air. Nicholas rang up to say that he would be late.

"Don't bother about a meal — I shan't want it."

She could not keep the old solicitude from her voice. She heard it there, and in some curious way it reassured her.

"Do you mean that you are dining out? You must have your food."

He said easily, "That's all right — I'll be having something here," and rang off.

Her heart sank. Another of those dreadful meals with Henry not speaking. There had been so many of them, and she had not noticed or minded. Now she saw them stretching out in an endless unendurable vista. And then, quite suddenly like the jab of a knife, there was the thought that there might be no future for her to dread. If she had fallen at the trip-cord on the stair last night she would not be here now, thinking about having supper alone with Henry and being frightened. Suppose there was something else that was planned to happen. Perhaps now. Perhaps later. It might be that she and Henry would sit down to one last meal. Perhaps nothing would happen until after that. Henry would want his supper — and there would be the washing-up —

How foolish, how dreadfully foolish to let such thoughts come into her mind. She mustn't let them come. She must think about getting supper and washing up afterwards. There were herrings to fry, and she must remember that Henry liked his crisp. And the toast too. That was the sort of thing she must keep her mind on. And then Nicholas would be coming home, and — and — "I can always lock my door."

CHAPTER
THIRTY-ONE

Up at crewe House Rosamond moved as if she were in a dream. The night lay before her like the river of Jordan, dark, and narrow, and fleeting. She had only to cross it, and she and Jenny would be free of their house of bondage. Only those twelve dark hours to cross, and the promised land would be theirs. Sometimes her thoughts were so light and joyful that she felt as if they had the power to lift her over a longer, darker passage than this. Sometimes she looked towards the morning and found it very far away. She had not as yet said anything to Jenny, either about her going to school or about Craig. Since Jenny would not now be going to the school which Lydia Crewe had chosen for her, there was no need to trouble her about it. If she were not afraid, she would be angry, and in any case violently disturbed. Rosamond wanted her to sleep and be ready for what she would have to be told next day. It wouldn't disturb her, she would be very much excited, and she must have a good night's rest.

Her efforts to get Jenny to bed early were extremely unsuccessful. Jenny wanted to listen to the wireless, she wanted to finish her book, she wanted to talk, she rejected with vehemence the idea of being sleepy. Her eyes sparkled and her tongue ran nineteen to the dozen.

"There's the kind of night you want to rush into bed and snuggle down and get into a nice comfortable dream, and there's the kind when you want to go out and dance in the wind. There's a lovely swoopy sort of wind tonight. I can hear it whooshing round the house like a lot of mad galloping horses. I expect it's what used to make witches get their broomsticks and fly up the chimney. Mustn't it have been fun! I'd have loved to be a witch and go rushing over the housetops!"

"Jenny, it's getting late."

Jenny put out her tongue. Her eyes danced and her hair glittered.

"Oh, no, it isn't. You know, Rosamond, what's the matter with you is that you're a born fuss. Come and have breakfast — come and have supper — come and have lunch — come along to bed — all day and every day! And if you think I don't get bored with it, you can think again! I get as bored as being stuck in the middle of a mud swamp and nothing to do except wonder how soon an alligator will come and eat me. Darling, wouldn't Aunt Lydia make a lovely crocodile!"

Rosamond was just going to say "Jenny!" again, when Lydia Crewe's bell rang. Jenny said, "Blast!" and was reproved with a shake of the head as Rosamond ran out of the room.

Lydia Crewe didn't like being kept waiting. Even now she was not in the best of tempers. She was in her chair, sitting bolt upright and tapping on the arm of it with bony fingers.

236

"I wished to ask you if you had spoken to Jenny."

"Not yet, Aunt Lydia."

"And why not?"

Rosamond came a little farther into the room.

"I didn't want to upset her."

"Why should she be upset? It's high time all this spoiling and cockering came to an end! Do you imagine that Jenny can go through the world in cotton wool?"

"I thought it would be better for her to have a good night's rest."

Miss Crewe said sharply, "If she would give herself the chance! You will remember to lock her in. Fortunately, there is no way in which she can get out of the windows. You were both very much annoyed when I had the bars put in. As I told you at the time, I do not approve of young girls sleeping on the ground floor without proper protection. I suppose you will now admit that I was right."

"Aunt Lydia —"

"Well?"

"It — it would upset her dreadfully to be locked in."

"Why should she know anything about it? She won't unless she tries to go out, and if she does that she will deserve to be upset. You don't really imagine that she can be allowed to run about the fields by night?"

"No, of course not."

"Then you will do as I say! You can lock the door after she is asleep and open it before she wakes in the morning. It is all perfectly simple, and you will see that it is done. You can go and get my hot milk now, and then I don't suppose I shall be wanting you again."

By the time she had heated the milk and brought it up Miss Crewe was in her bedroom. She put a hand round the communicating door to take the cup and shut it again at once. There was to be no more talk. And this was the last time that Rosamond would do this errand and get no more than that harsh good night for thanks. The thought startled her. It didn't seem as if the endless service could be ending here. She picked up the tray with its other two cups of milk and went along the passage to Jenny's room.

When she came in, there was no Jenny — just a hump in the bed and a stifled giggle from under the eiderdown. Then, as she turned to set down the tray, back went the bedclothes and Jenny was up like a jack-in-the-box, her bright hair tossing.

"Say I've been quick! I have, haven't I? And my things all neatly folded! 'Virtue Rewarded, or the Piece of Chocolate' is what I should call it if it was a story I was writing! Like those heavenly books that belonged to Aunt Lydia's mother when she was a Sweet Young Girl! *Darling* — can you imagine Aunt Lydia as a sweet young girl, or a nasty little one, or all wrapped up in long clothes like they used to with babies! And woollen veils over their faces because of the fresh air being so deadly! There was one in the photograph album Aunt Lucy brought to show me, and I don't see how the baby could breathe at all! No wonder such a lot of them died!"

Jenny drank her hot milk, and then suddenly in the middle of her chatter she began to yawn and was

238

pleased to allow herself to be tucked up and kissed good night.

Rosamond went back to her own room and thought about locking the door. She hadn't said she wouldn't, and she hadn't said she would. She had never done such a thing before, and she didn't want to do it now. If Jenny woke in the dark and found that she couldn't get out, it might do something dreadful to her. There was something about being locked in that could bring up all the prisons in the world and loose their dreams upon you. She made up her mind to leave the door alone. Now that Jenny was in bed, she could put some of their things together — not really pack them, but sort them out and get them ready to pack. She moved to and fro in the room. When there was no more to do, she undressed and lay down in her bed. She had no thought that she would sleep, but no sooner was her head upon the pillow than she had no more thought at all. All that had come and gone with her was lost in a formless mist.

CHAPTER
THIRTY-TWO

Jenny had absolutely no intention of going to sleep. Her mind was in an extremely quick and lively state. Ever since Rosamond had come in from the wood she had been quite sure that something was going on. It was very stupid not to tell her what it was. She could, of course, have got it out of Rosamond by being cut to the heart and allowing a few effective tears to trickle down the cheek, but on the whole she considered that she would get more amusement out of playing a guessing game and trying to catch Rosamond out. She might have had her back to the chest of drawers, but she was perfectly well aware that certain things had been carried away. Her thoughts, conditioned by the romantic novels of Gloria Gilmore, leapt to something very near the truth. They were going to elope with Craig Lester, and that would mean they wouldn't have to live with Aunt Lydia any more. The prospect was far too dazzling for her to waste a single minute in going to sleep. Rosamond could have half an hour after she had stopped moving about next door, and then Jenny meant to see to her own treasures. She wasn't going to leave her manuscripts to anyone else, or her books. The very things which you would die rather than leave behind were the ones that somebody else might leave behind, and she just wasn't going to have them left.

She heard eleven strike, and then the quarter, and the half hour. Sometimes the church clock sounded quite loud, sometimes you couldn't hear it at all. It just depended on which way the wind was blowing. When there hadn't been sounds from Rosamond's room for quite a long time, she got up and put on her warm blue dressing-gown. She had grown so much that it was nearly up to her knees, but it still met across the chest. She tied the cord round her waist and began to put all her manuscripts together in the top long drawer. There oughtn't to have been room for them there, but there was, because Rosamond had taken such a lot of things out.

When she had got all the papers together she started on the right-hand drawer at the top. It had her pencils in it, and some peppermint creams which gave the whole drawer a lovely smell, a pair of gloves with a hole which she had forgotten to mend, a compass, a ruler, a fountain pen, a bottle of ink, a brown hair ribbon, a warm scarf, a Chinese box, and a lot of odds and ends of the kind which other people have a most unfair way of describing as rubbish. Jenny didn't care what anyone said, everything in this drawer was precious and she was going to take it with her. The Chinese box was the most precious of all. There was a secret way of opening it. If you didn't know the trick, it just stayed shut. She opened it now. There was the pearl brooch which her godmother had bestowed on her at her baptism, after which she departed to Australia and never took any more notice. There was a pin with a blue glass bird on it, and a string of beads made out of bright red seeds with a black spot at one end. There was a silver thimble that had belonged to her grandmother, and a coin with a peacock on it. There was a blue Venetian bead.

She didn't want to look at it, but her eyes became fixed. She hadn't forgotten about it, but she had locked it away. Now it was there in front of her with the gold and silver flakes catching the light. She put out a finger and touched it. There it was, quite solid and real. Why hadn't she left it lying on the grass verge in Vicarage Lane? Why hadn't she thrown it away in the fields, or on the road? Why had she brought it home? She had a dreadful feeling that none of these things could be escaped from. There was something about the bead that fascinated her. Slowly, reluctantly she picked it up and set it on the palm of her hand. As she turned to get the light upon it she saw that the door was open, and that Lydia Crewe stood on the threshold looking in.

There hadn't been any sound at all. The door had been shut, and now it was open. There hadn't been anyone there. Now there was Lydia Crewe, all tall and black, with a black scarf over her head and a cloak that came down to her feet. It was a quite dreadful moment, like something out of the worst kind of dream. Jenny stiffened herself against it. There are people who collapse when they are frightened, and there are people who get angry. Jenny was one of the people who got angry. Under Miss Crewe's cold stare her colour flamed and her eyes blazed. Words were jerked out of her.

"What do you want?"

Lydia Crewe came into the room and shut the door.

"What are you doing out of bed like this?"

"I got up."

"So I see." Lydia's tone was cold and measured. The look was dark. "Where did you get that bead?"

"I found it."

"Where?"

Jenny went back a step. She closed her hand upon the bead and put it behind her.

"I just found it."

"And I asked you where."

"Why do you want to know?"

"Why do you not want to tell me? Shall I tell you? Because you have been getting out of the house at night and running about, you don't care to say where."

Jenny's eyes met hers and wouldn't give way. She was made of harder stuff than Rosamond. When people tried to bully her it got her back up and she didn't care. There was defiance between them, and for a faint faraway moment there was something in Lydia Crewe which felt a spark of pride. Jenny had the Crewe blood, if she hadn't the name. Something stirred and was gone again. She went on harshly.

"You must be quite aware that this sort of thing can't continue. I don't intend it to continue. I have made all the arrangements, and you will have to go to school. Rosamond will take you there immediately."

"I don't believe it!"

Miss Crewe said coldly, "Rosamond should have told you. But of course she thinks she knows best. I advise you to be sensible and to make the most of the advantages I shall be giving you. Since you will have your living to earn, it is very important to make up for all the time you have lost. And now give me that bead!"

As the dark figure advanced, Jenny could go back no farther. The chest of drawers was behind her, and the wall upon her right. What she could do she did. With her hand clenched on the bead she dodged an outstretched arm and ran towards the window. When she was a yard away from it her hand came up and the bead went flying. It was all over in a moment. The blinding anger that was in Lydia Crewe was like lightning in the room.

But there was no thunder. That formidable will could hold it back, and did. There was a terrible silence. Jenny leaned on the window-sill, the cold night air about her. Her heart knocked at her side. Lydia Crewe went to the door and took the key. Then she went out and the door was shut without sound or haste. The sound came afterwards — the little sound of the key turning in the lock and shutting Jenny in.

CHAPTER
THIRTY-THREE

Lucy Cunningham sat behind her locked door. She had gone up early, but she had not undressed. She was waiting for something to happen, she did not know what. The feeling that she must wait was heavy and cold inside her. It wasn't a thing about which she could think or reason, it was something felt and to be endured. Like fear, or grief. It was fear itself. With what remained of her conscious thought she tried to cover it up. Nicholas would be coming home — she wouldn't be alone with Henry any more. When she had heard Nicholas come in and lock the door she would go to bed, and perhaps she would sleep. And in the morning everything would be different.

There are always some to whom the morning does not come. She could almost have thought that someone had said that aloud — here in the room with her. There wasn't anyone of course. It was only her own frightened mind playing tricks. She got up and began to move about. It was a mistake to sit and listen to the silence. The church clock struck eleven . . . and then the quarter . . . and the half hour —

Nicholas was late. She wondered what was keeping him. He had never been as late as this before, not at

Dalling Grange. Why, everyone must have gone home hours ago. She felt as if she could not stay here waiting any longer. If anything was going to happen, it was better to let it happen and get it over. The sensible everyday Lucy Cunningham spoke in a sensible everyday voice and asked her what she was afraid of. Or of whom. Since there was only one other person in the house, there was the answer —

Henry.

Put like that, it shocked her into courage. She couldn't be afraid of Henry — not really. She had let her nerves take charge and frighten her into a nightmare. And the way to come broad awake was to go down and do what she ought to have done hours ago — have it out with Henry — tell him that someone had tried to trip her, and see what he made of it.

She went to the washstand, sponged her face, and felt the better for it. The dreadful helpless feeling was gone. But she put on the landing light and stood looking down the long flight of the stairs before she set foot upon it. And she put on a second light in the hall. Then she went along to the study and opened the door. Nothing could have been more ordinary than the littered table, the strong overhead light, and Henry with his back to her leaning forward above the specimens laid out before him. The table was so large that it took up nearly half the room, but every inch of it was occupied. There was a tray of fine instruments with a row of little bottles, there were cardboard sheets upon which were displayed the corpses of moths, butterflies, caterpillars, and spiders. There appeared to be rather

246

more of the spiders than of any of the other creatures. Most of them were large, and some of them were hairy. Even at this moment Lucy found herself capable of a shudder. Things with more than four legs had that effect on her — she didn't like them, and she never would. But as far as Henry himself went there was nothing that was in the least out of the way. With one of those fine instruments in his hand he was bending over the table and doing something to the corpse of the largest and most repulsive of the spiders. It might have been any evening of any day, and the specimen might have been a butterfly, a moth, or even a lizard or a frog, but the general effect would have been the same, and the prevailing smell of antiseptic.

At the sound of the opening door Henry Cunningham made his accustomed protest.

"If you don't mind — I'm busy."

Lucy had often minded before, but this time she was making no bones about it.

"I'm sorry, Henry, but I've really got to speak to you."

He said in a mild worried voice, "Some other time, don't you think?"

"No, Henry — now."

He sighed, laid down the fine instrument, and sat back in his chair, where he pushed his glasses up and ran a hand across his eyes.

"I thought you were in bed."

She went round to the other side of the table and pulled up a chair.

"Well, I'm not."

He sighed again.

"So I see. But it is very late, and I am really very busy. I have these specimens to get off to a Belgian correspondent. He is giving a lecture on spiders, and I am able to supply him with the specimens he needs for it. Slides will be prepared and thrown upon the screen greatly magnified. The series illustrates Lelong's theory — but that won't interest you."

Lucy Cunningham said, "No."

Since he appeared to be about to relapse into concentration upon the spider, she repeated her precious remark, only in a louder and firmer tone, "Henry, I must speak to you."

He sat back again and said, "I am really very busy. What is it?"

"Henry, someone tried to kill me last night."

His spectacles were half way up his forehead. He peered at her and blinked.

"Someone tried to kill you! What do you mean?"

As she leaned towards him, one of her hands was on the table. They could both see that it was shaking. She snatched it back into her lap and said in a voice that he would hardly have known,

"Someone tied a string across the stairs. Then a bell rang in the hall. I thought it was the telephone, but it could have been an alarm clock or any electric bell. I was running to answer it, and the cord caught me just above the ankle. The mark is still there. I had my hand on the balustrade, or I couldn't have saved myself. If I had gone down head-first upon those flagstones I should probably have been killed. Don't you think so?"

248

Henry looked bewildered.

"My dear Lucy!"

"Don't you think so, Henry?"

He had taken up the fine steel instrument. He laid it down again and flexed his fingers; perhaps they had closed upon it with a cramping pressure. He said, "Someone must have left a piece of string lying about and you caught your foot — Nicholas — or Mrs Hubbard. Very careless — very dangerous. I remember in Constantinople —"

She said abruptly, "This is Hazel Green. The string was garden twine. It wasn't left lying about. It was stretched across the stairs and fastened to the balusters. It wasn't there when I went to bed. After that there were only two other people in the house — you and Nicholas. I want to know which of you tied that string across the stairs."

"Lucy —"

"One of you put it there. If it wasn't you, it was Nicholas. If it wasn't Nicholas, it was you. I want to know why."

"You don't know what you are saying!"

"I ought to — I've had all day to think about it. Someone tried to kill me."

"Lucy, you can't be well! Don't you think if you were to go to bed — perhaps a cup of tea and an aspirin —"

All at once the fear touched again. He was just Henry messing about with his specimens. But some of the things in those little bottles were poison. A cup of tea and an aspirin . . . She heard him say, "You'd much better get to bed. I'll make you some tea and bring it up."

There was concern in his voice. Concern about what? She didn't know. He had never made a cup of tea for anyone else in his life. He forgot his own meals unless he was called to them. She remembered picking up a book at a railway bookstall, and it was called *Death in the Cup*. The row of little bottles swam before her eyes. She took hold of the edge of the table and stood up.

"Yes, I'll go to bed. I can't sleep. I won't have any tea — it might keep me awake — I'll just get to bed."

But on her way to the door she turned.

"Why is Nicholas so late?"

Henry Cunningham was already adjusting his glasses, picking up the long sliver of steel. He said vaguely, "Nicholas — he's often later than this —"

"But he telephoned from Dalling Grange and said he had been kept."

"Oh, well, he will have gone on somewhere."

He bent forward over the table, and she went out of the room.

As she stood in the hall, it came to her that she had only to lift the telephone receiver and she could speak to anyone she liked — to Mrs Stubbs at the Holly Tree — to Marian Merridew and her friend, that little Miss Silver — to Lydia Crewe. She could say what she chose to say — that she was ill, that she was nervous — that she had had a fall, a fainting fit. None of them lived more than a few hundred yards away — any one of them would come . . . Would Lydia? She turned her back on that, and in the next moment on all of it. To make herself the talk of the place — to rouse a friend from her sleep because she couldn't sleep herself? It was too late, much too late for that. The church clock struck midnight as she went slowly up to her room.

CHAPTER
THIRTY-FOUR

Miss Silver, conscious of having neglected a kind hostess, did her best to make amends. A good deal to her relief, she found on returning to the drawing room that Mrs Merridew had fallen into a comfortable doze from which she did not immediately awake. When at last she opened her eyes and sat up she really had no idea of the time, and it was not until quite half an hour later that she looked at the clock and exclaimed. Even after that there was some lingering conversation. By the time the round of the house had been made and doors and windows tested it was well on the way towards midnight.

Refreshed by her sleep, Mrs Merridew was pleasurably shocked. She really didn't know when she had been up so late. From an irresponsible past she recalled an illicit feast in the dormitory at school, and how Cecilia had so narrowly escaped being caught.

"Do you remember, Maud?"

Miss Silver remembered — disapproval tempered by indulgence.

"It was all a very long time ago."

Mrs Merridew sighed.

"Yes — I suppose so. But sometimes it doesn't seem as if it were. We haven't really changed very much, have we — any of us? Not in ourselves. Of course we don't look the same — but then you change so gradually that you don't notice it. But I really should have known you anywhere — and Cecilia too, though we used to call her Cissie and she has grown rather stout."

The goodnights finally said, Miss Silver closed her bedroom door and prepared to embark upon the settled routine of undressing. Advancing to the bedside table, she took off the watch which she wore pinned to the left-hand side of her dress, wound it, and laid it down. The next step should have been the removal of the hairnet which she wore in the day and its replacement by the much stronger sort which she assumed at night. No matter at what hour alarums and excursions might occur — and Miss Silver's experience had included some of a quite violent nature — she had never yet been seen with a single hair out of place. The arrangement at night would be different, the plaits a little tighter, but order and neatness would prevail. Tonight she had got as far as putting up a hand to remove the hairpins which controlled the net, but at that point something stopped her. The hand came down again, the hairpins remained where they were.

She stood where she was for several minutes and became immersed in thought. It might be Marian Merridew's talk about the old days when a rule could still be a challenge, or it might be something a good deal more important than that. There was a sense of uneasiness, of urgency. She looked at the comfortable bed which was waiting for her, and knew that it could offer her no rest until this disturbance in her thought was quieted. It came to her that there was a not too difficult course which might afford relief. Marian Merridew was not at all deaf, but she did not possess the acute hearing that Miss Silver herself enjoyed. Her bedroom looked to the back of the house. It had a delightful view of the garden. There would be no difficulty about a careful descent of the stairs or the opening of the front door. It would, in fact, be perfectly possible to leave the house without having to embark upon an explanation of her movements.

At this point in her meditations Miss Silver picked up her watch and pinned it on. After which she assumed her coat, her second-best hat, and a pair of outdoor shoes. Fastening the aged fur tippet, cherished companion of many winters, firmly about her neck, she extinguished the light in her bedroom and found her way down the stairs and out of the house without making any sound at all. The air was cold, but there was no sign of rain. Miss Silver felt gratitude for her tippet and for the fact that the night was fine, but even if it had been raining heavens hard, she knew now that her errand would have taken her out in it. Before she could sleep she must at any rate walk past the Dower House and look up at the windows. She did not know what she was to do when she got there. By now the house should all be dark. Darkness did not mean safety. A phrase from the Scriptures slipped into her mind — "They that are drunken are drunken in the night". There was more than one sort of drunkenness. Men

254

could be drunk with pride, with passion, or with power. They could be drunken with hatred, or with the lust of gain.

She walked down the dark and silent street and made no plan. If there was something for her to do, when the time came she would know what it was. The entrance to the Dower House was not more than a few yards away when she heard a step behind her. There was no moon, but the night was clear. Someone large loomed up. The height and breadth induced her to take a chance with his name.

"Mr Lester —"

Even in his astonishment he could not mistake her voice.

"Miss Silver! What are you doing here?"

She said composedly, "I might ask you that, might I not?"

He laughed.

"I didn't feel like sleeping. I thought I would come out and walk."

He wondered if she would guess him fool enough to go up to Crewe House and gaze at the dark square of Rosamond's window, appropriately barred since Miss Crewe would not have considered it safe to sleep on the ground floor without taking every precaution. He did not really mind whether Miss Silver thought him a fool or not. A bridegroom is entitled to wear motley if he will. He was in the mood to shout Rosamond's name abroad, or to carve it on the trees. This was his hour — and hers. He heard Miss Silver say, "I have been feeling extremely uneasy about Miss Cunningham."

He was taken completely by surprise. Rosamond and himself — Jenny and Miss Crewe — to any of these his response would have been instant. But Lucy Cunningham . . . He stared through the dark and said, "Why?"

"I believe that an attempt was made on her life last night. I did not feel that I could sleep without coming as far as the house."

He said bluntly, "What can you do?"

"I do not know. I shall at least feel that I have done what I can."

They were standing still in the shadow at the side of the road, their voices muted, the last cottage behind them and all the village asleep. He said quickly.

"What do you mean? There's been an attempt on her life!"

She told him plainly and precisely.

"But that would be someone in the house —"

"Yes, Mr Lester."

He gave a faint half laugh.

"That damp drip Henry! I can imagine his being crooked. He's the sort to slide down the drain, but I shouldn't have thought he would hurt a fly. That leaves Nicholas. She brought him up. It's not pretty."

"Crime very seldom is, Mr Lester."

"What do you propose to do?"

"Miss Cunningham was kind enough to take me over the house this afternoon. Her room is at the back. There are two windows. She informed me that she always slept with them open. If her light is out and they are open now, it will be some indication that things are normal. In the ordinary way I should not anticipate that a second attempt would be made so soon, but there might be some special reason for silencing her without delay, and I could not disregard my own uneasiness."

Some of it seemed to have communicated itself to Craig. He had found himself startled, sceptical, and now a good deal disturbed. He said, "I'll come with you if I may."

There was a slight but significant pause. He was being weighed. A laugh just touched his voice as he said, "I shan't make any noise. I can walk like a cat if I want to."

"Then I shall be very glad of your company."

The Dower House had no drive leading up to it. It stood fronting on to the road with a stone wall screening it and the Victorian edition of a glazed passage covering the bare dozen feet from the gate to the front door. As Craig lifted the latch and stood aside for Miss Silver to pass, the church clock struck the quarter after midnight.

CHAPTER
THIRTY-FIVE

The house appeared to be in complete darkness. On either side of the passage running up to the front door the windows on both floors showed nothing. A narrow glass door on the left led from the passage into the garden. It was locked on the inside. Miss Silver producing a very serviceable torch from her coat pocket, the key was located and turned. Feeling a good deal like a burglar, Craig preceded her, and found himself on a gravel path between two banks of shrubs. Closing the door behind her, Miss Silver followed him. She extinguished the torch, put it back in her pocket, and began to walk along the path with as much composure as if she had been an invited guest.

At the corner of the house the path turned, the shrubbery widened out. A blackness of trees appeared behind it. There was still no light anywhere. The mass of the house towered over them like a cliff. Craig bent to say, "Do we go all the way round?" and could discern that she inclined her head.

It was at this moment that they heard the sound. It came from the front of them and to the left — the small crisp sound of a snapping twig. He felt Miss Silver's hand on his arm, drawing him away from the path and

258

towards the house. A couple of steps, and they stood amongst bushes, listening. Someone was coming through the shrubbery on the other side of the path. If it had not been for the snapped twig, they would all have come together a little farther on. Miss Silver stood motionless remembering the lie of the land. This wall of the house did not run straight back from front to rear. It broke, to form a small paved courtyard, rather damp and gloomy at this time of the year, and with what she considered an excessive number of creepers. She remembered an old magnolia, a good deal of Virginia creeper, and one or two dark cypresses growing far too close to the house.

Someone came out of the shrubbery on the left and entered the courtyard. Miss Silver's hand came down with a warning pressure upon Craig's wrist. Then, quite soundlessly, she was gone. He could be in no doubt but that he had been told to remain where he was — the clumsy man whose big feet would naturally betray him if he moved. Since he had served as a paratrooper and time and again risked more than his own life upon his silence, he could afford a private grin over that. Nevertheless he stood where he was, since it wasn't his show, and in any event two people made more noise than one.

Time goes slowly in the dark. It goes slowly anywhere when you wait and wonder what is going on. When something stirred in the gloom ahead of him he stepped to meet it. Miss Silver's hand came out and touched him. As he bent to her, she said in an almost soundless voice,

259

"Someone has just come from Crewe House and entered the Dower House by a concealed door. I believe that we should follow."

"How do we get in?"

If it was breaking and entering, he was definitely prepared to put the male foot down and keep it there. In a good cause any woman would break any law with an unruffled conscience, but he was not prepared to celebrate his wedding by being arrested.

Miss Silver's reply was lucid and succinct.

"She unlocked the door, but I did not hear her lock it again."

He found a Gilbertian echo in his mind — "Who the deuce may *she* be?"

Lucy Cunningham? But why the melodramatic secret door?

Jenny? He wouldn't put it past her. But how would she come by an illicit key?

It wouldn't be either of these — oh, no. It would be Lydia Crewe. And that set such a danger signal ringing that he hadn't a word to say.

Miss Silver kept her hand on his arm. The stones of the courtyard were damp and soft with moss. Where the added blackness of a tall cypress pressed against the dark wall of the house she stepped before him. Her hand groped, found what it felt for, and reaching back, invited him to follow. There was no more than room to pass. He scraped the wall and was buffeted by twigs and branches. There was a cold aromatic smell. And then they were in a narrow, a very narrow passage. He was to learn afterwards that it ran between two of the

260

rooms. His shoulders touched it on either side. He wondered how many cobwebs he would collect before they were through. The place reeked of dust.

Ahead of them there was a line of light. It cut the darkness like an incandescent wire — as narrow and sharp as that. As they came up to it, he saw that there was a door — no, not a door, a sliding panel. Someone had gone through that way and pushed it to carelessly, leaving that shining crack. Where light can pass sound passes. Lydia Crewe's deep, harsh voice spoke from beyond the panel.

"Really Henry — what a story! Lucy must be going off her head!"

It was Henry Cunningham who answered her. He sounded nervous and fretful.

"She says there was a string across the stairs. She says it nearly tripped her up. She thinks there was only Nicholas in the house — and me."

Her voice came leaping at him, strong with anger.

"And I suppose you told her I was here!"

She must have made a move towards him. The chair grated as he pushed it back. The picture of a man who cowers from a blow flashed into Craig's mind, but he didn't think that the blow would have been a physical one. As the chair scraped, the nervous voice tripped over itself with hurry.

"No, no — of course I didn't. I didn't say a word. She doesn't know you come. I've never told her that. Or anything."

Lydia Crewe said, "You'd better not. It would be the end if you did."

"I don't see why."

"She knows too much already."

"She doesn't know anything from me."

She said with impatience, "What does it matter how she knows it! If she knows anything at all, it's too dangerous!"

"I don't know what you mean. What did you do last night? You went through into the house. What did you do? This story of Lucy's — why should you try to trip her up?"

"Perhaps I thought she would be better out of circulation — for a time. Perhaps I thought it would be good for her to have a nice long rest."

He must have stared at her, for she said with a scornful laugh, "Don't look at me like that! My dear Henry, you had really better leave all this to me. Keep your head in the sand and don't ask questions. You are very good at your own job, and you had much better stick to it. Pack the Melbury rubies inside those disgusting spiders of yours, and we'll get them out of the country under everyone's very nose. Your Belgian correspondent is a godsend. He can give another lecture after a reasonable interval, and we can get the diamonds off too. It was those big rubies which were the bother. I give you marks for thinking of the spiders."

He said, "Yes, yes," in a peevish way. Then, with a sudden energy, "Why should you want to get Lucy out of the way?"

There was the sound of a chair being moved. It seemed Miss Crewe was tired of standing. She said in a conversational tone, "I thought I told you not to ask questions."

"I've got to ask this one."

"Well then, here is your answer! And don't blame me if you don't like it. Lucy knows too much. She may know enough to ruin us."

"What does she know?"

"Mrs Bolder found that Holiday woman in my room on Sunday afternoon. She must have picked up an envelope there — a very important envelope. It came into Lucy's hands afterwards, and she brought it back to me. Anyone who saw what was inside that envelope could ruin us all. Well, you know what Lucy is."

Henry Cunningham's voice said, "She is my sister."

"She's a babbling fool. She has only to open her mouth once and it's the end for all of us."

"Why should she open her mouth? She is your friend, isn't she — she always has been?"

She made some quick movement.

"Henry, you *are* a fool! She wouldn't do it purposely — I'm not saying that she would. I don't suppose the Holiday woman took that envelope purposely. It must have slipped down the side of my chair. Mrs Bolder found her poking about there, and I expect she had it in her hand and just stuffed it into a pocket." She went on in a measured way. "Yes, that is what must have happened, because when Lucy met her at the bottom of the drive she was tugging to get her handkerchief out from under her coat, and the envelope came out too and fell down between them. Lucy picked it up, saw that it had my name on it, and said that she would take it up to the house and give it to me. Which she did. It was —" She paused and drew a long breath. "It was something of a shock."

"Why?"

"If you must know, there was my first sketch of the Melbury necklace inside that envelope. I work to scale, but I make a rough sketch first. And that envelope was open. It was a used one, and I had pushed the sketch inside. Someone had come into the room — I think it was Rosamond. Just one silly accidental happening after another!"

"I don't see what all that has got to do with Lucy."

She said with an odd quietness, "You never do see very much, do you? Now listen! The envelope was open. If Lucy took one look, just one look inside it —"

"She wouldn't!"

"Are you prepared to gamble on that? I'm not! Have you ever thought about going to prison, Henry? You like wandering about — when you like, where you like — picking up your moths, your butterflies, your cocoons. That spider everybody thought was extinct — you got a lot of pleasure out of finding a couple of specimens and breeding from them, didn't you? You like your easy life — no one to harry you, and nothing to do for it except a little of the one thing you really are good at. That is all that is asked of you, and it is all you need to know anything about."

He said on a shuddering breath, "Miss Holiday —"

"Well, Henry?"

"She's dead . . ." Then, after a frightening pause, "Like Maggie —"

"Really, Henry — what a thing to say! Maggie got bored with Hazel Green and those exigent parents, and went off, as no doubt she would have said, to better herself. As to Miss Holiday, she was always touched in the head, and I'm afraid she got the rough side of Mrs Bolder's tongue on Sunday. A very faithful creature, Mrs Bolder, and properly scandalized at anyone poking about in my room. It was, of course, unfortunate that Miss Holiday should be upset to the point of committing suicide. Or was it? I wonder!"

"Lydia —"

"My dear Henry, don't you think you have asked enough questions? There is an excellent proverb about the shoemaker sticking to his last. You stick to your specimens! Miss Holiday committed suicide, and that is all there is to it."

CHAPTER
THIRTY-SIX

Nicholas came in through the gate and up to the front door. It was very late and he had walked from Dalling Grange, but it was only now, on his own doorstep as he slipped his key into the lock, that he was aware of fatigue. It was a purely physical sensation separate from himself, from the Nicholas who had emerged from a nightmare. Until the whole thing was over he had never let himself relax from taking just the one inescapable step which lay before him, looking neither to the right hand nor to the left. It was not until now, when the strain was over, that he could let himself think of Henry and feel ashamed because he had not dared to think of him before. If Brown hadn't cracked, sticking to his superior pinnacle until it looked as if he had an unshakable footing there and then suddenly, horribly plunging from it, he supposed that the nightmare might have been going on still. It came to him there and then how heavy in cross-examination are the odds against the guilty man, and how with one single slip he may be precipitated into disaster. It is only the bedrock truth that cannot be shaken.

He knew now how much afraid he had been. About Henry. With every stammering word of Brown's, he had waited for Henry Cunningham's name. And it hadn't come. It hadn't come. Nicholas was to have been framed to account for the leakage, but Henry didn't come into it at all. Things had been getting too hot, and a scapegoat had had to be found. Nicholas had been cast for the part. The incriminating notes had been planted. If he had done anything else than what he did do, disaster would have been sure enough. But he had gone straight to Burlington. And poor old ramshackle Henry didn't come into it at all. He wondered now why he should ever have thought that he might. Something about the way he drifted through life — something that would make him an easy tool — the lost twenty years —

All these thoughts were in his mind as he turned his key in the lock. The door swung in, swung back. He let it go, and it made more noise than he had meant it to. There was a light still on in the hall. He turned to shoot the bolt.

Back in the study Lydia looked up.

"What was that?"

Henry Cunningham gazed in his vague way.

"It will be Nicholas — Lucy said — he wasn't in —"

"Is that door locked?"

"Oh, no — I never lock it."

She might have been young again, she moved so quickly. The key turned before he had finished speaking. Her breath came sharply. It was a moment before she could control it. She came back to the table. Then, almost soundlessly, "I didn't think even you would be such a fool."

He looked mildly through his glasses.

"He won't come here — he never does."

"Suppose he did?"

"He would think it very odd that I should have locked the door."

"Keep your voice down!"

She went back to the door, unlocked it, set it ajar, and looked down the hall. There was a light in the dining room. The door stood open. She said over her shoulder, "Does Lucy leave a tray for him?"

"If he is late."

Lydia Crewe shut and locked the door again. Henry said, "You needn't do that. He won't come here."

"I'm not taking chances. And you shouldn't. Where are the rubies?"

"Oh, in one of the drawers."

"Just lying about loose, I suppose!"

"No, I don't think so. I believe — in fact I'm sure — I put them . . . Now where did I put them? No, not this drawer — it must have been one of the others —"

He was pulling drawers in and out as he spoke, jerking them out and jerking them in again. Her voice was a mere bitter thread.

"An unlocked drawer! Do you know what they are worth?"

He said peevishly, "I never lock anything up. It's much safer not to. And I should be sure to lose my keys. Yes, here they are. I remember now — I put them in the middle of the cotton wool for packing the spiders. They are perfectly safe there. Neither Lucy nor Mrs Hubbard would touch one of my drawers if you paid them. There was a live grass snake once, and Mrs Hubbard wouldn't do the room for weeks. So the stones are perfectly safe."

She stood there looking down at him, frowning. His vagueness had always irritated her. It was a danger, but there were moments when she could see that it was an asset too. Who was going to suspect a man so genuinely absorbed in scientific pursuits, so careless with his belongings — everything just left lying — not even a locked-up drawer? Too much had been left lying a year ago, and Maggie Bell had had to go. She wasn't squeamish, but these things were a risk, and it was Henry's carelessness that had made it necessary to take the risk.

She maintained her frowning silence. She was not at the moment in a position to rebuke him. She had been careless herself, and the risk had had to be taken all over again with Miss Holiday. And this time with much more annoying consequences, since it left her short of a daily maid. And no one anxious to fill the gap. She had had to fall back on that half-witted Winnie Taylor who went about looking like something out of an asylum, though she wasn't too bad at her work.

She pushed in the drawer which held the Melbury rubies in an untidy mess of cotton wool and said,

"Well, I must go. Give me time to get to the end of the passage before you unlock the door. And you had better get off to bed yourself. You look tired."

He passed a hand across his forehead.

"Yes — perhaps I will. Lydia, you're quite sure about Maggie?"

"Of course I'm sure! She had just got to the point where she had to have a change. She told me so, and I gave her the money to go away. But you had better keep that to yourself. There — does that make you feel better?"

He took off his glasses and wiped them. She found it ridiculous that his eyes should be full of tears.

"Yes — yes — I think it does. And, Lydia, you said this was to be the last job."

"Of course. Only don't worry. It's not good for you."

He said, "No, it isn't. Sometimes — I do — feel ill —"

Her hand came down on his shoulder and pressed it.

"Just go off to bed and leave everything to me. All you've got to think about is your spiders."

On the other side of the panel Miss Silver had been moving inch by inch. The passage went on past the opening to the study. It would be interesting to know where it came out, but this was neither the time nor the place for anything which did not bear directly upon the present emergency. Craig following her, she moved to leave the way clear for Miss Crewe's retreat. They had indeed no more than a bare margin of safety when the panel slid and a rectangle of light lay on the passage floor. If Lydia Crewe had looked to her right she might have seen them. She held an electric torch. If she had turned it in their direction she must have done so. She looked neither to right nor left. As Henry shut the panel behind her, she followed the beam of the torch along the passage by the way she had come.

When all sound of her going had died away Craig bent to Miss Silver's ear.

"Well, what do we do next?"

She answered him, not in words but by a light pressure upon his arm, in obedience to which he began to move before her down the passage. But when they came to the door by which they had entered they found it locked against them. Craig allowed himself an almost noiseless laugh.

"Well — what now? I suppose we go back and see where the other end comes out. Have you any idea of where that may be? You know the geography of the house, and I don't."

She said in her usual composed manner, "It would be in the hall or in the drawing room, I should think. Both have panelling of a character very similar to that of the study."

They retraced their steps. As they approached the panel which had been ajar, it was momentarily startling to see that light still came from it. Henry Cunningham had closed it — they had heard the click of the spring from where they stood, a yard or two away on the other side. But almost as Craig touched Miss Silver in a warning gesture they could both see that the light now came, not from the edge of the panel, but from a round knot hole some five foot up from the floor. There was no doubt about its purpose. Anyone who approached through the passage could make sure that the coast was clear before stepping into the room.

Miss Silver had to raise herself a little in order to make this peephole available. She had a good view of the writing table, and of Henry Cunningham leaning over it. In front of him on a sheet of white paper lay the spider which he had been dissecting, a sight which she found repulsive in the extreme. In his right hand he held a pair of tweezers with which with meticulous care he was inserting a large red stone into the cavity which had been made in the spider's body. She could not doubt for a moment that she was looking at one of Lady Melbury's lost rubies — probably, from its size, the central stone of her diamond and ruby necklace. It disappeared into the body of the spider and the tweezers were laid down. Another small instrument was then dipped into a saucer in which there was something black and glutinous, and drop by drop the stone was covered and the body rounded out again. Henry Cunningham's hand was steady, his absorption complete.

After a minute Miss Silver yielded her place to Craig. Both received the same impression. For this time at least, Henry Cunningham was in a world of his own. It was a world in which he was hampered by neither doubt nor inefficiency, a world in which there was no moral law and therefore no crime. There was only his own skill and the means of exercising it. The moment in which the thought of Maggie Bell had troubled him, the moment in which he had said of Lucy Cunningham, "She is my sister," belonged to a different world altogether, and it was one from which he shrank, and from which he must at any cost escape.

Miss Silver began to move forward along the passage. It came out, as she supposed it might, in one

272

of the darker corners of the hall, and the panel slid as silently as the other had done. Lydia Crewe would have seen to that. There was still a light burning. It striped the darkness as the panel slid back, seeming much brighter than it really was. The pressure of Craig's hand upon the wood stopped suddenly. The dining room light clicked out and Nicholas Cunningham came into view. The gap in the panel showed his easy, confident air. He crossed the hall and went soft foot up the stairs. A door opened and shut on the landing above.

CHAPTER
THIRTY-SEVEN

Miss Silver suggested that they should leave by way of the back door. In Miss Cunningham's probable state of mind she would not be able to recall with any certainty whether she had ever locked it. Besides, by the time she came to consider the matter at all too many other things would have happened for it to be of any importance.

They came out on to the paved yard and by way of a gravelled path to a garden gate. As Craig closed it behind him, the church clock gave four warning strokes to announce the hour, and then struck one. The night air was cool and soft. After the dusty passage and the airless shut-in feeling of the kitchen and scullery it had a living quality. Craig filled his lungs with it. To creep by stealth through another man's house in the middle of the night was not an experience that he had enjoyed, or one that he would wish to repeat. And where was it going to land them? That was what he wanted to know. As far as he could make out they were very comfortably situated between the devil and the deep sea. If Miss Silver made tracks for a telephone and informed Frank Abbott or the county police that she had located the Melbury rubies, the balloon was bound to go up. That wouldn't have mattered if Lydia Crewe wasn't bound to go up with it, in which case he could see that he was going to have trouble with Rosamond, who was practically certain to say that she couldn't marry him tomorrow. No, not tomorrow — tomorrow had already become today. It had become his wedding day, and he saw Rosamond slipping away from him into some damned nonsensical Cloud-cuckoo-land where she wouldn't marry him at all. If he could only get Miss Silver to hold her hand until after half past ten, as far as he was concerned she could go ahead and have the whole lot of them arrested.

They walked, and the light moving air went with them. He said, "What are you going to do?"

She stopped and turned to face him.

"I do not know. I think we must go back."

"Into the house?"

"No — that should not be necessary. But I am not easy about Miss Cunningham. I believe that her life is in danger."

"Her life!"

"Mr Lester, you heard the conversation between Miss Crewe and Mr Cunningham. Did it leave you in any doubt as to her intentions with regard to his sister?"

"I suppose not. It seems incredible all the same."

She said soberly, "Murder must always seem incredible to the normal mind. The murderer has lost his balance. His own desires, his own plans, his own safety have come to outweigh normal control and the moral law. With each further step he becomes more

275

justified in his own eyes, more inflated with his own importance, and more certain that he can carry out his plans with success. This would not be Miss Crewe's first step into crime. Whether or not she took a personal part in the removal of Maggie Bell and the death of Miss Holiday, I have not the slightest doubt that she was cognizant of both those murders. We may never know just what happened to Maggie, but working as she did at the Dower House, it seems probable that she saw something which might have been dangerous if she were given time to put two and two together and think about the result. It is quite certain that this is what happened in the case of Miss Holiday. In Miss Crewe's absence she went prying into her room. Surprised by Mrs Bolder, she pushed a chance-come envelope into her overall pocket. As Miss Crewe herself suggested, it had probably slipped down between the seat and the side of a chair. The whole thing was due to no more than idle curiosity and to the instinctive movements of a maid who is tidying a room. She would shake up the cushions and run her hand round the side of any chair which had been occupied. But you know what that envelope contained — a sketch of Lady Melbury's diamond and ruby necklace. The first sketch in fact from which a copy was to be prepared."

"Yes, I heard that. I don't know anything about the necklace. Has it been stolen?"

"Yes, Mr Lester. A few weeks ago Lady Melbury discovered that the necklace in her possession was a copy. Neither she nor anyone else had the least idea as to when the substitution had been made. I gather that she would not have made the matter public, but Lord Melbury had been less discreet, and it is now an open secret. With the result that half the county believes Lady Melbury to have sold the necklace herself."

Craig whistled softly.

"I see. A very pretty kettle of fish! And the unfortunate Miss Holiday threatened to upset it."

"Just so. The envelope she picked up was open. It had Miss Crewe's name on it, and it contained a sketch of the Melbury necklace — the first sketch for a detailed plan which would be drawn to scale for a jeweller to work from. Any chance that Miss Holiday had seen it and would talk of what she had seen was too dangerous to be risked. The poor woman dropped the envelope when she pulled out her handkerchief, and Miss Cunningham picked it up and returned it to her friend. In doing so she also came under suspicion as a possible danger. She might not suspect her brother or her friend. She would not intentionally give them away, but she has an artless, affectionate mind and a tripping tongue. There was no knowing what she might say — so there was a trip-cord across the stairs."

"And now?"

"I am afraid that Miss Crewe may return — not immediately, but at some time during the night. She will give Mr Henry and Mr Nicholas enough time to make sure that they are asleep, and then I think that there will be another attempt on Miss Cunningham's life. It is, at any rate, a possibility which must not be neglected. Believe me, I feel very much for your position in the matter. You would naturally wish to take

Miss Maxwell away before any arrest is made, but in the circumstances I think you must see that there can be no delay in informing the police."

He said, "No."

Miss Silver resumed.

"The entrance to the passage should not be left unguarded. Miss Crewe must not be allowed to reach Miss Cunningham. If you will remain on guard there, I will go back to the White Cottage and ring up Inspector Abbott."

CHAPTER
THIRTY-EIGHT

Lydia Crewe made her way back by the winding path which threaded the two shrubberies. She had no need of a torch. Her feet had taken this way so often — by sunlight, twilight, moonlight, and in the dead of the night as now. She knew every turn, every bush that brushed her shoulder, every bough to which her head must stoop, every jutting root. She had walked it when hope was high and the illusion of youth still lingered. She had trodden it when hope was gone and her formidable will drove her along another path from which there was no turning back.

She passed through the gap which separated the two gardens, and beyond it under overarching trees to the gravel sweep before the house. The door by which she would gain admittance was here, but Rosamond's and Jenny's room and her own were on the farther side. She crossed the front of the house, walking quickly and with no special precaution. All these front rooms were empty, where they had once been filled with sons and daughters, guests, and up in the attics the maids and men who served them. No need to walk softly for the ghosts of a bygone splendour.

She turned the corner and came to the barred windows on the ground floor — her own, Jenny's, Rosamond's. Her own were shut, Jenny's and Rosamond's open. She stood by Jenny's window and listened. There was no sound at all. There had been time enough for her to cry away her temper and fall asleep. It was from this window that Jenny had thrown the blue Venetian bead. She switched on her torch and sent the beam travelling.

Immediately under the window a border set with wallflower and tulips against the spring. The bead wouldn't be there — Jenny had thrown it with all her might. Nor would it be on the gravel path which continued round the house. But beyond the path where the rock garden opened out, that was the place to search. The beam went to and fro over moss which carpeted the stones amongst neglected lavender, overgrown rosemary, tangled rock rose, campanula and thyme. It crossed the pool in the centre of the garden, the water too clouded, too muddy to see whether the bead lay there or not. She thought it would hardly have come so far, but these things were incalculable. If it was in the pool it would be safe enough.

She came back from the garden slowly, letting the light go to and fro. Tomorrow by daylight there would be a better chance, and at least if she couldn't find it, no one else would be likely to — there was always that. She switched off the torch and heard a long groaning sigh come out of the dark. She said sharply, "Who's there?" and it was a dead woman's voice that answered her.

280

"You won't find it. It's mine — you won't find it."

It was so faint that she could tell herself afterwards that she hadn't heard it. But whether she heard it or not, she knew the voice and she knew what it said. She found herself pressed up against Jenny's window, holding to the bars, her heart shaking her. There was a rushing noise in her ears. If the voice had spoken again she would not have heard it. But it did not speak again.

Inside the room Jenny lay with her back to the window and a corner of the pillow stuffed into her mouth to stifle the laughter which bubbled up in her. She had done it really well. She had very nearly frightened Aunt Lydia into a fit. Poor old Holiday was easy enough to do, with her genteel accent and her whiny-piny voice. Jenny thought she would very nearly have had a fit herself if she had heard it like that in the dark when she was looking for something which had belonged to a poor dead thing.

All at once she *was* frightened. The beam of the torch came into the room. It struck the wall beyond her and caught the glass of a picture, and then the shiny round disc at the end of it came dancing to and fro about the bed. It was really horrid, but the worst part of it was that she had begun to be frightened before the beam came in. It might have been her own trick, or it might have been Aunt Lydia hating her out there beyond the bars. But she was frightened before there was even the faintest shimmer from the torch. She had been laughing, but the laughter was gone. There was a choking sob in her throat, and tears were running down into the pillow and soaking it.

The torch went away. Aunt Lydia's footsteps went away. Everything was nice and dark and quiet again. And then all of a sudden the darkness and the quietness stopped being nice and began to terrify her. She slipped out of bed and ran to the door, quickly in case there was something that might be going to pounce — a black bat with ragged wings like Aunt Lydia hating her, or Miss Holiday all white and wet come back to find her blue Venetian bead.

And the door was locked. It was the most dreadful moment in Jenny's life. Worse than the one just before the accident, when she knew it was going to happen. Worse than coming round in the hospital and feeling all smashed up. Because with Jenny the things that happened in her mind would always be worse than anything that could happen to her body. She stood flat against the door and made herself stiff, so as not to beat upon it with her hands and scream for Rosamond. If she did that, Aunt Lydia would come, and she would know that it was Jenny who had tricked her. It took every bit of strength, but she did it.

And then all of a sudden the key turned, and the handle, and the door began to move. She had been pressed against it, but at the very first sound she went back inch by inch on her bare feet, her hands at her throat to stop the scream which was there. The door went on moving, and suddenly, blessedly, there was Rosamond in her white nightgown with the passage light behind her. She saw Jenny, her hair standing up in a rumpled halo and her eyes staring. When she held out her arms Jenny ran into them, gasping for breath and all at once a dead weight to be carried to the bed and laid down there.

When Rosamond had shut the door she came back to kneel down and listen first to a wordless sobbing, and then to half-stifled words. Some of them were to come back to her afterwards. At the time she could only think of Jenny's clinging hands and the trembling of her body. They were there together in the dark. A movement to put on the light had brought a more agonized shuddering than before, and a gasp of "No — she'll come!"

When the sobbing died away Rosamond's almost inarticulate words of comfort began to take form.

"Jenny, listen! . . . Yes, you can if you try. Something lovely is going to happen, and I'm going to tell you about it. There isn't anything to be frightened of. We are going away." Jenny gave a rending sniff. "Wait till I get a handkerchief and I'll tell you all about it."

She made her way to the chest of drawers, came back again, and sat on the bed.

"Here you are. And don't cry any more, or you won't be able to listen."

"I'm not crying — I'm blowing my nose." Then after an interval, with no more than a catch in her breath, "Where are we going?"

"We are going away with Craig. I'm going to marry him."

"When?"

"Tomorrow — no, I expect by this time it's today."

"I'm coming too?"

"Of course! Oh, Jenny, I wouldn't leave you!"

Jenny said, "I should think not!" And then, "Aunt Lydia locked me in."

"I know, darling. Nobody shall again. Only you mustn't go out at night — you'll promise, won't you?"

"Who said I went out at night?"

"Aunt Lydia saw you. And Craig did too. You mustn't, darling — it isn't safe."

Jenny's voice went stiff.

"I don't want to any more." Then, with sudden energy, "Rosamond —"

"What is it?"

"Suppose she comes back!"

"Aunt Lydia?"

Jenny was gripping her wrist.

"Yes — yes! She was out there! She came and looked in and shone a torch!"

"Was that what frightened you? I thought I heard someone in the garden — someone talking. Was that Aunt Lydia?"

"The talking part wasn't. Rosamond, she shone her torch to see if I was awake. Suppose she comes along the passage and tries the door!"

"Why should she?"

"She might. Let's go into your room. We can lock this room again and she'll think I'm here, and we can lock ourselves into yours. And then we'll run away tomorrow and marry Craig and live happy ever after."

CHAPTER
THIRTY-NINE

Lydia Crewe went back to her room and put on all the lights — not only the big chandelier with its many-faceted lustres, but the gilt and crystal sconces on either side of the chimney-breast and between the windows, until every inch of the crowded room sprang into view. The curtains hung across the windows in dark straight folds, but this was the only darkness which remained. There was no place for shadows under the blaze of those unsparing lights. She sat down in her chair, stiffly upright, rigidly controlled. Her heart still beat more heavily than it should have done. She set her will to steady it. The dark garden was shut away from her by a barrier of walls, a barrier of lights. If it was her nerves which had played her a trick, they should learn that she was their mistress. If it was Jenny —

She held her anger in a leash and would not let it go. Jenny could wait. This was no time to take an extra risk. It was Lucy who was the danger, not Jenny, playing with a blue Venetian bead which no one would ever see again. It was gone, and tomorrow Jenny would be gone to the school which Millicent Westerham had described as "a bit rough and ready, but the discipline is excellent and the fees really low". Jenny wasn't going to like the excellent discipline of Miss Simmington's school. It might perhaps be left to deal with her, at any rate for the present.

She came back to Lucy Cunningham, who was the real danger. After that interview with Henry it would be safer to wait, but she couldn't risk it. And in a way it would be all to the good, because he would be able to say in the most truthful and convincing manner that poor Lucy had been in an extremely nervous state and had complained about not being able to sleep. Only of course he must stick to that and not go beyond it. He had neither the nerve nor the clarity of mind to lie convincingly.

Well, it must be done tonight. More people than Henry would have noticed that Lucy hadn't been herself all day. When she was found in the morning, it would be just one more case of an elderly woman who couldn't sleep and had gone beyond the safety line in the matter of a drug. Her mind began to busy itself with the details. Henry and Nicholas must be asleep. Lucy had often complained that nothing woke either of them once they were off. They must have time to be so profoundly asleep that no one would ever know that she had returned to the Dower House. No one except Lucy, and Lucy would not be in a position to tell what she had known. It would have passed with her into the silence from which there is no coming back.

The voice which she had heard in the garden whispered at the edge of consciousness and was refused. The dead could not return. They had no power to harm. You were safe from them. When Lucy was dead she would be safe from her . . . Time went by.

When at last she rose to her feet she was steady and resolved. Her bedroom lay beyond with a connecting door. She went through to the bathroom on the other side, a converted room with some of the furniture which had belonged to it still taking up what should have been clean, clear space. She went to the small bureau in the corner and lifted the flap. There were a number of pigeonholes behind it, all stuffed with papers — old bills, old correspondence, things she had never troubled herself to deal with. When she had cleared the second hole from the left she felt for the spring which disclosed a small inner compartment. It was empty except for just one thing — a glass bottle very nearly full of white tablets.

She put everything else back, tipped a number of the tablets into the palm of her hand, and contemplated them. They were more than twenty years old — nearer thirty. Old Dr Lester had prescribed them for her father in his last illness. One, or at the outside two if the pain became severe. On no account more. She wondered if the drug would have kept its strength. She had never heard anything to the contrary, and she would just have to chance it. Better make the dose a stiff one — say ten tablets. She counted them out and put them into a tumbler to dissolve with a little hot water. She would need a small bottle for the liquid. After some deliberation she selected from a cupboard a three-parts-empty bottle of ipecacuanha wine, washed it out carefully, and when the tablets were fully dissolved corked them up in it.

She stepped out into the passage, resolved and confident, and enough at her ease to walk back as far as Jenny's room and try the door. If it had been open, she would have locked it again and taken the key. She had not been at all satisfied with Rosamond's response when the matter was discussed, and she did not intend to be flouted. But the key was turned and the door fast. She passed down the passage and across the hall. And so by the side door and the dark familiar path to the Dower House.

CHAPTER
FORTY

Craig Lester kept his watch. After some reconnoitring he decided on a vantage point where an old apple tree rose among the shrubs which lay between the side of the house and the gap by which the garden could be entered from next door. In the darkness, and still bare of leaf, he could not know what kind of a tree it was, but Lucy Cunningham could have told him that it would have a wealth of rosy bloom in May and be weighed down with rosy apples in September.

Lydia Crewe could have told him more than that. For two hundred years there had been an orchard here between the houses. Then the taste in gardening changed, became more formal. Shrubs took the place of pear and cherry, apple and mulberry and quince, to suit the whim of Sophia Crewe who had brought a fortune into the family's already depleted coffers. She was beautiful, stubborn, and extremely well dowered, and Jonathan Crewe had let her have her way. But he would not part with the tree which provided his breakfast apple for ten months in the year. He had boasted about it for too long, and his middle-aged foot came down and stayed that way. He had been gone for a long time now — and Sophia and her dowry — but the apple tree remained. It had low spreading boughs. When Craig was tired of standing he could sit comfortably enough, and when he was tired of sitting he could stand again. What he could not do was to walk about. He found it remarkably like old times.

He began to think about Rosamond. He could not believe, he would not let himself believe, that anything could go wrong now. Whatever happened or didn't happen tonight, they must be married as he had planned. He hoped with all his heart that nothing would happen. He supposed Miss Silver was bound to ring up the police, but somehow he didn't see the county people rushing over in the middle of the night to arrest Henry Cunningham on the word of an elderly spinster. There would have to be a search warrant, and a search warrant meant recourse to a higher authority. Higher authority didn't take kindly to being knocked up in the small hours. He considered there would be some weight behind the argument that if the Melbury rubies were in Henry Cunningham's drawer they could very well stay there for a few hours longer. As to Miss Cunningham being in any danger, he felt that a good deal of scepticism could be expected.

He began to feel a good deal of scepticism himself. If he had not stood behind the panel and heard Lydia Crewe say, "Lucy knows too much," the scepticism might have been complete. As it was, the words stuck in his throat — "Lucy knows too much." And how did it go on — "She knows enough to ruin us." He could tell

290

himself that she was putting a case to Henry Cunningham, and that anyhow people said a lot of things they didn't really mean. But the words stuck, and the voice that carried them. It occurred to him quite suddenly that he had never disliked anyone as much as he disliked Lydia Crewe.

If his ears had not been trained to listen, he might not have heard her when she came. The path ran close beside his tree. If he had taken one step and stretched out a hand he could have touched her, but she went past with what was hardly a sound. The air moved, something went by. Since he knew where she must be going, he did not hurry to follow her. He had unlaced his shoes; now he slipped them off and left them hanging on the tree. He came in his stockinged feet to the edge of the little courtyard as she slipped behind the bush which screened the secret door. The key turned, the door swung in, and she was gone. He could neither see nor hear these things, but he knew that they were happening.

And then Miss Silver was saying, "She has just gone in, has she not?"

"Yes."

"She must be followed, and at once."

The tall figure of Frank Abbott loomed up. He said in the almost soundless voice which the others were using, "There's a delay about the search warrant. It may be some time before it gets here."

Miss Silver was already on her way towards the house. Frank followed her.

"My dear ma'am, we can't just go in!"

He considered that her reply exhibited the Victorian tradition at the point where the sublime transcends the ridiculous. It was not so easy to achieve dignity without emphasis, but she achieved it.

"My dear Frank, I am on visiting terms with Miss Cunningham, and I feel no difficulty about entering her house. You and Mr Lester will, of course, do what you feel to be right." With which pronouncement she too stepped behind the bush and entered the passage.

Standing for a moment to listen, she could hear nothing. There was need for haste, but there was also a need for caution.

Lydia Crewe passed through the study, leaving the panel open. A small light burned in the hall. After some consideration she left it as it was and went up to the bedroom floor. If she had to make a sudden retreat it would be useful to be able to see her way. Lucy Cunningham's door was the first on the right at the top of the stairs — Henry opposite on the left, and Nicholas at the back of the landing. She had no fear that they would wake, but if either of them did, Henry had alarmed her about Lucy and she had slipped over to see that all was well.

She tried the handle of the door and found it fast. Her brows met in a frown. She lifted her hand and knocked. After a moment a voice said,

"Who's there?"

She would hardly have known it for Lucy's voice, it was so hoarse and strained. She made her own voice smooth.

292

"It's Lydia, my dear. Henry was concerned about you. He said you were not well. He was concerned enough to ring me up."

Lucy Cunningham was startled right out of her fear.

"Henry rang you up!"

"Yes. You can tell how worried he must have been. Let me in — we can't talk like this."

She heard Lucy come up to the door and turn the key. A triumphant sense of power took hold of her as she stepped into the room and pushed the door to behind her. She did not stop to latch it. She would not be here for long. What she had to do could be done without delay. She looked at Lucy, still in her afternoon dress, and said in a shocked tone, "But, my dear, you are not undressed. Do you know how late it is?"

Lucy shook her head.

"It doesn't matter — I can't sleep. Did you say Henry rang you up?"

Lydia Crewe nodded.

"He's terribly worried. I told him I would come over and bring you a sleeping-draught."

"*Henry* rang you up?" Incredulity struggled through the flat fatigue of her voice.

"That is what I said."

"*Henry?*"

"Would you be glad to know that we have made it up again?"

"*Glad?* Oh, Lydia!"

The tears began to run down her face. She put out her hands gropingly. Lydia Crewe took them, guided her to the bed, and sat there beside her, speaking to her soothingly.

The sound of this soothing voice reached Miss Silver as she came to the top of the stairs — that and the sound of Lucy Cunningham's sobs. They made it quite safe to approach the door, which was ajar. Standing there, she heard Miss Crewe say, "Now, Lucy, there's nothing to cry about. Henry and I are just where we were, and you ought to be pleased about that. But he is terribly worried about you, so I want you to take this sleeping-draught. What you need is a good night's rest. Henry can ask Mrs Hubbard to let you sleep on in the morning, and when you wake up you can tell us how glad you are that we can all be friends again. Of course you and I always were. We never did let anything come between us, did we, and we never will."

All the time that she was speaking Lucy wept, not loudly but in an exhausted fashion as if she had come to the end of her strength and could do no more. Lydia and Henry had made it up — Lydia was being kind — there was nothing to worry about any more. But she was too tired to be glad. All she wanted was to lie down and sleep. She was conscious of the removal of Lydia's arm and of her getting up and going over to the washstand. There was the chink of glass against glass.

And then Lydia was back again, standing in front of her and holding out a tumbler.

"Now, Lucy, drink this. And then we'll get your clothes off and you can go to sleep."

294

Miss Silver pushed the door an inch or two wider. Lucy Cunningham was sitting on the side of the bed, her face wet with tears, her eyes blurred. Standing over her with her back to the door was Lydia Crewe. There was a tumbler in her hand, half full. She held it out to Lucy and said in a tone of authority, "Come now — drink it up!"

Lucy gave a last tired sob and said, "I don't — want it, Lydia. Now you've come — I shall sleep."

The tone of authority became harsher.

"You will drink it at once and no nonsense about it! What you need is a good long rest!"

Lucy Cunningham put out her hand half way and took the glass. And saw Miss Maud Silver come into the room with her black cloth coat, her fur tippet, her second-best hat, and her warm woollen gloves. It was such a surprising sight that it shocked her broad awake. The impact of Lydia's will was blunted. Her face changed, she drew back her hand.

Miss Silver gave a slight arresting cough and said, "I think it is extremely wise of you to resist a sedative, Miss Cunningham. Natural sleep is always to be preferred."

Lydia Crewe turned stiffly round. She had had one shock already. She had surmounted it. Now there was this. In a moment she would be able to think, to plan, to know what she must do. Just now, in this instant of time, she could only stand there and stare.

With a purely instinctive movement Lucy Cunningham leaned sideways behind Miss Crewe's back and set the tumbler down upon the bedside table. There was no design in what she did. There was a tumbler in her hand, she set it down. Something had brought Miss Silver into her room in the middle of the night. She got to her feet, passing Lydia, standing away from her, because all at once the room was full of fierce currents. She didn't understand them, but they were there. Lydia who had been kind was not kind any longer. Her voice shook with a sound which Lucy knew and feared beyond anything else.

"What — do — you — want?"

Miss Silver did not appear to be impressed. She said in her usual composed manner, "I want you to go home, Miss Crewe. I believe that you had better do so. Miss Cunningham should rest."

Lydia Crewe made a great effort. She controlled the rage that shook her. She controlled her voice to say, "I found she had dissolved some tablets for a sleeping-draught — they are some she had by her. I was just waiting to see her take them and help her to bed."

And what must Lucy say, the babbling fool, but "Lydia, I've never had any sleeping-tablets. I don't like them — I don't need them. It was you —"

There was a silence. Lydia Crewe gathered her remaining forces. She said, "Very well, I'll go. Since you don't need that draught, we can throw it away." Then suddenly, sharply, "What have you done with it? . . . Ah!"

She had not turned in time. Miss Silver had moved between her and the bedside table, and at that her control broke. She made a dreadful sound and reached for Miss Silver's throat.

Lucy Cunningham screamed at the top of her voice, and in a moment the room was full of people — Frank Abbott, Craig Lester, Nicholas. And at long last Henry Cunningham, his shaking hands to his ears, because now it was Lydia Crewe who was screaming — dreadfully.

CHAPTER
FORTY-ONE

Rosamond lay dreaming. She walked in a spring garden with Craig. The dark wood was a thing of the past, she didn't seem to remember it any more. This was a spring garden. There were apple trees rosy with bloom, there was cherry blossom. The path where they walked was set on either side with daffodils and coloured primroses. There was a blue sky overhead, and the sun shone. She woke to darkness and a voice that called her name.

"Rosamond! Wake up!"

It was Craig's voice. The sweetness of the dream was still round her. She sat up beside Jenny in the wide old-fashioned bed and called softly, "What is it?"

"It's Craig. Come over here to the window. I want to speak to you."

They kissed with the bars between them. He held her.

"Darling, I hate to wake you like this, but we've got to push the time on a bit."

"What is it?"

"I'll tell you afterwards. Look here, it's nearly six o'clock. I want you to wake Jenny and get dressed — both of you. If you'll let me in by the side door, I'll be getting you some tea. I don't want to start our married life by starving you. I suppose there'll be eggs?"

"There ought to be. But Craig —"

"My sweet, there's not time for any buts — you've just got to do what I say! Put on your dressing-gown and let me in, and I'll wrestle up some food while you get packed."

She did what she was told. It might have been part of the dream — darker than the one from which she had come and full of questioning thoughts. They did not pass her lips. There was a sense of urgency, of fear. If Lydia Crewe should wake — She shrank appalled at the threat of what scene would follow and of what the bitter tongue might say. The thoughts came and went. There was no time to dwell on them. The sense of urgency persisted. It was in Craig's clasp and kiss when the garden door swung open to let him in. It was in the quiet haste with which he sent her back to dress as soon as she had shown him the way to the kitchen.

Jenny was awake when she got back, and the light was on. There sprang up in her a picture of Lydia Crewe standing at her window to look out and seeing that bright rectangle printed on the path. It was her custom to sleep with windows closed and curtains drawn, but in the picture Lydia stood at the window to watch the light from Rosamond's room. She might have stood there to listen when Craig spoke from the other side of the bars. Rosamond did not know that Lydia Crewe would never stand at those windows to listen and watch again. She made haste to draw the curtains across her own.

Jenny was stretching and yawning.

"Darling, it's the middle of the night. Where have you been?" Rosamond said soberly, "It's after six. Craig wants us to come with him now. Hurry up and get dressed! He's making tea in the kitchen."

Jenny stopped yawning to blow her a kiss. Her eyes sparkled, the sleep all gone from them.

"Ooh! Lovely! We mustn't make any noise, must we? Suppose *she* heard us and came along snorting out fire and forbidding the banns!"

Rosamond was stepping into her clothes. She said briefly, "We should go all the same — she couldn't stop us. But hurry!"

As they turned from the side passage which served their room and Lydia Crewe's, Jenny looked back. Words came tumbling out of her mouth in a whisper.

"What do you say when you are going away from a place you hate with all your might? It can't be 'Goodbye', because that means. 'God be with you', and it can't be 'Farewell'. It had better be 'Horrid, horrible place, I hope I shall never, *never, never* see you again!'" She caught at Rosamond's arm. "Run, before it comes after us and pulls us back!"

Rosamond could feel that the hand was shaking. She steadied her own voice to say, "I can't run with two suitcases. And there's no need — no one will come after us."

It was whilst she was saying it that she could feel for the first time that it was true. They crossed the hall. She had left one light burning there. It did very little with the darkness except to show how the shadows clung about the stairway, and how black was the upper landing and the mouth of every passage. Somewhere in the gloom above their heads the ancestral portraits watched them go. It was a relief to pass the baize door at the back of the hall and find bright lights beyond. Craig seemed to have switched on everything as he came to it.

He was fishing eggs out of a boiling saucepan as they came into the kitchen. There was a cloth spread on the table. Cups and saucers, butter and a loaf, stood ready. He called over his shoulder, "Get out the salt and pepper, and the knives! Oh, and the milk — the kettle is just going to boil!"

It wasn't romantic, but it was extremely reassuring. When the baize door fell to they had left the haunted shadows behind them. Kitchens don't have ghosts. Or at least no more alarming ones than the lingering aroma of bygone meals. They ate and washed up what they had used. Mrs Bolder would miss the eggs and know that the bread and the butter had been cut, but she wouldn't be able to say that they had left their cups and plates for her to deal with.

It was striking seven when they let themselves out of the side door and walked down the drive to where Craig had left his car. It was a still, cold morning, and the darkness had begun to thin away.

CHAPTER
FORTY-TWO

Mrs Selby woke up. She had heard the clock strike quarter after quarter all through the night, and then quite suddenly she was asleep. Or was she? She didn't know. The clock had stopped striking. Everything was very still and very cold. She was quite alone — there wasn't anyone or anything. It was more frightening than the most frightening dream.

Then into the emptiness and silence there came something that must have been a sound. She didn't know where it came from, but it woke her. She sat up in bed and heard a car come down the lane. It was quite dark in the room. She didn't care about having windows open and the night air coming in, and she kept her curtains drawn. Horrid and damp the night air was in the country, and she didn't hold with letting it in. Besides there were bats, and if a bat got into the room she would go crazy. Fred, now, he liked his windows open — said the room got stuffy if they were shut and he couldn't sleep. Well, she couldn't sleep with them open, so he had his own room, and she had hers. It wasn't what she thought they would ever come to. Married people ought to sleep together, and that was a fact. But have those windows open on the ground floor and cats and bats and goodness knows what coming in, she couldn't and she wouldn't. There hadn't been any unpleasantness over it — she would have liked it better if there had been. What she didn't like was the feeling that Fred was just as well pleased to have it this way. He ought to have been put about and have made a fuss, instead of just smiling to himself and saying, "Have it your own way, my dear."

She sat up in bed and heard four men get out of the car. She knew that there were four, because she heard them talking, and not troubling to keep their voices down neither. They came up to the door and she heard the buzz of the electric bell. Well, she wasn't opening doors in her nightgown — Fred would have to go. But she got out of bed and went to the window. With the curtains pulled a little to one side to make a peep-hole she could see that it wasn't dark any more, just the grey of the early morning, and the clouds so low that they would be bound to have rain before you could turn round. Funny how you got to notice the weather down here in the country. When they lived in town she never noticed it unless it was snow, or hail, or a thunderstorm, or one of those hot spells when it didn't seem as if there was enough air to go round.

The electric bell went again. This time the man kept his thumb on it. She could see him now, and the others, standing round the door and waiting for someone to come. Policemen! She let the curtain fall and stepped back, cold and shaking. What did the police want, coming here like this before anyone was dressed? Fred would have to go to the door. They would have to wait.

She reached for her dressing-gown, clutched it about her shoulders, and went in barefoot to the room at the back where he slept. The draught from the open window met her. He lay facing it with his back to her and the bedclothes huddled up around his ears. She had to pull them away and shake him before he roused, flinging out an arm and grumbling, "What's the matter?"

"The police, Fred!"

He said, "Nonsense!" And then, sharply, "What do they want?"

"I don't know. I can't go to the door like this."

He gave the bedclothes such a shove that they fell over on to the floor and hung trailing. Someone was banging on the door now. He threw her an angry look and went padding down the passage to open it.

Mrs Selby stood where she was. She got her arms into her dressing-gown and did up the buttons. There was talk going on, but she couldn't hear what was said. It would be something about Miss Holiday. She didn't want to hear what it was. Every time she thought of that poor thing going down the well it made her feel giddy and sick.

There were footsteps in the passage, and Fred came back into the room. He looked as if he might be getting a chill. A raw morning like this he ought to have his clothes on. There was one of the policemen with him. He cleared his throat and said, "You'd better go back to your room, ma'am. Mr Selby is going to get dressed."

And Fred said, "Yes, my dear. Better get your clothes on, and then you can make us some tea. The police just want to go over the premises again, and as I tell them, I'm sure we've no objection. We've got nothing to hide,"

The constable coughed behind his hand. Like a stabbing knife the thought came into her mind, "What has Fred been up to?" He had a smile on his face, and to anyone who didn't know him like she did his voice was just the jolly, friendly voice he'd use for company. But it couldn't take her in. There was something wrong, and he was trying to put a face on it.

She went into her own room and put on the first clothes that came to hand, a royal blue skirt and jumper and a purple cardigan. She dragged a comb through her hair and tidied it. The bright colours gave her a ghastly look, but she didn't think about that. She put on her stockings and a pair of quilted slippers with a fleecy lining that were warm to her feet. She took a little pleasure from the warmth.

Fred came out of his room, and there was a trampling of feet through the house and out by the back door. Mrs Selby went into the kitchen and put a kettle on the oil stove, but it had boiled, and come off the boil, and cooled, and gone back on a low flame, before anyone came into the house. The rain was falling in a steady drizzle when she went to the back door and looked out. Sometimes there was nothing to see except the rain falling on the hen-houses, and the hens, rather draggled, pecking and scratching in their runs. Sometimes the men came into view, crossing from one shed to another. There were two good sheds on the place. She couldn't think what they wanted with them.

In the end the trampling feet were back in the house again. Only one of the men came through into the kitchen, the Inspector from Melbury. He came right up to her with his hand shut down over something and stood there, the kitchen table between them. Then he laid down his hand on the bright checked cloth and opened it, and there in the middle of his palm was one of Miss Holiday's beads. There was no mistaking it — bright sky-blue, with those gold and silver flakes mixed in under the glass. Her mouth opened, and before she could stop herself she said, "But that's one of Miss Holiday's beads!"

The Inspector said, "Sure about that, Mrs Selby?"

"Oh, yes — of course I'm sure. Why, she —"

There was a chair beside her. She sat down on it and stared at him.

"Mrs Selby, when you gave us a description of what Miss Holiday was wearing on Sunday night you included a string of blue beads. Do you identify this bead as having formed part of that string?"

Her voice had sunk away. She could hardly hear it herself when she said, "Yes —"

He said,

"When Miss Holiday's body was taken up out of the well the string of the beads had broken, but some of them were discovered in her clothing. This bead has just been found in the last of the sheds we searched. It had slipped inside the mouth of an old sack. Is there any way in which you can account for its being there?"

She said, "No."

"Miss Holiday was alive when you saw her last?"

"Oh, yes."

"She was wearing these beads?"

"Oh, yes."

"The string wasn't broken?"

"Oh, no."

"Did you see her again after she left this house?"

He had taken her back to the Sunday evening — sitting there with Miss Holiday in the lounge — seeing the blue beads and thinking how pretty they were when the bits of gold and silver sparkled under the light — going to the door with her and seeing her out. Everything else seemed to have slipped away. It was just saying goodbye on the Sunday evening that was real. She could see Miss Holiday going out of the front door, and herself shutting it and turning the key. She said, "I let her out, and I locked the door. I never saw her again."

CHAPTER
FORTY-THREE

When Lydia Crewe stopped screaming she began to talk. She talked through all that remained of the night, and she was still talking when they brought Fred Selby into the station and began to question him there after cautioning him that anything he said might be taken, down and used in evidence. Lydia Crewe had been cautioned too, but it made no difference, she just went on talking. Something — some control, some check, had slipped. Frank Abbott was reminded of a clock belonging to his grandmother, the redoubtable Lady Evelyn Abbott. It had started striking in the middle of family prayers and no one had been able to stop it. Her look of surprise and disapproval merging into outraged rebuke remained with him as a pleasant memory.

But there was nothing pleasant about Lydia Crewe's performance. Plainly enough, she had passed the bounds of sanity whilst remaining dreadfully and convincingly lucid. First and foremost there stood out pride in her own achievements. To preserve Crewe House, to endow it with new wealth, were objects which justified all that she had done, and she took great pride in the doing of it. When they told her that her

308

conversation about the Melbury rubies had been overheard by two witnesses and the rubies themselves recovered, two from the bodies of spiders freshly mounted by Henry, and the rest from his table drawer, she ran off into telling them exactly how she had changed the stones.

"What was the good of them to Felicia Melbury or to anyone else kept locked up in a safe? How many times do you suppose she wore them last year? Exactly twice — at the County Ball and the Melbury Hunt Ball! So I rang her up and said could I come over — we are connected by marriage, you know — and when I got there she told me she was wearing the famous necklace, which I knew already, and she was quite pleased to show it off. So I had my chance. You wouldn't understand the process, because I invented it myself — paper specially prepared to take an exact impression. It has, of course, to be supplemented by a keen colour sense and a photographic memory, both of which I possess. I had only to invent a pretext for getting her out of the room for a moment. I said that I had forgotten my handkerchief, and she went into her bedroom next door to get me one. By the time she returned the impression had been taken and the paper was safe in my bag. To make a finished sketch from which a jeweller could work was a business requiring a great deal of skill. The stones for the substitute necklace came from Paris to my specification. Selby has an extremely clever workman in his shop in Garstin Street. You didn't know he had a jeweller's shop, did you —

but no one expects the police to be clever. We outwitted you every time."

The Melbury superintendent said nothing. A massive man, not given to change of countenance. Frank Abbott said, "Not this time, Miss Crewe."

She went on as if he had not spoken.

"It's just a shabby shop in a shabby street — pins on brooches, and watches to mend — cheap strings of pearls for the local girl to put round her neck and think she looks like somebody. You didn't know Selby had a shop like that, did you? He retired from the business he used to run with his brother, but he stuck to his little jeweller's shop and the clever Hirsch — a very industrious man and actually very trustworthy. When the necklace was ready I had only to wait for the Hunt Ball and go over to Melbury Towers again. Felicia doesn't like me, but she is afraid of my tongue. I go there when I choose, and she is always very polite. There is very little I don't know about most people in the county. I went over, I admired the necklace, and I changed it for the one which Hirsch had made. She was actually in the room at the time. I had called her attention to something in the garden, and the change only took a moment."

The harsh voice went on and on. She was asked about Miss Holiday. She took up the tale of the envelope thrust carelessly into an overall pocket by a frightened woman and dropped again for Lucy Cunningham to pick up and bring back to Crewe House.

"So then, you see, she had to go. She might have looked inside and seen the sketch for the necklace. Selby managed very cleverly."

The Superintendent said, "How did he manage?"

Her eyes looked past him, pleased like a cat with a bird.

"I went across the fields and let him know. He said she would be coming down to see his wife as soon as he went past to the Holly Tree. She was frightened of men, you know! Such a fool! He said he could slip out and catch her just before nine, when she would be going home. She always went at the same time because the old woman locked up then. He said no one would miss him if he slipped out for a minute or two like that. It's no distance. So that is what he did."

"He killed Miss Holiday?"

"Oh, no, he only stunned her. And we put her in one of the sheds at the back of the bungalow. You see, we couldn't put her down the well until quite late in the night in case of there being anyone awake. It wouldn't have done for Mrs Selby to notice anything, or old Mrs Maple."

The Superintendent put his hand to his chin.

"Miss Crewe, you have been warned that what you say is being taken down and may be used in evidence. Am I to understand that you were present when Miss Holiday was first stunned and at some time later thrown into the well at the bottom of Mrs Maple's garden?"

Her glance flickered over him, dry and bright.

311

"Oh, yes — he couldn't possibly have managed without me. There is a most convenient path across the fields which comes out at the stile in Vicarage Lane quite close to the Selbys' bungalow. I can assure you the whole thing was extremely well organized. I spared no trouble. You must understand, Superintendent, that the controlling mind has been my own throughout. Selby has been useful, but he has always taken his orders from me. He is quite incapable of working out the intricate plans which have made our enterprise so successful. I must insist that you are clear on this point."

"And Mr Cunningham — what was his position?"

She said, "Oh, Henry!" Her hands gestured as if letting something fall. Her rings flashed under the light. Frank Abbott thought, "They'll take them away, and she'll mind like hell." An odd irrelevancy which came and went in between one breath and the next.

"Henry!" she said. "Why, he couldn't plan anything if he tried! All he could do was to mount the stones in his specimens. And we never told him anything we could help. He liked doing the work, but the other side of it worried him. He really made some excellent models of caterpillars. Some of them are quite large, and he was very clever about packing them with diamonds. You can get quite a number of diamonds into one of those big caterpillars. He used some stuff like plasticine and painted them when they were dry. They were supposed to be used for instructional purposes abroad."

Frank Abbott's light sardonic gaze rested upon her.

"Very ingenious, Miss Crewe. The whole thing must have given you a great deal of thought. May I ask whether the disappearance of Maggie Bell was another instance of your ingenuity? I suppose she saw something she wasn't meant to see at the Dower House, and when Henry Cunningham told you about it you took the matter in hand?"

Her brows drew together in a frown.

"What do you know about Maggie Bell?"

He leaned back in his chair, his pose negligent, his voice easy.

"Well, if you ask me what I think, I should say Henry was careless. Let me see — you had already got away with Lady Melbury's necklace. You may have intended to get the stones out of the country a year ago, and then have decided to wait. Henry may have had some of them to pack into a specimen. At a guess he probably left them lying about loose on his blotting-pad while he went out of his room, and when he came back, there was Maggie Bell looking at them."

"She had no business in his study," said Lydia Crewe severely. "She had been told she must never interrupt him when he was working. If people disregard orders they must take the consequences."

"May I ask how you induced her to — er — take them? How did that clever planning brain of yours deal with what must have been quite a dangerous situation?"

"Naturally I saw at once that the matter was urgent. Maggie would not be likely to mention anything she had seen to her parents — very disagreeable people and interested in nothing except themselves and their

313

ailments. But Maggie used to slip down to that cousin of hers who works for Mrs Merridew, Florrie Hunt. Lucy Cunningham happened to mention that she was going there that evening. Lucy always mentions everything — a tiresome habit, but sometimes it is convenient. I told Selby to have his car ready and to pick me up. The Hunt's house is the last in the village, and we drew up beyond it. I went back, and when Maggie came along I was waiting for her. I said I had a note for Mrs Hunt, and she walked with me to the car to get it. Really a very stupid woman though quite an efficient worker. I told her to get into the car, as there was something I wanted to explain about the note. When Selby had dealt with her, we disposed of the body and went home. There was really no risk about it at all. Selby posted two cards which I had prepared and everyone thought she had just got bored with Hazel Green and gone off."

"What did you do with the body?" said the Superintendent.

Lydia Crewe bridled — there was no other word for it. The effect was ghastly.

"Ah!" she said. "You never found out, did you? If you had found a body, people wouldn't have believed she had run away, would they? So I took good care that the body should not be found!"

Frank Abbott raised his eyebrows and said, "Well we have only your word for it that she didn't run away, haven't we? All that clever plan of yours that you've been telling us about rather goes by the board without any evidence to back it up. Personally I shan't believe a word of it unless you can provide the body. If you really disposed of it as you say you did, then you will be able to tell us what you did with it, and when we have found it you can expect us to believe your story. At the moment I don't feel particularly credulous."

She went on talking.

CHAPTER
FORTY-FOUR

Miss Silver was quite ready when Craig called for her at a little after half past nine. She wore the hat which had been her best for no more than two winters, a black felt with a bunch of pansies on the left-hand side. Frank Abbott has always maintained that during the years he has sat at her feet, Maudie has only possessed two hats, labelled respectively Best and Second-Best, but that periodically, like the Phoenix, they renew their youth and rise on stepping-stones of their dead selves to higher things — these being exemplified by new black or purple ribbons and fresh bunches of the more sober kind of flower. It is, of course, so far true that her hats are always of the same shape, and that they are always made of black felt or black straw, according to the season. The current hat carried a black ribbon edged with purple, and the stalks of the pansies were controlled by a small jet buckle. She had in readiness to put on the pair of grey suede gloves which Cecilia Voycey had sent her for Christmas. She considered them far too light to be practical, but for a wedding they would be most appropriate. From her composed and serene appearance nobody would have guessed that she had been up all night.

After a search of the study at the Dower House had disclosed the presence of the Melbury rubies the arrest of Henry Cunningham had, of course, been inevitable. Lucy Cunningham's distress had been painful to witness, and it had not been possible to leave her until she had fallen into an uneasy sleep. Nicholas had been really helpful, and she had come away towards morning feeling that Lucy might safely be left in his care until Mrs Merridew could relieve him.

Fortunately, Marian had slept through the hours of the night without any suspicion that the front door was unlocked and her guest absent. By the time she awoke to these facts they could no longer be considered of the first importance. The arrest of Lydia Crewe, of Henry Cunningham, of the good-natured Mr Selby, dominated everything.

"Oh, my dear Maud, those poor girls — what will they do! And Lucy! She will feel it quite dreadfully, poor thing! I must go to her! Poor Henry — it doesn't seem possible! He was such a good-looking young man. Of course Lydia has always been strange. It isn't really good for people to live in the past as she has done. After all, these old houses and pictures, and furniture — they don't matter as much as people do and we oughtn't to let ourselves think so. But Lydia did — one couldn't help seeing it. And whatever happened, she had to have her own way."

Hazel Green buzzed with talk. But for once Florrie was not first with the news. She found Mrs Merridew and Miss Silver already informed, and very little inclined to talk of what they knew.

Mrs Merridew's, "It's all very sad, Florrie, and I must hurry and get dressed so that I can go to Miss Cunningham," was as much as she could get from her, and Miss Silver had taken her cup of tea into her own room and shut the door.

When Craig arrived Mrs Merridew had already gone over to the Dower House and Miss Silver was ready. She waited until the village was behind them before giving him anything but a grave "Good morning." Then she said, "How have they taken it, Mr Lester?"

There was a touch of defiance in his answer.

"They don't know."

"You have told them nothing?"

He shook his head.

"Not a word. As soon as it began to get light I called through their window and told them to get dressed and come along. They didn't ask any questions. I think there must have been some kind of a scene with Miss Crewe. Jenny looked odd. She wasn't in her own room — she was in with Rosamond. I didn't ask any questions either. I thought I'd leave well alone until we were married. Rosamond is perfectly capable of saying she can't go through with it because that mad woman has been arrested. But once I'm her husband I'll be able to deal with that, and with anything else that crops up. I don't mind telling you I'm like a cat on hot bricks until I've got her safe."

"Where have you taken them, Mr Lester?"

"Well, I thought about my uncle's house. Highly respectable and all that, but it would have made too much fuss. Elderly maid, nurse companion, everything going like clockwork — you know the sort of thing. It wouldn't have done. So I took them to the Station Hotel — they're used to people arriving by early trains. They'll stay in their room — or at least I hope they will — until we come for them. I don't think Jenny had had much sleep, and Rosamond would be trying to keep her quiet."

Miss Silver sat silent and thoughtful. News flies fast in the country. The case was a sensational one. The arrested persons had been taken to Melbury to be charged. There might already be talk in an hotel, where the staff would be coming to work. The Melbury rubies would set tongues wagging. She hoped indeed that Rosamond Maxwell would remain in her room.

At Craig's knock on the door Rosamond opened it. If he too had had misgivings, they were swept away. She was wearing the blue jumper in which she had come to tea with Mrs Merridew. It wasn't new, but it deepened the sapphire blue of her eyes. When she looked at Craig they were full of light.

He said "Miss Silver has come to see us married," and she turned at once and put out both her hands.

"How kind of you — how very, very kind!"

Jenny was feeling rather grand because she was wearing a skirt and jumper of Rosamond's. Her own clothes were all up over her knees, and you can't go to your sister's wedding like that. These things weren't new — none of their things were new — but she could feel the skirt swishing against her legs in a perfectly grown-up way, and though it was just rather a dull old tweed and the jumper was brown, they did show up her hair. Odd that when Miss Silver looked at her she should feel as if she wanted to cry.

They went down to the Register Office in Craig's car. Jenny thought it was a very dull way to be married. Rosamond would have looked so nice in a long white dress with a train behind and a lovely floating veil. And Jenny would have been bridesmaid, in a white dress too, with a wreath of flowers on her hair. And an organ, and singing, and a lot of flowers in the church. Dull, that's what this was, and all over whilst she was still thinking how nice the other sort of wedding would have been. She hadn't really got as far as deciding whether she would have snowdrops and ivy leaves or grape hyacinths in her hair before the Registrar was saying, "Let me be the first to congratulate you, Mrs Lester," and it was all over.

Craig and Rosamond didn't kiss. They looked at each other. There was something in the way they looked which gave Jenny a curious shaky feeling. It wasn't flowers and a white dress and music that made a wedding romantic. It was something else — something which was between the two people who were marrying each other. And just for a moment when Craig looked at Rosamond and she looked back at him Jenny had seen it.

CHAPTER
FORTY-FIVE

"She never stops talking," said Frank Abbott. "It's pretty grim. They've got her in the Infirmary — she just goes on and on and on. Detailed accounts of everything for the last twenty years."

Miss Silver sighed.

"An extremely shocking case," she said.

It was the evening of a crowded day. They sat in the drawing room at the White Cottage, Frank stretched out in the largest chair, Miss Silver primly upright with her knitting in her lap. Mrs Merridew was still with Lucy Cunningham, and would remain there until she had seen her settled for the night. The coffee tray stood at Frank's elbow, and a pleasant fire burned upon the hearth. He said, "The Chief Constable wouldn't believe it, you know. Said she had gone off her head, and the whole thing was just a painful delusion. Even the sight of the Melbury rubies didn't shake him. There had been Crewes at Crewe House for three hundred years, and so forth and so on. If there was a villain in the piece it would be Henry Cunningham. The Cunninghams, you see, have only been here about thirty years, and as to Selby, a mere chance-come Londoner, well naturally he might be anything. Odd, you know, because he is quite an able man. But that sort of thing is dyed in the wool — the old county family can do no wrong."

Little Josephine's leggings were very nearly completed. There had been just enough of the cherry-coloured wool. She said, "And pray, how did you convince him?"

Frank poured himself out another cup of coffee. He sugared it extravagantly.

"Well, you know, when she said that Maggie Bell's body was in the old sand pit just off the road down the second lane to the left on the way to Melbury and it was there under a tangle of nettle and bramble, he had either got to credit her with second sight or come round to the idea that she had helped to put it there just as she said. She told us with a good deal of pride how she had intercepted Maggie on her way to the Hunts and got her into Selby's car by saying there was something she wanted her to explain to Florrie's mother. After which it was quite easy for Selby to knock her on the head, and so to the sand pit. Exit Maggie who, like the unfortunate Miss Holiday, had seen too much. Very regrettable, and a lot of trouble for Lydia Crewe. Henry had been careless enough to leave stolen diamonds lying about on his table when he went out of the room and returned to find Maggie looking at them. Naturally after that there was only one thing to be done, and Selby and Lydia did it. I gather they didn't tell Henry. All he did was to pack the stuff in his specimens."

"That is so. Mr Lester and I overheard her assuring him that Maggie had gone away because she was bored, and that Miss Holiday had committed suicide. He was

322

uneasy, but only too anxious to be convinced. A weak man, and very much under her influence."

Frank finished his cup and set it down.

"You know, what got everyone all wrong was the original assumption that the disappearance of Maggie Bell had anything to do with the leakage of information at Dalling Grange. If Maggie hadn't been working for the Cunninghams, and Nicholas Cunningham had not been employed upon highly confidential work at Dalling, the two things would never have got mixed up. The Security people couldn't get it out of their minds, and it coloured the whole approach. For instance, they investigated Selby and found he had retired from a perfectly respectable garage business in which he and his brother were partners. If they had found out — which they didn't — that Mrs Selby's father used to have a small jeweller's shop which he left to his daughter, it really wouldn't have meant anything to them at all, but that is where all the funny business went on. Mrs Selby didn't know anything about it — I gather Selby was pretty lordly about her affairs. He picked up a very clever jewel-faker chap — French Jewish refugee — and they got going on substituting new stones for old. What I want to know is, how did you tumble to it?"

Miss Silver reprehended the expression. A slight cough conveyed the fact. Frank blew her a kiss.

"Apologies and regrets! Evil communications corrupt good manners. My cousin has a lamentable vocabulary. After which honourable amend you will, I am sure, relent and tell me all."

She smiled with indulgence.

"My dear Frank, you talk extravagantly. What is it you want to know?"

"How you got on to the jewel business."

Her needles clicked. She pulled on her cherry-coloured wool.

"It is a little difficult to say. Miss Crewe affected me in a very disagreeable manner. She was closely and curiously linked with the Cunninghams. There had been an engagement between herself and Henry Cunningham. Mrs Merridew made it clear that he was completely dominated by her. Then a valuable piece of jewellery was missed in circumstances which threw suspicion on Mr Cunningham, and he lent colour to it by leaving the country. After more than twenty years he returned, a quiet depressed recluse, interested only in natural history. And Lydia Crewe went out of her way to advertise the fact that there was a complete breach between them. She would cut him dead in the street. She did so on the occasion when she came here to tea. Mrs Merridew was very much distressed about it, and told me that it was her invariable practice. The conversation at tea turned upon Lady Muriel Street having discovered that the stones in a brooch which she had always believed to be valuable were imitations. It was Mrs Merridew who introduced the subject, but Miss Crewe pursued it in rather a curious manner, instancing a similar discovery on the part of Lady Melbury which need never have been made public if it had not been that Lord Melbury had most indiscreetly talked about it among their friends. She went on to say that if all were known, it would be found that a great deal of historic jewellery had been copied and the originals sold, and that sensible people kept these things to themselves. There was something in the way she spoke which I find difficult to describe. It left a certain impression. Her tone was disagreeably censorious, yet it evinced a kind of pleasure. The subject undoubtedly pleased her. She dwelt upon it. I fancied I could detect some personal pride — I cannot get nearer to it than that."

He was watching her with interest from between half-closed lids, those light eyes of his intent.

"Yes — go on."

"When Miss Holiday disappeared, and after the discovery of her body, I went back over these first impressions and found in retrospect that they were considerably intensified. For one thing, it was impossible not to connect this latest disappearance with that of Maggie Bell a year ago. But I could not accept a theory which would link the murder of Miss Holiday with a leakage of military secrets from Dalling Grange."

"May I ask why?"

She inclined her head.

"I was becoming convinced of a sinister connexion between Miss Crewe and the tragic death of Miss Holiday. Miss Cunningham met this poor woman coming away from Crewe House on Sunday evening. You informed me that the police had obtained a statement from a young woman who happened to pass them on her bicycle. She said that one of them dropped a letter and Miss Cunningham picked it up. Miss

Cunningham's explanation was that this letter was one which Miss Holiday pulled out of her overall pocket when she used her handkerchief. Seeing that the envelope had been opened and was addressed to Miss Crewe, she considered that it had been picked up by mistake, and offered, as she was going there, to take it up to Crewe House. In that brief episode the motive for the murder of Miss Holiday became plain. The letter contained something so dangerous to Miss Crewe that she would stick at nothing to ensure that it went no farther. When the murder of Miss Holiday was followed by an attempt upon Miss Cunningham, I felt convinced that Miss Crewe was engaged in something of a criminal nature, and that Miss Cunningham's life was in serious danger. But I was not prepared to accept any theory which involved Miss Crewe in the sale of secrets to a foreign power."

Frank Abbott opened his eyes.

"You surprise me."

Miss Silver's gaze rested on him in a disappointed manner.

"My dear Frank, you are not really thinking. Miss Crewe is an evil and ruthless woman, but it is never safe to neglect the motives which prompt a criminal. In the case of Lydia Crewe they are not difficult to discern. She has an implacable pride of race, a passion amounting to idolatry for her family, its traditions, its exploits, its accumulated possessions. Since the Crewes were an integral part of the county, and the county an integral part of the nation, she would no more be a party to anything of a treasonable nature than she

326

would neglect to rise to her feet when the National Anthem was played. But in the business of robbing her neighbours she was probably well within the family tradition. History presents one with a continuous picture of the rise and fall of great families — lands lost by adherence to a losing cause — lands acquired at a neighbour's expense through the chance of being found upon the winning side. I have no doubt that the Crewes had their ups and downs in just such ways as these, and that Miss Crewe's depredations appeared to her in this guise. Everything fitted into this picture. The complacency which I had observed when she was talking about the jewel robberies, the touch of personal pride, her assumption that the conversion of valuable heirlooms was now widespread — all these things left me in very little doubt as to what had been going on. But it was Miss Cunningham's danger which made the situation so urgent. After you had left me I became more and more uneasy on her account. In the end I felt impelled to go the Dower House. I thought I would see if there was a light in her bedroom. Beyond that I had no plan. As you know, I most providentially encountered Mr Lester, and as we were making our circuit of the house we saw Miss Crewe go in by the secret door."

He passed a hand over hair already mirror-smooth.

"My dear ma'am, you are always in the right place at the right moment. In fact, the complete reply to that dreary fallacy, 'Never the time, and the place, and the loved one all together'."

"My dear Frank —"

He hastened to forestall rebuke.

"Miss Cunningham owes you her life."

Miss Silver was casting off. As the last cherry-coloured stitch dropped from the needles, she said, "It has all been a terrible shock to her. I do not think she had many illusions about her brother. She knew him to be weak and drifting, but she had no suspicion that he was involved in a criminal enterprise, and no idea at all that the breach between him and Lydia Crewe was no more than a sham and that in reality he was seeing her constantly and was as much under her influence as he had ever been. His trial and all that must come out at it will be a terrible experience for the poor woman."

He hesitated for a moment. Then he said, "Keep this to yourself. Selby's for it, of course, but Cunningham isn't at all likely to stand his trial. He has had some kind of a seizure. I gather he is not expected to come round. It would save his sister and young Cunningham if he didn't. By the way, the Dalling Grange affair has been cleared up — the Security people let us know this morning. An attempt was made to frame Nicholas, and apparently he turned the tables. The real villain of the piece was Burlington's trusted private secretary, Brown. It's the same old story — a minor indiscretion to start with, a glass too much, the temptation to magnify his own importance by appearing to be well informed. Then pressure, the threat of exposure, blackmail — the whole bag of tricks — you know how it goes. Fingerprints on a compromising letter which had been planted on Nicholas finally gave him away. When confronted with them Brown collapsed — one of

328

Kipling's 'brittle intellectuals who crack beneath a strain'! So that is that. I hope you went to bed and slept this morning after being up all night?"

Miss Silver smiled.

"I was more pleasantly engaged."

"And now what have you been up to?"

She laid her knitting-needles down upon little Josephine's completed leggings.

"I attended a wedding. I was giving away the bride."

"How extremely versatile! Who was it?"

"Rosamond Maxwell. Miss Crewe was sending Jenny away to school today and Mr Lester had persuaded Rosamond to consent to this sudden wedding in order that he might have the right to act for her in the matter. The two girls were entirely financially dependent on Miss Crewe. Owing to Jenny's long period of invalidism following upon an accident, Rosamond had been unable to earn anything. The situation was, in fact, so difficult that an immediate marriage seemed to be the only solution. Mr Lester asked me to be present because he felt that Rosamond should have some support, and they did not like to involve any of Miss Crewe's friends in what she was bound to consider an affront."

Frank whistled.

"Poor old Craig — he's run into something!"

Miss Silver coughed reprovingly.

"I can assure you that he considers himself extremely fortunate to have won the love of so good and charming a girl. As Lord Tennyson so aptly says:

'If I were loved, as I desire to be,
What is there in the great sphere of the earth,
And range of evil between death and birth,
That I should fear — if I were loved by thee?'

Frank sat up laughing.

"Oh, if it's that way of it, there's nothing more to say, is there! What is a mad murderous aunt or two when you and Lord Tennyson approve! She's raving, so they won't hang her anyhow. All that remains is to offer one's felicitations, select a suitable gift, and hope for the best. It's a mad world anyhow."

Miss Silver smiled.

CHAPTER
FORTY-SIX

"Craig, I must go back."

She sat looking at him, all the bloom and radiance gone. It made him feel like an executioner. Twenty-four hours, and he had had to bring that tragic look to her face! Even the brief respite had been hard to achieve. The evening paper had to be suppressed, a chance taken with the possibility of some ghastly poster headline, some friendly encounter. Well, they had had their twenty-four hours. The arrival at this house, old Nan's welcome, Jenny's excitement, Rosamond's quiet delight, the feeling that they had reached a place where all the things they had dreamed of would come true — And now, in the grey morning with rain beating on the windows and a cold wind blowing, he had had to tell her about Lydia Crewe.

He knew her so well that he had known what she would say. Now he heard her say it.

"Craig, I must go back."

"My darling child!"

She put out her hands to him and he took them.

"Oh, you ought to have told me before! You oughtn't to have let me marry you!"

Her hands were strongly, warmly held.

"Darling, don't be stupid! Now, will you just listen to me! You are about to produce all the old cliches, and I don't want to hear them. Instead, you will listen to the voice of common sense. To start with, nowadays people stand or fall by what they do themselves. Nobody cares two hoots about their relations. Most people have one or two whom they don't exactly brag about, you know. To go on with, no one is going to connect you and Jenny with Miss Crewe unless you make a point of it."

A sudden colour came into her face.

"Craig, don't you see I can't just turn my back and pretend she doesn't belong? She did take us in when we had nowhere to go, and she is a relation — my mother was a Crewe. I can't walk out and say it's got nothing to do with me. Someone must see about the legal part of it. I can't just run away and let her think I don't care. I must go back."

He said, "She won't thank you."

Rosamond pulled her hands away.

"What does that matter?"

He smiled suddenly.

"No it wouldn't — to you. All right, darling, we'll go back. Jenny can stay here with Nan. You don't want to drag her into it, I suppose?"

"Oh, no!"

Jenny had no wish to return to Hazel Green. The things which had happened there were things she never meant to think about again. Neither now nor at any other time would she call back the hour when she had kneeled behind the stile which led into Vicarage Lane and watched the beam of a torch slide over something which lay upon the grass verge beyond — a long, dark something covered with sacking. She would never let herself think about the blue bead she had found there. The dark hours were gone. The bead was gone. She didn't care whether Aunt Lydia was mad, or whether she was in prison. The only thing she cared about was that she need never, never, never see her again. She had Craig for a brother, and this darling house to live in, and Nan, all comfortable and rosy and about two yards round the waist, to look after them. Nan was going to let her make an apple turnover. She was *nice*.

Rosamond and Craig drove through the rain. He knew now he had always been sure that Rosamond would go back. She was gentle, but she was resolute. He laughed suddenly and said, "You know, my sweet, what you've got is a strong, persevering Scottish conscience."

"Do you mind very much?"

"I shall get used to it. One of my grandmothers was a Scot, which will help me to keep my end up."

It was still raining when they drove up to Crewe House to find the police in charge there.

Later in the day they were admitted to see Lydia Crewe. Rosamond had not Jenny's gift of being able to shut the door upon what she did not choose to remember. The interview which followed was to haunt her — the bare room with its white-washed walls and its smell of varnish — the long yellow table with Aunt Lydia at one end of it and herself and Craig at the other — the two policewomen who stood one at the door, and the other behind Aunt Lydia's chair. Afterwards

333

she was to remember with a shudder that there were two. At the time it gave her a vague sense of security. The mad incessant talking had stopped, but there might still be an outbreak of violence.

Lydia Crewe sat at the far end of the table, her back stiff, her eyes hooded. Rosamond's hands held one another tightly. She said, "We have come to see what we can do, Aunt Lydia. You will want to see a solicitor."

"A solicitor?" Miss Crewe's tone was haughty in the extreme. "Do you imagine that I am not already provided with a legal adviser? Mr Hawthorn of Hawthorn and Monkshead has done all my business for years."

Craig said in a low voice, "They won't touch the case — not in their line. They'll recommend someone, I expect."

Lydia Crewe said sharply, "Don't mumble, Mr Lester! It's a deplorable habit! And may I ask just what business this is of yours?"

Rosamond flushed.

"Aunt Lydia — we are married —"

She lifted her lids and fixed them with a long cold stare.

"Indeed? So this is how you repay all that I have done for you and Jenny! You seem to have been in most indecent haste!"

Craig said in his pleasant voice, "I thought that Rosamond and Jenny needed someone to look after them, Miss Crewe. Now Rosamond and I have come here to see whether there is anything we can do for you.

We are not allowed to stay very long, so perhaps you will let us know."

She kept that staring look, but it had become unfocused. She said, "Married —" And then, "I do not know that I should have objected if I had been properly approached. The important thing is that the name should go on. You will, of course, take immediate steps to entitle you to call yourself Crewe. Major Maxwell always refused to do so. A most stubborn person, and quite unappreciative of the honour we did him in admitting him to the family."

When Craig made no reply, she said with extreme sharpness, "You will take the name — immediately!"

"I think not, Miss Crewe."

She stood up then, leaned forward with her hands at the table's edge gripping it, and began in a low shaking voice to rehearse the bygone glories of the Crewes — Sir John who died with Philip Sidney at Zutphen — Charles, his brother, who sailed against the Armada — Bevis, the saintly bishop — James, the witty courtier beloved of Charles II — name after name, generation after generation, whilst her voice rose and a fire kindled in her eyes. She looked at Rosamond and said, "My house — my people. And thanks to me they will not die. The great houses are going down — the life blood has been drained out of them. But not the Crewes — oh, no, not the Crewes! They are going to be greater than ever! The old glories will come back! I have seen to that, you know! There will be money enough!" She

335

repeated the word in a whisper, "Enough —" and stood there empty and shaken.

The two women closed in on either side of her and took her away.

Rosamond and Craig did not speak. They went back to the hotel where they had taken a room. When Craig had opened the door and stood aside to let her pass Rosamond went over to the window. She stood there looking out but not seeing anything at all. When Craig came to her she put out both her hands to keep him away. He had seen her pale, but never as pale as this. She said, low and quite steadily, "I'm so ashamed — so ashamed —"

He took the hands and found them icy cold.

"My darling, if we start being ashamed of what other people have done, we've got our work cut out. And she is mad. You do realize that, don't you?"

"Is she?"

"I don't think there is any doubt about it. I should say she's been heading that way for years."

A shudder went over her. He came nearer and held her close.

"We're not going to let it spoil things for us. Do you hear, my sweet? If you think I'm going to let you go about in sackcloth and ashes, well, you've got another think coming. You know, happy people have got something to give to the world. That sounds a bit grandiloquent, and I wouldn't have the nerve to say it except just to you. But it's true. We love each other, we've got a right to be happy, and if you go round disseminating gloom, I shall probably beat you, after which you will be able to divorce me. And what a lot of good that is going to be — especially for Jenny!"

"Jenny —"

He put his cheek against hers.

"You know, it strikes me that Jenny can do with a bit of happiness. She has been living at an abnormal pitch, and she is a lot too old for her age. What she wants is to relax and be part of a family circle. And live a normal life — I think probably a day-school to start with, and a home background to give her a sense of security."

He could feel the tension going out of her. She leaned against him now instead of stiffening and drawing away. He went on in a quiet everyday voice.

"That's what she wants. And that's what you want too. You won't bother about that, but I'm afraid you'll just have to give it a passing thought. Unless you are happy, Jenny won't be happy, and that would be very bad for Jenny. And quite damnably bad for me. Now are you going to come off it?"

"You make me sound a most frightful prig."

"There's a slight danger in that direction, but it shall be corrected."

"Oh, Craig!"

"That, darling, was a joke. The first step towards a successful marriage is for a wife to laugh at her husband's jokes. So now is your chance!"

Her lips began to tremble. He suddenly pulled her close and kissed her.

"Oh, my darling sweet, you are going to be happy — you *are!*"

337

There was a sense of release, of things that slipped away into the past where they belonged. They were in a light place. The sun shone on them. Rosamond lifted her face and said, "Yes."

Through the Wall

Patricia Wentworth

There are bitter scenes in the Brand family when Martin Brand dies and leaves his large estate not to his widowed sister-in-law but to Marion, his young niece whom he had only met once in his life.

For Marion, the prospect of sharing her new home with Martin's predatory relations is not a happy one, and when a battered body wearing her coat is found on the beach her unhappiness turns to panic. Will Miss Silver find the murderer before the next killing?

ISBN 978-0-7531-8648-0 (hb)
ISBN 978-0-7531-8649-7 (pb)

Anna, Where Are You?

Patricia Wentworth

Thomasina Elliott never expected to keep in touch with lonely orphan Anna Ball after they left school. However when Anna wrote to her, she felt obliged to reply. The correspondence between them was constant for years until Thomasina found herself waiting for a letter that never came.

Thomasina has no particular reason to believe that anything has happened to her old friend, but when she makes some enquiries she discovers Anna has disappeared without a trace. Deeply concerned, Thomasina turns to Detective Inspector Frank Abbott, who asks Miss Silver to investigate.

ISBN 978-0-7531-8122-5 (hb)
ISBN 978-0-7531-8123-2 (pb)